Night Owl

Night Owl

M. Pierce

St. Martin's Griffin ♞ New York

This is a work of fiction. All of the characters, organizations, and events portrayed in this novel are either products of the author's imagination or are used fictitiously.

 Printed in the United States of America. For information, address St. Martin's Press, 175 Fifth Avenue, New York, N.Y. 10010.

www.stmartins.com

The Library of Congress Cataloging-in-Publication Data is available upon request.

ISBN 978-1-250-05823-2 (trade paperback)
ISBN 978-1-4668-6228-9 (e-book)

First published in the United States by M. Pierce through Amazon Digital Services, Inc.

First St. Martin's Griffin Paperback Edition: July 2014

10 9 8 7 6 5 4 3 2 1

For Anna, of course

For a breath of ecstasy
Give all you have been, or could be.

SARA TEASDALE, "Barter"

Night Owl

Chapter 1

MATT

I lied to Hannah about the picture.

I lied to her about a lot of things.

No relationship should be built on lies, but I was in no relationship—at least not with Hannah. She was a girl I met on the Internet. Bethany was my girlfriend, who shared my apartment, my bed, and my life.

Hannah got the scraps.

"No pictures," I told Hannah on Skype. "No specifics, no last name, no phone number. Nothing. I don't want to know you, and I don't want you to know me. We write together online, that's it. I'm not looking for a new friend. I'm looking for a writing partner."

"Got it," she replied.

I remember staring at the text on my laptop and wondering if she was hurt. It was impossible to tell, the words hanging there with no tone.

Hannah broke two of my rules within a month when she sent me an e-mail from her personal address, hannah.catalano@xmail.com. Beside the e-mail was her account picture. A picture of her.

I glared at the tiny square image, then at her last name, then back at the picture. I should have gotten on Skype and chewed her out then and there, but I didn't. I clicked on the picture, which took me to her Google+ page and a larger version of the image.

She was wearing a strapless cream-colored top with a fringe of black lace along the neckline. Deep cleavage disappeared into the lace. Her skin was incredibly pale, flawless, and her hair fell in thick black-brown curls around her face. She wore dark-rimmed rectangular glasses with little gems on each side. She was blowing an air kiss at the camera. *At me.*

I should have closed the window immediately.

Instead, I stared at Hannah's picture—and stared at it—until I felt my cock getting hard in my slacks. I tried to ignore it, but the longer I looked at Hannah's picture, the harder I got. She was beautiful. And I was furious with her, for foisting her picture and last name on me.

I slid my hand between my legs and closed my eyes.

That was the second time I got off thinking about Hannah.

The first time was a week before. Bethany had just left on a tour of Brazil. I could have joined her, but I had no desire to sight-see in South America with Bethany's parents in tow.

I found myself chatting with Hannah every day.

It was late—about 2 A.M. Hannah's boyfriend had gone to bed. That meant Hannah was alone in their basement office. As for me, I was on my laptop in the guest bedroom of my Denver apartment.

"I sent you a few paragraphs," I typed, "but don't worry about replying tonight. Aren't you tired?"

Little.Bird: Not yet. I haven't been sleeping well.

Little.Bird was Hannah's Skype name. Mine was Night.Owl.

Night.Owl: You could take something. I don't know, melatonin?

Little.Bird: Never works for me.

Night.Owl: Well, damn.

We were in unknown territory with this conversation. As a rule, we dialogued about our collaborative story and nothing else.

Our story was an ongoing fantasy. We e-mailed pieces back and forth. That was how we met, and why: on a fiction writers' forum, seeking writing partners.

Hannah's character was a human with supernatural powers, and mine was a demon.

She was Lana. I was Cal.

Little.Bird: Sometimes I smoke a little bit of Mick's weed to help me sleep.

Night.Owl: Is that right.

Little.Bird: Yeah. *Shrugs* Mick smokes 24/7 and drinks every day, too. I'm not like that. Anyway, it's legal here.

My stomach clenched. Colorado had recently legalized marijuana for recreational use. So had Washington. God, did Hannah live in my state? Why did that possibility have my stomach flip-flopping?

Night.Owl: Yeah, it's legal here, too. I'm in Colorado.

Little.Bird: Okay, Mr. Secret Agent No Specifics.

I smirked. Oh, so Hannah wasn't going to volunteer her whereabouts. I deserved that.

Night.Owl: I'm allowed to break my own rules.

Little.Bird: Just ask.

Night.Owl: What? Ask what?

Little.Bird: Oh please, Matt. You're waiting for me to tell you where I live.

Night.Owl: Then tell me.

Little.Bird: Seattle.

I felt a funny twist in my gut. Washington, not Colorado.

Night.Owl: Ah. I've never been out that way.

Little.Bird: You should visit sometime. Great food, great atmosphere.

Night.Owl: Your boyfriend sounds like a real charmer.

Little.Bird: Lol. Sure. Doesn't matter, I won't be with him much longer. Brb.

Hannah was gone for ten minutes. Fuck, had I upset her?

Little.Bird: Back.

Night.Owl: Wb. Are you okay?

Little.Bird: Yeah, I'm fine. I wanted to change into something more comfy.

I stared at the screen for a full minute before forcing my fingers to type what my brain was screaming. After I typed it, I stared at the words for another minute before hitting Enter.

I must have been losing my mind. Or turning into a creep. Or both.

Night.Owl: So what are you wearing?

Little.Bird: Lol! All the walls are coming down tonight . . .

Night.Owl: Haha. God, sorry. I have no idea why I just typed that. Ignore that. Such a creeper right now.

Little.Bird: No, it was funny, that's all. You're not a creeper, trust me. I'm a girl who used to play online games. I know what creepers are.

Night.Owl: Well, whatever.

I felt my face heating. Hannah and I were having our first actual conversation, and I asked what she was wearing.

I, a successful and very taken twenty-eight-year-old man, had become the equivalent of a horny fourteen-year-old. Real smooth.

Little.Bird: Matt, I said trust me. You. Are. Not. A. Creeper. You're like the anti-creeper. That's why I laughed. It's like suddenly Mr. I'm Not Looking For Friends So Don't Piss Me Off With Details About Your Life wants to know what I'm wearing. Do you still want to know?

My blush of embarrassment was rapidly turning into a flush of anger.

Night.Owl: Yes, I still fucking want to know. That's why I asked, so either tell me or drop it. I don't need you to make me feel like a dipshit for asking.
Little.Bird: Okay! I'm sorry. Don't get angry. I'm wearing a blue bathrobe.
Night.Owl: A bathrobe . . . ?
Little.Bird: Yes. It's a soft fuzzy blue bathrobe. Hits me about midthigh.
Night.Owl: Is that all?
Little.Bird: Yes.

I felt a throb between my legs. At the time, I had no idea what Hannah looked like, but that fact didn't seem to matter to my dick. I slid the laptop off my thighs and onto the mattress. I pressed a hand to my sex. And I waited. Where was this going?

Little.Bird: Do I . . . get to ask what you're wearing?
Night.Owl: Lounge pants.
Little.Bird: Is that all?
Night.Owl: Yes.
Little.Bird: Yummy . . .
Night.Owl: Hannah. You should let your robe hang open.
Little.Bird: All right.

My mouth gaped. My erection pushed against my palm. *All right?* She took my order so calmly and without hesitation. Was she really doing it?

I conjured up an image of a young woman seated at a computer desk, her small robe hanging open and her full breasts bared to the screen. I shoved my pants around my hips and freed my shaft. My whole body was tingling.

I needed to tell Hannah to stop and that I wasn't single and that we were going to ruin our pleasant anonymous online friendship.

Night.Owl: Describe your body. Spread your legs. God, my heart is pounding.

Little.Bird: Mine too. I spread them. Telling you this stuff is making me wet.

Night.Owl: God, Hannah.

I began to pump my cock with one hand, pausing to swirl my thumb over the head. I could feel the lean muscles along my thighs and arms locking up—tensing in excitement or else willing me to stop. I needed to stop.

Little.Bird: My breasts are . . . big. 34DD. They sit high on my chest for natural breasts. My nipples are dark pink. They're really sensitive. I'm curvy. Hourglass figure I guess.

I was ready to come. Already. I let myself moan into the silence of the apartment and rocked my hips into my hand. *Oh God oh God oh God.* I groped at the laptop keyboard.

Night.Owl: Help me come.

Little.Bird: I shave my legs all the way up. And I'm . . . really tight. And wet. So wet. I'm making a mess.

Night.Owl: God, you're a slut Hannah.

Little.Bird: I am. My legs are spread so wide it hurts. I wish you were pounding into me right now.

My orgasm took me by surprise, the pleasure unfurling all at once. I gasped and sat up sharply. I came into my hand with a groan.

I'm making a mess.

I wish you were pounding into me right now.

I collapsed against the pillows. My chest was heaving. A rivulet of sweat trickled from my dirty-blond hair to my jaw.

What just happened? I stared at the laptop and waited. I couldn't log off; I had to say something. Thanks? Sorry?

Night.Owl: I should go.

Little.Bird: Wait. That was all right, Matt. If you're going because you feel awkward, don't. We don't have to talk about it.

Finding the words "I should go" had been difficult enough. I had nothing else to say. I needed to think, or not think. I most definitely needed to get away from Hannah.

Little.Bird: Listen. I don't normally do this. I don't want you to think I'm like that.

Night.Owl: No. Neither do I.

Before Hannah could type a reply, I closed Skype and shut my laptop.

I didn't log back on for a week.

And what a week it was. Thoughts of Hannah invaded my mind. I woke up thinking about her, often hard, and I went to sleep thinking about her. I thought about her in the shower. I thought about her when I tried to work, my latest project open on the computer screen and my head locked in a daydream.

Hannah, Hannah, Hannah.

Over and over I turned the few details she had given me. Large breasts, a curvy figure, a tight cunt.

A friend took me out to lunch on the weekend.

"What do you know about Seattle?" I asked, striving to sound nonchalant.

"Seattle? Why?"

"I'm putting it in a story. Figured I'd ask. I've never been, no idea about the place."

"Well, I've been to the Pacific Northwest a few times." My friend chewed and watched me thoughtfully. I stared at my plate. I had hardly touched my meal, but under his careful gaze I shoved a forkful of risotto into my mouth.

"Tons of hipsters," he said. "All that unflattering facial hair. And I'll tell you what, it's depressing as *fuck,* the weather out there. It's gray. I mean if you like that kind of thing, it's great. But it's *wet,* Matt, it's basically wet all the time."

I slammed down my fork. I nearly choked.

Wet. So wet. I'm making a mess.

Hannah e-mailed a story installment after two days. Usually she replied within hours. Maybe she was having second thoughts about me.

Hell, I'd be having second thoughts about me.

Her writing was perfectly normal, though.

Our characters were traveling to a port city in search of information to help Lana harness her powers. I could feel my character falling for Lana as we wrote. I tried to steer him away from it, but Hannah wrote the girl in such a clever, engaging way. She was quirky and strong, a lover of laughter, by turns tomboyish and then disarmingly feminine.

Hannah. Lana.

I began to make connections.

She described Lana as buxom, short, and curvy. An hourglass figure. Was Hannah playing a thinly veiled version of herself? And for that matter, was I? Like me, Cal was tall and fair-haired, cynical in the extreme, and neurotically secretive.

I booted up my laptop a week after *the bathrobe incident* with the intention of continuing our story. Or maybe with the intention of logging on to Skype to chat with Hannah. I missed her.

That's when I saw the e-mail from hannah.catalano@xmail.com.

The e-mail with her picture.

The picture that made me hard.

Subject: Come back . . .

Sender: Hannah Catalano

Date: Tuesday, June 25, 2013

Time: 11:15 PM

Matt, hey. I really hope you read this. You haven't replied to my post. I miss the story. And I miss talking to you.

I can't stop thinking about what happened.

I met Mick through WoW (I'm a reformed nerd) and we cybered like twice over private messages. He's a really bad writer. It was really bad. Then we started dating long distance and I used to do things with him over video chat. That's all.

I don't know why I'm telling you this stuff, except that I want you to know that what happened between us isn't normal for me. I liked it, though. Knowing you were getting off turned me on.

Speaking of Mick, I'm leaving him. My sister is flying out here on Thursday to help me pack and we're driving back together. I'm moving in with my parents for a while. Pretty awesome, since I'm 27.

I guess the point is, we'll be on the road for two or three days and I'll only be online on my phone.

Hannah

After jerking off to Hannah's picture like a desperate juvenile, I must have reread her e-mail three times. I mentally filed the new information.

Hannah has a sister.

Hannah is twenty-seven.

Hannah is leaving her boyfriend.

Hannah liked helping me get off; she can't stop thinking about it, and it turned her on.

And now she had a face and a name, both of which I expressly asked never to know.

Hannah Catalano.

So she was Italian. That explained the knockout figure and the dark, heavy hair.

I logged on to Skype.

Night.Owl: Hey.

Little.Bird: Hey! That was quick, lol. I sent you an e-mail like fifteen minutes ago.

Night.Owl: Don't I know it.

Little.Bird: Haha . . .

Night.Owl: Let's get one thing straight, Hannah. I'm not sure what you think it means that you helped me get off with your rudimentary descriptive skills, so let me clarify. It means nothing. It definitely does not mean you can now assault me with your life story.

Little.Bird: Wow. Wow . . .

Night.Owl: Use your words.

Little.Bird: You . . . are such an asshole right now.

Night.Owl: You say this like it's news.

Little.Bird: It's news to me. God, I'm SO SORRY that I decided to tell you I'd be gone for a few days. We WERE telling a story together basically every day, but since you haven't replied to my last post, I guess that's off.

Night.Owl: It's not off. Don't get all hyperbolic on me, Hannah. However, let's pause and consider the distance between 1) telling me you're going to be MIA for a few days and 2) forcing your name AND picture on me.

Little.Bird: . . . what?

Night.Owl: Yes, shocking but true. Our minor indiscretion does not suddenly negate my wish to preserve mutual privacy. No full names, no pictures, etc.

Little.Bird: Wtf. I didn't send you my picture. Or tell you my name.

Night.Owl: Okay hannah.catalano@xmail.com.

Little.Bird: omg

I rolled my eyes and sat back in my chair. Maybe I had been a little harsher than necessary, but I got my point across. I was angry. I was angry with Hannah for plaguing my thoughts, and angrier that she was gorgeous and forced me to know it.

Somehow, my life would be easier if I could imagine Hannah as a fat pimply stranger on the Internet, or even a faceless stranger on the Internet. Anything but that dark-haired beauty blowing a kiss at me with her pink, pouty lips.

Five minutes passed and Hannah said nothing.

I fiddled with the desk calendar.

Night.Owl: Do you have anything to add to that stirring articulation?

Nothing.

I opened my e-mail, then opened Hannah's e-mail. Her account picture had changed. Gone was the tiny portrait of Hannah Catalano, replaced by a purplish swirl of galaxy and stars.

Panic chilled me.

It was gone. Her picture was gone.

I clicked on the galaxy and it took me to a larger picture . . . of the galaxy.

I already couldn't remember the details of Hannah's face.

Night.Owl: What the fuck. You just changed your account picture? You do realize I have already seen it . . .

Little.Bird: Matt, I am so, so sorry. I know you're never going to believe me, but this is the truth. I e-mailed you from my main account by accident. I am so embarrassed right now, I want to die. I would never infringe on your boundaries like that. God, everything's been so insane in my life lately. I was worried I'd scared you off. I sat down to write you an e-mail, and bang.

Night.Owl: Oh . . .

Little.Bird: Yeah, I . . . I'm so mortified. I'm so sorry . . .

Night.Owl: I . . . really thought you did it on purpose. Obviously. Wow.

Little.Bird: No, I would never. I swear. I love writing with you. I respect your privacy. Or I try to . . .

I frowned and considered the words on my screen. It was an accident. And thanks to my overblown reaction to that accident, I had lost access to my only image of Hannah, the girl who was steadily setting my mind on fire.

I ran a quick Google image search on Hannah Catalano.

Nothing.

Night.Owl: Do you even want to know what I thought?

Little.Bird: What you thought?

Night.Owl: Of how you look.

Little.Bird: Oh. Um. It doesn't matter.

Night.Owl: Doesn't matter?

Little.Bird: Yeah. It's . . . no big deal. I'm just so embarrassed.

Night.Owl: Well, in that case, you'll be pleased to know I barely looked at it. It was a tiny picture and as soon as I realized what it was, I closed the window.

Little.Bird: Oh . . . okay . . .

Night.Owl: Yeah. And thanks for changing it so promptly. I appreciate that.

Little.Bird: Sure. So . . . I should . . . probably get back to packing.

Night.Owl: Mm. Good luck with that. I'll reply to your post soon.

Little.Bird: Sweet. I'll reply when I can.

Night.Owl: Don't worry about it. I know you've got a lot going on, and you'll be tired after the move. What state are your folks in?

Little.Bird: Oh . . . didn't I tell you? Haha. Gosh. Super awkward night.

Night.Owl: Huh?

Little.Bird: Nothing. They still live in the house I grew up in. In Colorado . . .

Chapter 2

HANNAH

Leaving Mick's hairy ass was the best decision I'd made in the last five years.

Leaving my job as a teller at Bank West was the second-best decision.

The guy and the job didn't respect me—and they didn't deserve me.

No matter how I asked or what I threatened, Mick refused to quit smoking and drinking. He had an infuriating habit of groping me in public, and lately the sex was, well, not sex. More like a six-thrust *oops!*

When I looked at Mick, I had to force myself to remember that I used to love him. I used to find his nerd humor funny. I used to be attracted to his jawless pointy-chinned face and scruffy receding hairline.

Sort of.

As for the bank, I had stayed on as a teller for three years while my favorite boss got canned, my friends gradually left, and I was passed over time and time again for promotions.

Good riddance to them both.

And hello to three days on the road going fifty-five with a U-Haul hooked to my Civic, spacing out and thinking about Matt.

"Hellooo?" My sister waved her iPod in my face.

"Huh? What?"

"For the . . . third time." She turned down my Lana Del Rey playlist. "Can I puh-lease change the music?"

"Oh, yeah. Whatever."

I stared ahead at the highway.

I felt Chrissy watching me as she plugged in her iPod.

"Sooo." She plopped her feet on the dash, and hip-hop blared from the speakers.

"So what?" I glanced at her. As always, I was struck by my sister's beauty. She's twenty-one and has a dancer's fit little body. Much to our parents' chagrin, she was saving for an apartment and putting herself through dance classes by working at a strip club. She claimed to love it, but I wasn't so sure.

"So, who's the new guy?" She arched a perfectly plucked eyebrow.

Our father calls us both heartbreakers, but Chrissy and I are practically opposites. My style is natural. I let my hair grow long, prefer glasses to contacts, wear very little makeup, and work out only enough to define my soft curves.

My sister is punk. She has tats, half a dozen piercings, lives in eyeliner, and dyes her pixie haircut black and blond.

And when it comes to me, she has always been uncannily perceptive.

"New guy? There is no new guy," I said. "Can you turn this shit down? Or at least find a song that doesn't make my ears bleed?"

"Girl, you better get used to it." Chrissy grooved in her seat, lifting her arms. Bracelets clanked down her wrists. "It's what we'll be listening to when I teach you how to twerk."

"Excuse me?"

"I've seen you dance, Han. You need a little help. And then you can show your new guy; it'll drive him nuts. Is he in Colorado?"

Yes. Yes, he is.

"What? No! I mean, no, there is no guy. You're ridiculous."

"H'okay," Chrissy laughed. "All I know is, you would never have ditched your job and boyfriend without some motivation. Sorry, Han, your balls just aren't that big."

I swallowed and focused on the yellow lines rolling ahead of me in the night. I wanted so badly to talk about Matt. I thought about him nonstop while we packed and drove.

Spread your legs. Help me come. God, my heart is pounding.

But what could I tell Chrissy? *You're right, Sis, I met this guy named Matt. Online. I know exactly three things about him. He lives in Colorado, he's an awesome writer, and he gets off talking to scantily clad strangers on the Internet. Love at first Skype.*

Yeah, that would go over well. Lots of laughing and eye rolling would ensue, and of course the inevitable question: *Do you know what he looks like?*

God, no, I didn't know what Matt looked like.

I knew what Cal looked like—tall, blond, handsome, lean—but Matt could be a three-hundred-pound basement dweller. Ugh, he probably was. Stereotypes exist for a reason, and Matt happened to be an Internet-trawling male of an indeterminate age who came inside of five minutes when I told him I had big breasts (and who also had a convenient no-pictures rule).

What a depressing line of thought.

I gave my sister a flat look.

"Be useful," I mumbled. "Help me look for a motel."

We stopped at 3 A.M. in the Cascades. My sister flung herself onto the motel bed and passed out. I sat in the bathroom and checked my e-mail for the one hundredth time.

Finally! Two e-mails from Matt. One was a reply to my post. The other had no subject.

Subject: (no subject)
Sender: Matthew S.
Date: Saturday, June 29, 2013
Time: 2:46 AM
Hi, Hannah,
I just sent you a post. How's the move going? You're a brave little bird. And hey, you're invading my state. Small world, right?
I want to say that I hope you don't think less of me after what happened (the bathrobe incident, as I like to call it). I know it was seedy as fuck. I wouldn't be surprised if you did think less of me. I don't know what to think of myself.
Sorry I was a dick about the picture.
I haven't seen you on Skype so I assume you're on the road. I'm going to break another one of my rules. If you want to call, my number is 555-774-5761.
Matt

Subject: Seedy as fuck
Sender: Hannah Catalano
Date: Saturday, June 29, 2013
Time: 3:20 AM
Hey, are you still awake?

Subject: Re: Seedy as fuck
Sender: Matthew S.
Date: Saturday, June 29, 2013
Time: 3:21 AM
Yeah. I'm waiting.
Matt

I felt my breaths grow shallow as I read Matt's reply. *I'm waiting.* How could a guy seem so sexy and confident when he was only words on a screen?

He was waiting. Waiting for me to call. He didn't need to say it; I knew it.

My hands shook as I added Matt to my contacts and called the number.

Panic set in as I listened to the ring.

I'm about to talk to Matt.

I'm about to hear his voice.

I don't even know this guy.

What the hell am I doing?

He could be a psycho stalker.

We shouldn't cross this line.

I can hang up.

I can hang up now.

Yeah, I'm going to h—

"Hannah?"

I swallowed and slid down the bathroom wall.

"Hannah, is that you?"

Matt's cool, clear voice swirled in my ear. It was distantly accented—New Jersey, maybe New York—and a little husky.

He sounded sleepy.

He sounded sexy as hell.

I had the overwhelming urge to ask him to keep saying my name. *Hannah, Hannah, Hannah. Help me come.* Warmth bloomed between my legs.

"Okay, then." He laughed softly. I felt my reason melting at the sound. "We'll play the one-sided conversation game. I'm Matt, it's nice to—" Again, he broke into quiet laughter. His voice was rich with amusement, but not warm. He sounded contemptuous. He sounded ready to laugh at anything, simply for the pleasure of laughing with his silky voice.

I couldn't help but picture the devilish eyes that must have accompanied that voice.

Green eyes, I decided. Dark green, secretive and deep like a forest.

"I was going to say it's nice to meet you," he went on, "but I guess we've technically met online. Now we're meeting on the phone. Maybe . . ." He trailed off. I heard some shuffling. "God, if this is you trolling me, Nate, I swear I'm going to break your fucking—"

"Hey! Sorry, I—" I scooted over to the bathroom door, opened and closed it, then sat back against the wall. Brilliant. *Sorry, I was soaking my underwear while I listened creepily to your voice.* "—sorry, yeah. I had to go into the bathroom. My sister is asleep."

Matt was silent for a moment.

"Is that why you're whispering?" he said.

"Yeah. She's really tired. We're at a motel, we just stopped. Pretty sure the wall between this bathroom and her bed is a piece of plywood, so . . . "

"Well . . . damn. I wanted to hear your voice. I mean, your regular-volume voice." He chuckled. "Do you think you could risk a few words? I'll deal with your sister if she wakes up."

I smirked, imagining a conversation between my hotheaded sis and this glib personality.

"I think that would be a bad idea. But, um. Sure. What should I say?"

"With your normal voice? How about: 'The quick brown fox jumps over the lazy dog.' "

"Okay." I cleared my throat. I was suddenly painfully self-conscious about my voice. "Um. Okay. The . . . the quick brown fox—"

Laughter exploded on the line. It was loud and sharp, nearly cruel.

"Oh . . . my God, Hannah." I heard a clatter, then some scuffling. "Oh, fuck. You were really saying it. The quick . . . brown fox . . . oh, God." Matt dissolved into laughter again.

I glared at my knees.

"What's so fucking funny?" I whispered.

"Hannah. Hannah, I'm sorry."

I heard him take a few calming breaths.

"Okay," he said. "I'm sorry. Ignore me, seriously. I have a weird sense of humor. That . . . that struck me funny. You have a lovely voice. Go figure."

Go figure? What did he mean by that?

"Look, is there a reason you wanted me to call, or were you just looking for some late-night entertainment?"

"Pretty sure this classifies as early-morning entertainment, Hannah."

"Okay. Well, whatever. Look, I'm not sure why I—"

"I can't stop thinking about you."

His words stopped me cold.

His words, and something in his voice. Honesty.

"What we did," he continued. "Or, what you did to me . . ."

My throat went dry. *What I did to him.* It should have grossed me out, the thought of a stranger beating off to a few details about my body, but it didn't. It intrigued me. The heat between my legs pulsed.

"You know what I'm talking about," he insisted. An edge came into his voice at the slightest provocation.

"Y-yeah," I managed. "Yeah."

"You enjoyed it."

"Yeah."

"You said you wished I were pounding into you."

"Yeah . . ."

I couldn't believe this smooth-talking stranger was dictating to me how I felt.

I couldn't believe I was blindly agreeing.

And I couldn't believe my considerable vocabulary had suddenly been reduced to "yeah."

"Hannah, you made me come so hard. And I did it again, thinking about you. Let me return the favor."

His words hung in the silence between us.

Return the favor. *Help me come.*

"Yes," I whispered. My voice was a thread of sound.

"God, Hannah. Tell me what you're wearing."

Shivers raced up and down my spine as I locked the bathroom door and glanced at myself in the mirror. My skin was flushed. I must have been biting my lips because they were swollen and bright.

"A baby blue cami and jeans."

"Get out of those jeans. What else?"

My eyes fluttered closed. I jerked at my jeans with one hand and shoved them down, stepping out of them. I kept watching myself in the mirror. I expected to see confusion on my face—*Was I out of my fucking mind right now?*—but all I saw was a glazed look of arousal.

"A gray push-up bra and a blue thong with a black lace waistband."

"Fuck, a thong? Perfect. God, you're perfect. Lie down. Put the phone near your ear. I want you to have both hands free."

I obeyed automatically. I was putty in this stranger's hands. Not even his hands! His sexy, soft voice, demanding and encouraging.

I grabbed two clean towels from the rack and spread them on the bathroom floor, then stretched out on top of them and set my iPhone beside my ear.

"I bet your breasts look damn good in that push-up bra, Hannah. Why don't you lift your cami and show them off. How do they look, hm? Pressed together, nice and high? You like to show them off? Squeeze them for me. Spread your legs. Is that the kind of girl you are, teasing men with your beautiful tits? I bet you like it. You liked driving me mad in your bathrobe, making me get hard."

"Yes," I gasped. Yes, yes, yes. I pulled my tight cami up, bunching it high around my chest and baring my bra and breasts to the empty bathroom. I imagined Matt hovering over me. I imagined him smirking and telling me I liked to show off my tits. *Was it true?*

I squeezed the cups of my bra and bit my lip to suppress a groan.

"Your nipples are sensitive. You told me that." Matt laughed softly. "Twist them, Hannah. Rub them and pull on them. Don't spare yourself the pain. I bet you're drenched."

"I am," I whispered. "God, Matt . . . I can feel it, how wet I am."

I could. I could feel the slick, oozing sensation of desire between my legs.

Matt drew a sharp breath.

With trembling hands, I unclasped my bra and slid the cups off my breasts. I pinched a nipple between my fingers and gasped. So sensitive! An arrow of pleasure shot down to my sex. *Don't spare yourself the pain.* I twisted my nipple and yelped.

"Hannah!" For the first time, I heard a quaver in Matt's voice. He was losing control. He was losing control *with me.* I began to tremble.

"Do it with me," I whispered. "Matt, please."

"I am. I have to. I can't help it. Hannah . . . God, do it. Spread your pussy, rub your clit. Come with me. God, I need this. What are you doing to me?"

My nipples were already stiff and aching. I shoved aside my thong and began to slide my finger over my clit. Everything between my legs was soaked.

"So wet," I breathed. "Everything. So wet. Matt, God."

"S-say my name again. Again."

"Matt, God, Matt, I . . . I'm close."

I heated with embarrassment. On my own, it could take upward of twenty minutes to get a good orgasm. Now, with Matt's insistent voice in my ear, I couldn't stop the pleasure from spiraling upward.

"Oh, God, Hannah. Fuck, I'm c—"

"Coming!" I panted.

Matt gave a ragged moan. My pussy throbbed and pleasure rolled through my body like a shock wave. I shook on the floor. Fluid squirted around my fingers. *Bliss.*

I don't know how long I lay there breathing, feeling the little aftershocks of ecstasy. My heart slowed to a sluggish pace. I thought I could sleep forever. On the line, Matt sighed and took one deep breath after another. Finally his voice broke the silence.

"Is blue your favorite color?"

"What?" I smiled lazily. "I mean, yeah. How did you know?"

"Good guess," he murmured.

"What's your favorite color?"

"Don't have one."

"Oh, that's a little sad somehow."

"Nah." He chuckled. "I actually have one. You'll laugh, though. I'm not telling."

"What? No way, I won't laugh." Except I did laugh, and I heard my satisfaction and happiness in the sound. This felt like pillow talk. This felt like the kind of thing Mick and I used to enjoy when we first hooked up. Too bad nothing lasts. "It's probably something ridiculous, like . . . hot pink. Am I right?"

"Not telling. Hey, it's late."

"Pretty sure this classifies as early, Matt."

He laughed. "Touché, little bird. You looking forward to being home?"

"Yes and no. I miss my family. I miss Colorado; it's where I grew up. I'm pretty sure I'll be lonely, though."

"Lonely? You'll have your family."

"Not that kind of lonely."

"Ah." I could hear the smile in Matt's voice. "But there's no such thing as loneliness. There is only the idea of loneliness."

I blinked and sat up.

There is no such thing as loneliness. There is only the idea of loneliness.

"Matt, did you seriously just quote from *Ten Thousand Nights*?" I laughed. "Are you a Pierce fan?"

I heard a click, then silence.

"Matt?"

I frowned at my phone. He was gone. And it was close to 4 A.M. for me, 5 A.M. for him. I sent him a text.

> *Think our call got dropped. Or you awkwarded out and hung up. It's late anyway. I mean early. ;) Good night. Good morning. And thanks.*

The motel mattress was like a slab of concrete, but I dropped into sleep within seconds. My sleep was full of dreams. My dreams were full of laughing green eyes, whispered demands, and hushed moans.

Chapter 3

MATT

Hannah said my name for the first time in a motel bathroom somewhere between Washington and Colorado.

God, Matt . . . I can feel it, how wet I am.

It did something to me. It turned a feeling like a key inside me.

Then she asked if I was a fan of my own books.

That did something to me, too. It made me hang up.

I stalked through the apartment at 5 A.M., considering my rash of stupid decisions.

Stupid decision number one: giving Hannah my phone number.

Stupid decision number two: quoting from my own book. What are the odds Hannah would have read my books? I groaned and buried my face in my hands. Pretty fucking high, considering I'm a national bestseller four times over.

Stupid decision number three: phone sex with Hannah. I didn't even know the girl. I had a picture (one that was rapidly fading from my memory), a name and age, a few other minor details, and a growing fixation. And a girlfriend.

What kind of girl was Hannah, anyway? What kind of girl has phone sex with a stranger she met on the Internet?

I had no room to judge. After all, what kind of guy has phone sex with a stranger he met on the Internet? At least Hannah was single. Maybe I could consider the bathrobe incident an accident, but the phone sex was clear-cut cheating.

I was heading into scumbag territory, fast.

I grabbed my emergency Dunhills and lit one on the balcony.

I "quit" smoking five years ago, along with drinking and drugs, but I always kept a pack of smokes handy for situations like this.

At 7 A.M. I was still smoking and staring into the city. The morning was cool and clear; I could tell the day would be a scorcher. The city came alive around me. Joggers crisscrossed the street, dogs barked, and car horns sounded.

I had calmed considerably, and I had pretty much reasoned away my stupidity.

Quoting from my own book: So what? No way would Hannah make the logical leap to me being M. Pierce. In the light of day, my minor freak-out seemed ridiculous.

Giving Hannah my phone number (plus phone sex): I was taking my psychiatrist's professional medical advice, "opening myself to new experiences," "letting myself need people," and "eschewing the confines of social norms." Good enough.

My phone chimed. There was a short e-mail from Bethany. She was in Gramado.

> Don't forget to water the lemon tree. Are you eating? I won't bother describing this place since you've been. Still wish you'd come. You better not be a skeleton when I get back. Remember, the stuff in the freezer is dated. Kisses, Bethany

That was my girlfriend, excessive maternal instincts and all. I'd reply later.

For now, I wanted to stay right where I was, lost in thoughts of Hannah.

I stripped off my T-shirt and flopped onto the living room couch with a sketchbook and a pencil. Laurence was up. His long ears swiveled toward me like satellite dishes. He stretched and hopped over to his litter pan.

"Hey, buddy," I said to the rabbit, tapping my pencil on a blank page.

I began to sketch what I remembered of Hannah's picture. I started with her eyes, which were large and dark, then her slender nose, moving down to her expressive full lips. I tried to capture the sweetness in her face, the oval shape of it framed by heavy brunette coils. I shaded in her glasses. Lightly, I drew the neckline of her top and hinted at her cleavage with a smudge.

I frowned at the portrait.

Not bad, but not quite right. I closed my eyes. I struggled to remember the picture. I remembered her voice on the phone. Not too high, not too low, velvety and feminine. *What's so fucking funny?* God, she was adorable in her anger.

Do it with me. Matt, please.

I drifted awake at noon. I was sprawled on the couch, my sketchbook open across my thighs and my dick hard. Of course.

I stared at the lemon tree until my wood relaxed.

Then I called Hannah.

She picked up after two rings.

"Hello?" she said. Her voice sounded a little huskier.

"Hey, little bird."

"Bird?" She giggled. "Sorry, babe, this is Hannah's sister. Hannah's driving."

I glowered at my sketch and considered hanging up.

"Maybe you should take a turn driving," I muttered, "or not answer your sister's phone."

"She gave it to me, Mr. Frostypants."

I heard Hannah's voice in the background. She sounded annoyed, but I couldn't make out what she was saying.

"What did she say?" I demanded.

"She said I should stop trolling you. She also said hi. Hey, are you Hannah's new guy?"

"Excuse me?"

I sat up. My sketchbook flopped onto the floor. New guy? Hannah had a new guy? Anger—and not a little jealousy—tightened around my chest.

"Yeah. New guy. Are you the new guy?"

"No, I . . ." My mouth worked speechlessly. Hannah told me she was leaving her boyfriend. She neglected to mention she was leaving him for another guy. I guess that made us both faithless assholes. Perfect.

So why did this hurt? Why did I feel used? It wasn't like I could have Hannah. I couldn't even meet her—couldn't risk my little obsession morphing into full-blown infidelity. I wasn't that kind of guy. Was I? I felt sick to my stomach.

"Earth to Mr. Frostypants!" Hannah's sister shouted.

"Fuck off," I said, ending the call.

Chapter 4

HANNAH

"Fuck off?" I stuck my hand on my hip and glared at Chrissy. "Just wait a minute. He said 'fuck off' and hung up?"

"Uh-huh. Yup. Unless it was an epically well-timed call drop. But um, Hannah, not sure about that guy. He was a *liiittle* bit of an asshole." My sister squinted as she emphasized the word "little." I couldn't help but laugh. "A little bit of an asshole" was putting Matt lightly. Still, I had to figure out why he got so mad.

My sister and I were stopped at a motel in Billings, Montana. It was 2 A.M. I had another hour of driving in me, but I wanted to talk to Matt, and I wanted to search for something in the U-Haul.

I blamed being on the road for thinking about Matt constantly. The endless highway, the repetitive scenery, tuning out my sister's bad music—oh, and our explosive phone sex last night.

God, ridiculous! I was infatuated with a guy I knew nothing about.

"One more time," I said, yanking open the back of the trailer. It rolled up with a clatter. "You called him . . . Mr. Frostypants."

My mouth twitched. "And he immediately said 'fuck you' and hung up?"

"Ohhh my God, yes! That is what happened, Hannah. What is your deal with this asshat?"

"He's a good friend," I lied, "and I think he's actually pissed. I texted him from Perkins and called and got nothing."

"Maybe he was out. I don't know. What are you looking for in there?"

"Oh, um . . . I wanted some clothes." I rubbed my neck. My sister stared at me. I got the sense that she had seen through both of my lies and possibly even heard me in the bathroom last night. "So. Yeah. I don't need any help. Gotta rummage, that's all. You can check us in."

"Mhmmm." Christine spun and headed into the motel.

Thank God.

At this point, I knew I would spill if she grilled me. I felt like a thirteen-year-old girl, bubbly with excitement and desperate to gab about my latest crush. He said this, he did that. Spare me. I was so much cooler than this.

I boosted myself onto the edge of the U-Haul and turned on my key chain flashlight, peering into the jam of boxes and furniture. After fifteen minutes of struggling, I managed to shift out the box I was looking for. It had the word BOOKS in black Sharpie on the side.

I dug out my worn copy of *Ten Thousand Nights* by M. Pierce. I flipped through its dog-eared and highlighted pages until I found the lines Matt quoted.

There is no such thing as loneliness. There is only the idea of loneliness.

I sighed and swung my legs from the edge of the U-Haul. God, what lines, and what a strange concept—that the fear of loneliness is the fear of a phantom.

In the back of the book I had printouts from the *LA Times* book blog and clippings from the *New York Times Book Review.* I flipped one open and perused the first few lines.

M. Pierce remains a mystery,
tops charts with "Harm's Way"

NOVEMBER 13, 2009

Almost two years after the appearance of national bestseller *Ten Thousand Nights, Harm's Way,* the new hardcover fiction from M. Pierce, has reached the top of the bestseller list. Like its predecessor, *Harm's Way* straddles (or obliterates) the boundary between genre fiction and literary fiction. Part thriller, part Kunderian inquiry and all page-turner, *Harm's Way* has critics going to bat . . .

I skimmed down a few lines.

Little is known about the author, who declines book signings, tours or any form of public appearance in connection with his or her fiction. Knopf's lips have been sealed since the 2007 release of *Ten Thousand Nights.* The author's agent is rumored to be at the Granite Wing Agency, though this has never been confirmed.

Perhaps, like other notable reclusive writers, including Thomas Pynchon and J. D. Salinger, M. Pierce fears the effects of publicity on his or her life and prose.

The author's decision to remain anonymous leaves fans wanting. "Official" M. Pierce fan pages have appeared . . .

I smirked, refolded the article, and tucked it away. God, leave the author alone.

I owned all four of M. Pierce's books—*Ten Thousand Nights, Harm's Way, Mine Brook,* and *The Silver Cord*—which had been published between 2007 and 2012. I didn't care if I never found out who the author was, and book jacket photos are universally depressing. I just wanted another M. Pierce novel, soon.

I studied my phone.

I'd told my sister I called and texted Matt from Perkins. I actually called twice. I texted four times. His silence gnawed at me.

Was he having misgivings about our . . . our what? Our friendship that wasn't a friendship? Our weird arrangement in which we helped one another get off?

"Fuck this," I muttered. I called him again.

The ringtone sounded twice.

"Hannah."

"Matt! Hi. Don't hang up, please. Did you hang up on my sister?"

"Yeah."

"I'm sorry. I shouldn't have let her answer. She's a little . . ." I frowned. Edgy? Abrasive?

"She's fine," Matt said. His tone was cool. "I was simply done talking."

"Oh. So is that your thing? You hang up whenever you feel 'done talking'?"

"Sure, why not." He gave an exaggerated sigh, like it was killing him to be on the phone with me.

"And hey, are you only in a good mood after you jerk off? Because it's starting to feel that way."

I heard Matt's hesitant, breathy laugh.

"You're funny, little bird."

"I don't feel very funny right now."

"God, you're too cute."

"What!" I spluttered. "Stop being crazy. I'm . . . I'm trying to—"

"Trying to figure out our situation? Give up. I don't think there are any rules for this kind of thing, or any helpful guidelines. Anyway, it doesn't matter."

There was a long pause. I held my breath. Doesn't matter? Somehow, this thing with Matt—"our situation"—*did* matter to me. I liked it. I wanted it. It made me feel a little out of control, but I liked that too.

"Doesn't matter," he repeated quietly. He cleared his throat. "So. Who's the new guy?"

"Huh? New guy?"

"Yeah, your sister said there was a new guy. Hannah's new guy."

"Uh . . . she did? I didn't hear that."

"Yeah. Well, no. She asked me if *I* was your new guy, which I'm obviously not, and which . . . obviously implies there is some . . . *new guy.*" Matt couldn't keep the feeling from his voice, and the feeling wasn't curiosity. It was simmering rage.

Realization hit me like a sack of cement.

Matt thought I'd gleefully helped him come and enjoyed our intimate chat on the phone, all the while cruising into my next relationship.

"Matt!" I snapped.

"*What?*" he snapped back.

"I would never have done those things with you if I had a new guy. God! Could you for one minute think better of me? I mean, first the picture thing, now this. I get that you don't know me, but seriously, you're projecting your assholery onto me. I'm not some backhanded psycho chick looking for a good time *on the phone* because I don't have the guts to cheat for real on my nonexistent new guy, *trust me.*"

I was gripping *Ten Thousand Nights* so hard my nails dug into the cover. Okay, so I kind of lost it right there. But he deserved it.

I listened to the silence. I checked my phone to make sure Matt wasn't "simply done talking." He was still on the line.

"Hello? Matt?"

He began to chuckle, the wry sound fanning my anger.

"Assholery?" he murmured.

"Yeah, well. Ugh. You know what I mean." I loosened my hold on the paperback. "And by the way, I know you plagiarized M. Pierce the other night. Nice try."

Matt was quiet again.

"Hey . . . I'm kidding. I mean you did quote from *Ten Thousand Nights.* But it was awesome. Pierce is seriously one of my favorite authors."

"Oh? I've only read that one book. Not sure why I bothered. It got a lot of publicity; I thought it would be better. I guess the line stuck with me. Personally I think the author is a bit of a windbag. What are you wearing?"

Matt's sudden transition from bored dismissal to my attire left me speechless.

"Clothes," he offered. "You have them on. I want to know what they look like."

"I'm outside," I said sheepishly, "sitting on the edge of the U-Haul."

"I don't care. I'm not angling for phone sex, though I wouldn't mind it. It's unusually easy to come with you, Hannah. Unusually satisfying, too."

I sighed and tilted my head against the cool metal interior of the trailer.

"Soon I'll be home. I'll have my own room, a door I can lock."

"I can't think about that now," Matt said. "Don't make plans. I'm not real."

"What?"

"You don't know me. I'm scared to have you close. Tell me what you're wearing."

"A . . . a little black dress with an empire waist. Black strapless bra, black thong."

"Another thong. Did you wear that for me? Did you know we'd talk?"

"Yes." I blushed. "And no. I wore it so I could tell you. I didn't know if we would talk. I hoped we would."

"Hannah . . ." For a split second, Matt sounded grieved. When he spoke again, his voice was level. "God, Hannah. I've been thinking about fucking you. It's like there's something wrong with me. I can't stop thinking about it. I want my body against yours, my cock inside of you. It's driving me wild. Does that frighten you?"

"No. No, I've . . . been thinking about it, too."

"Have you? Tell me."

"Yeah." I pursed my lips and swallowed. He wanted me to describe my fantasies? How totally awkward. "Um, I'm surprised

I haven't veered off the road yet, honestly. I just keep . . . daydreaming hard-core." Oof, word choice.

"Hard-core? How illuminating." Matt chuckled. "I'll tell you, then. Today when I showered, I thought about having you there. I thought about your soft body pressed against the cold tiles, my arm around your neck, your ass against my cock."

I closed my eyes.

"Go on," I whispered. My words pulled another little laugh from Matt. I found myself smiling at the sound, which was quickly becoming one of my favorite sounds.

"Greedy little bird, aren't you? I thought about your breasts pressed into the tiles. I wouldn't be gentle, Hannah. I would force your legs apart and finger you like I owned you."

A helpless moan slipped out of me. I clamped a hand over my mouth and glanced around the parking lot. I was alone. The only sounds were the wind and the occasional rumble of a truck passing on the highway.

"I'd make you moan a lot louder than that. Whether or not you were ready, I would push my dick up inside of you . . . and you would shake against me. I would slap your ass to feel you tighten up in surprise."

"God." I sighed. I had turned to jelly, slumped against the wall of the trailer. I would definitely need to change my underwear before I slept.

"I think that'll do for now," Matt said, his voice suddenly businesslike. "Believe it or not, I'm trying to be decent tonight. This morning, rather."

"Decent?" I felt myself spiraling back down to earth. God, this guy could breathe and get me wound up.

"Mm, decent. As in, trying to have an interaction with you that doesn't end with me whipping out my dick . . . even if jerking off is the only thing that puts me in a good mood."

I laughed and rolled my eyes.

"Fair enough, no more sexy talk tonight. But one night of decency won't clear your reputation, Matt. Sorry."

"Hey, I'm not usually like this. I usually play my depravity a little closer to my chest."

"Pfft, you're not *depraved.*"

"Tell that to my dick. I swear, it's like a dog lately—show it the slightest scrap of attention and it gets all excited."

I giggled, then blinked. *Did I just . . . giggle?*

"Um." I picked at the hem of my dress. "Yeah, so." No sexy talk. Great, fine, except I didn't know if Matt and I were capable of *normal talk.*

"Aha, not only is she a first-class phone sex partner, but her scintillating conversational skills will likewise leave a man breathless."

"Matt! Yeesh, I was thinking." I tucked a coil of hair behind my ear. "I wasn't sure if you wanted to go . . . or if we could talk for a little bit. Um, about decent things."

Matt stayed quiet.

I was coming to expect his silences, along with his fitful laughter and sarcasm.

"We can talk," he said finally.

And we did. Or rather, I did.

For an hour and a half I sat on the edge of the U-Haul and told Matt about Mick, my childhood in Colorado, my sister and brother, my parents, my job at the bank and shitty jobs before that, and dozens of other irrelevant facts.

Matt was an expert evader. He was a great listener, too. Every time I tried to steer the conversation toward him, he deftly turned my questions back at me. It should have been infuriating—I usually hated going on about myself—but this time it was a relief.

I needed this.

For the first time in years, someone wanted to hear about my thoughts and feelings in more than a cursory fashion.

And Matt wasn't just being polite. He laughed and asked questions; he reminded me where I was when I lost my train of thought.

By the time we were done, I had told Matt my condensed life story.

And I had gleaned a single new fact about him.

He was twenty-eight.

"We're in Billings," I told him at the end of the call.

Matt enthused about Montana briefly. He mentioned idolizing Norman Maclean and having done some hiking and climbing around Glacier—and then, as though he'd let go of two precious pearls, he shut down.

"Climbing, huh?" I ventured.

"Mm."

Mm seemed to be Matt's all-purpose noise, which could mean yes, no, let me think about it, I'm bored, I'm amused, I'm annoyed, I'm aroused—basically anything.

"That's cool. You must love Colorado, then. Are you super outdoorsy or something?"

"Mm."

"Cool . . ." I snapped up the new facts: Twenty-eight, Norman Maclean, outdoorsy.

Just what I needed to fuel my fantasies: the idea of a well-read young man with a lean, muscled climber's body. Yes, please.

"I better get to sleep," I said reluctantly. I glanced at my watch. 3:40 A.M. "Jeez, where does the time go?"

"*Optima dies,*" Matt mumbled, trailing off.

"What?"

"Latin. Never mind."

I frowned.

"Okay. Well. Yeah. Sleep. I think if we get going early and push it, we'll be in Colorado by evening. I'll reply to your post ASAP."

"No rush on that. You'll be busy when you get home."

"I know. I want to write it. I miss our story . . . a lot."

"Then I look forward to it," he said.

I heard a little electronic click and glanced at my phone. Matt was gone.

Note to self: Teach this man how to say good-bye.

Chapter 5

MATT

You're projecting your assholery onto me.

"The last pages you sent me," Pam said, leaning across the table, "are very nice. I do have some questions about the pacing. I see your main plot arc, and I want to say it must be a third of the way along. Am I right? Not to pressure you, but I want to mentally deadline this."

Pam's words pinged on the edge of my attention.

Nice. Pacing. Deadline.

Projecting your assholery onto me. How right Hannah was. Because I was cheating, I assumed she was cheating. I made a total ass of myself. I even had the nerve to get pissed about Hannah's imaginary cheating, meanwhile ignoring my own very real deceit.

This situation was getting fucked-up.

"Matthew?"

I felt a tug on my sleeve. I glanced down at Pam's perfectly manicured hand.

"Sorry. Ah, I—" I ran a hand through my hair and flashed a smile at Pam, who returned a tight-lipped, all-business smile. "I'm not sleeping well. Going nocturnal or something."

We were seated at a booth in Flight of Ideas, my favorite bookshop-cum-coffeehouse in Denver. Pam looked prim as usual, her frosted blond hair styled in stiff waves around her face. Pam was thirty-six, but she always looked closer to forty with her chalky makeup, dark lipstick, and austere skirt suits.

Pam had been my agent for seven years. I could almost say I trusted her implicitly, but I don't trust anyone implicitly.

"Sorry to hear that. Let's get back to this." She spread her fingers on her laptop. Most of the time, I appreciated Pam's work-centric drive. Today, though, I wanted nothing more than to daydream about Hannah in my air-conditioned apartment.

"I can't help you with the deadline," I said. "I don't know. It'll be done when it's done." I chewed on the end of my stirrer. "Also, Pam, help me to understand why we keep meeting out like this when I have specifically indicated my preference for phone calls, video chats, I don't know, the occasional meeting at my place?"

"It's a matter of convenience, Matthew. Unlike some present, I live on a tight schedule. You know I try very hard to comply with your requests. However, I believe they are still *requests,* yes? Or have they now become demands?"

I smirked and slouched in the booth, glancing around. That was another thing I liked about Pam; she wasn't a fawner. She gave as good as she got.

"Mm, they're still requests. I do sometimes like to emerge from my garret and see how the other half lives."

I smiled cheekily and lowered my voice.

"But Pam, don't think I don't know your game. In your desperately wicked little heart, it is your sincerest hope that one day we are spotted, eavesdropped on, whatever, and my identity comes out, and you are then free to turn me into the golden-haired, high-profile author of your dreams. I can practically see you trotting me around the globe like a dancing bear. Think of the publicity. Oh, and that would make you"—I pointed my stirrer at Pam, who was watching me with a tolerant smile—"Pamela Wing, agent to said high-profile author. Not too shabby."

"Are you done?"

"Sure," I laughed. "For now."

"Good. You should really restrict these theoretical flights of fancy to your fiction, where I can redline them on grounds of verbosity and excessive allusion."

"You know you're not my editor, right? Or are your delusions of grandeur expanding?"

Pam and I bantered like that for another half hour, after which I escaped home.

A run through the city or a ride out to the mountains might have done me good, but lately I couldn't break away from my phone and computer and a safe space in which to handle my daily hard-on for Hannah.

I took a stab at writing. The result was me slouched in my office chair and staring into space. Around dinnertime, I sent Hannah an e-mail.

Subject: Assholery
Sender: Matthew S.
Date: Sunday, June 30, 2013
Time: 7:37 PM
Hi, Hannah,
I enjoyed our conversation last night. In the future, you probably shouldn't be so lax with personal information. We Internet predators feed on such facts. For example, now that I know your superpower wish is to fly, I am ten times closer to discovering the location of your secret bunker.
And I want to project more than my assholery onto you.
(I was decent last night. All bets are off now.)
Call me when you get a chance. I'm bored.
Matt

I sent the message and roamed my apartment like a zombie.

I stared at the forty-plus Tupperwares crammed into the freezer, each labeled with a sticky note. Yes, my girlfriend had not only cooked and frozen about two months' worth of meals for me but planned the order in which I should eat them.

I picked out a frosty noodly-looking thing dated for the middle of July. I zapped it in the microwave for two minutes. Mystery dinner: beef stroganoff.

I was still poking at my food when Hannah texted.

> *9900 Sienna St. in Aurora. We have an open-door policy. Except for tonight, an old high school friend is taking me out. I'll have my phone. So excited to be home!*

I called her immediately.

"Hey!" she answered. I could hear a dog barking in the background and people talking over one another. "God, I'm s—"

"What the fuck is wrong with you?" I growled. "I cannot . . . believe you texted me your address. Are you insane?"

"Oh, don't start. I refuse your bad attitude tonight. I'm freaking stoked to be home and you are not going to do your Mr. Frosty-pants routine on my parade. Come *on.*"

"Hannah." My voice trembled with anger. "You don't even know me."

"Yes, you've pointed that out more than once. It's not for lack of trying."

"It doesn't matter. I could be anyone. You can't go around giving your address to strangers from the Internet, please. That kind of behavior is a terrible accident waiting to happen. Do you have any idea how much this troubles me?"

"I'm starting to get an idea." She yawned in my ear. Oh, that little devil.

"Fortunately for you I am not a psychopath, but I c—"

"Yes, okay, Matt. Point taken. I solemnly swear never to give my address to Internet randos in the future, et cetera et cetera. But this is my life, my life I'm *risking* or whatever. And I didn't give my address to some random weirdo, okay? I gave it to *you.* I want to meet *you.*"

I had meandered into the living room and was gazing at my sketch of Hannah. Every time she said my name, contentment spread through me.

God, Matt . . . I can feel it, how wet I am.

Compared to the eyes I remembered from Hannah's photo, the eyes in my sketch were lifeless. I could meet her. I could meet those dark, mischievous eyes.

I glanced at a framed photo on the wall—Bethany's face and mine squished side by side, both of us smiling broadly against a backdrop of Miami Beach.

Bethany. My girlfriend.

"You want to meet me," I repeated, testing the incredible weight of the words.

I had never felt such longing in my life. My whole body responded to the idea of Hannah near me. My shower fantasy flickered through my mind.

"Yes," Hannah said, "I want to meet you. The thought makes me nervous as hell, but I want to meet you."

"But not tonight."

"Um, unfortunately no. Not unless you want to meet my friend from high school."

"A guy friend?"

"Yes, Matt. A guy friend. A friend who is a guy. Don't get any ideas."

"I don't have any ideas," I muttered, "but he might. Where is he taking you?"

"I don't know. Some bar. I'm dirt-poor so he's buying."

"Great." My mood was souring fast. Hannah was going to a bar with some skeezy old high school friend. Given what she'd told me about her adolescence, I knew her high school pals weren't exactly young scholars. Mostly gamers and dropouts.

"Try to sound a little happier for me."

I made some kind of noise. Hannah giggled. Fuck, that sound. Why did she have to be going out with some dickbag tonight? Why couldn't she pant and moan on the phone with me until I came? I needed to come—with her. God, I needed it.

"You're cute, you know," she said.

"I prefer handsome. And yes, I know."

"Ha! Such a snob, too."

Someone in the background was repeatedly calling Hannah's name.

"I also know that. You're being summoned."

"Ugh, I know. Apparently the way to solicit attention in this house is to go full five-year-old. Anyway. Um." Hannah moved away from the background noise and lowered her voice. "I'll . . . I'll text you when I get home, okay? We can chat if you're still up."

"Mm."

"And I'm . . . wearing a baby blue satin thong," she whispered.

I exhaled and closed my eyes. My world slowed.

"Good," I said and hung up.

Chapter 6

HANNAH

After my brief conversation with Matt, the last place I wanted to be was at Lot 49 with Evan Rexer.

Don't get me wrong, the Lot was a hip little bar and I loved the Pynchon reference, but after Evan got one beer in him, it became apparent that Matt had been right—Evan had *ideas.*

He kept draping his freckled arm around my shoulders, squeezing my side, and "inadvertently" brushing against my breasts. Gross. I wouldn't have enjoyed it even if Evan were good-looking, which he wasn't. He was overweight and had a scruffy beard that reminded me all too much of Mick's body hair.

I shot Matt a text.

I grudgingly admit defeat . . . this time. Idiot friend is creeping on me.

Matt replied within seconds.

Are you all right?

I quickly answered.

Fine, just annoyed. This outing can't end soon enough. I didn't mean to worry you.

Matt's response came a few minutes later. Reading it, I could practically hear his sarcastic voice, laced with that strange mixture of anger and amusement.

Well, you did worry me. You'll have to make it up to me. Text me if you need a ride, though I make no promises to get you home.

I shivered and slipped my phone back into my purse. Powerful knowledge, that I could call my sexy stranger and he'd whisk me away from this crowded bar and pimply horndog.

Evan pinched my side.

I twisted away.

"That kind of hurts," I grumbled. I doubt he heard me over the loud, distorted music coming from the band.

I sighed and sipped on my Long Island. The drink was hitting me hard, probably because I needed dinner. When Chrissy and I got home, after hugging my parents and brother and dog, I shuffled around the house feeling depressed.

Moving home at twenty-seven is less than triumphant. I didn't even have enough money saved to get my own place.

My mother had promised to delegate some of her transcription work and pay me under the table until I got on my feet. While I appreciated the offer and would definitely appreciate the funds, it was a blow to my pride.

Was this really my life? How could I graduate summa cum laude, attend grad school on a full scholarship, and end up living with my parents and typing medical records?

I recognized the song floating above the voices in the bar. The band was doing a halfway decent cover of "Jigsaw Falling into Place."

"Perfect!" I laughed. I finished my drink with a big swallow.

"What? You want another?" Evan shouted.

"No! I'm going to dance!"

"Oh." His face fell. I almost felt sorry for him. I knew Evan would never join me on the dance floor. This was a guy who played Dungeons & Dragons and dressed up for opening night of the new *Star Trek* movie. "I'll finish my beer!" he shouted.

I slipped off my stool and melted into the small crowd in front of the stage.

The band guys and a few dancers eyed me hungrily, but I closed my eyes and tuned them out. God, I loved this song.

The tempo whirled higher and I began to dance. I lifted my arms into the air. I was wearing a pale tiered ruffle skirt and it rose off my thighs when I spun.

I let my mind drift back to Matt. I missed him. I'm not sure how I could miss someone I'd never met and had chatted with only a few hours ago, but I did.

I wanted him to be here.

I wanted him to be dancing with me, his hands on my body and his voice in my ear.

I missed our story, too. Writing with Matt had become the high point of my days, and despite our campy storyline, it challenged me. My prose was clunky compared to his. I got hung up on diction and syntax; I agonized over every word.

Matt's prose flowed effortlessly. He grabbed words without fear, however colloquial or antique, and sacrificed every rule of grammar in the pursuit of expression. And damn, did that boy know his grammar.

Once, he scathingly brought my attention to my "chronic misuse of apostrophes."

"How about your chronic use of sentence fragments?" I shot back.

"It's deliberate," he replied, "versus what you're doing—making clumsy mistakes. I'm sure you've seen Picasso's surreal stuff, but have you seen *Science and Charity*? Art is not an assembly of accidents. You have to master the rules before you break them."

I smiled and swayed to a stop as the song ended.

We left the bar around 10:30 P.M., mostly because I lied about having cramps.

Evan was ranting about an online game. He tried to take my hand as we crossed the street. I pulled away.

"Seriously, Evan," I huffed.

I was about to unleash on Evan when something caught my eye.

A few yards down, almost directly across from the Lot, a streetlamp illuminated the figure of a tall man. He stood at a slant and held a leash. At the end of the leash was a small lump with tall ears.

Evan snickered. "Oh, my God," he said, his beery breath too close to my face. "Is that dude walking a rabbit? What a faggot."

I drifted down the sidewalk toward the man. He ignored me, even as I stepped onto the grass. Even as I ogled him shamelessly.

His hair was dirty blond, carelessly mussed, and he wore a fitted gray T-shirt and jeans. Damn, this guy knew how to wear jeans. The light-wash denim clung to his lean thighs and tight ass, and I could see that the low waistline barely covered his groin. His handsome face was clean shaven. I stared up his body from his flip-flops to his hair.

Fuck. I hope Matt looks this delicious.

But this was definitely not Matt. No way. I may not have known Matt well, but I could say with near certainty that he would never, ever own a pet rabbit, much less take it for walks in the middle of the night on some kind of . . .

"Tiny harness," I blurted. I stared down at the bunny.

So. Cute.

Never mind the sexy guy and the ridiculous charm of the scene. The animal itself was adorable. It was the size of a football. Its eyes were big and round and black and its coat was patterned black and white like a tux.

The man stared off. Jeez, asshole wouldn't even look at me.

The rabbit hopped toward his feet.

"Sorry, I . . . am I scaring him? Him, he?"

The man's jaw tightened. He gave an almost imperceptible nod. He was staring at a splash of street art like his life depended on it.

Evan hovered on the sidewalk a few feet away, obviously intimidated by the young god and his rabbit.

"He is sooo precious," I crooned, crouching to get closer to the bunny. "Can I pet him? Will he let me?"

The man didn't move. What was his deal? Maybe he was stoned out of his gourd.

I reached toward the rabbit and it flattened itself to the ground.

Finally, the man crouched and collected the frightened animal. He gathered it against his stomach and began to stroke its head and ears. I smiled. When I didn't move, the man's dark eyes flickered over me. He smirked.

He reached for my wrist. I let him guide my hand along the rabbit's body.

"So soft," I whispered. I stared at the man's long fingers covering mine. The alcohol must have been working on me; desire shivered up the skin of my arm. I wanted to lean in and smell his clean scent. I wanted to press my hands to his chest.

I don't know how long I stayed crouched there, the man's hand over mine and the bunny's warm body beneath my palm. The stroking motion relaxed me totally.

The young god, on the other hand, grew more and more tense until I thought he would explode. Only his hand on mine was gentle. I could see the sinewy muscle clenching on his forearm and cording along his beautiful neck.

He frightened me.

I wanted him.

Guiltily, I remembered Matt waiting for me to get home and call. I pulled back just as the man stood. We stumbled apart.

The man hurried up the street, disappearing around the corner. I watched his hot ass go. Even his stride was sexy, prowling and sweeping. Damn.

Dazed, I returned to Evan.

"How was the rabbit whisperer?" he said, throwing a fleshy arm around my waist.

"Evan, eat a dick."

I shoved Evan back and stalked away, fishing for my phone in my purse and halfheartedly trying to hail a cab. I knew I could call Matt, but suddenly the city felt huge and anonymous, and the thought of meeting that demanding stranger scared me.

Besides, I was still reeling from whatever had just passed between me and the guy outside the bar. Why did that silent encounter feel so charged? Why wouldn't he speak? Why wouldn't he look at me?

A cab pulled up beside me and I climbed in gratefully.

When I got home, I saw Dad had already set up my bed in a room in the basement.

So I was going to be a genuine basement dweller now. I guess I couldn't complain. The basement was finished and would be cool all summer, not to mention private.

The room itself was bleak and impersonal at the moment.

Tomorrow I would start unpacking my books. Books can fix any room.

I flopped onto the bed and called Matt.

No answer.

I tried again after twenty minutes.

No answer.

I miss you, Matt.

I sent the text and stared at the ceiling. *There is no such thing as loneliness,* I told myself. A lump formed in my throat.

If there was no such thing as loneliness, what was I feeling?

Chapter 7

MATT

Come over tonight. I'll pick you up. I need you.

I looked at the text I had written.

I deleted it.

I wrote it again and deleted it again.

I couldn't think.

I ranged through my apartment, stripping off clothes, shoving down my jeans and boxers to free my erection.

"Hannah, God, Hannah," I whispered. I filled the rooms of my apartment with feverish pleas. I gripped my hair and stood aching in the dark kitchen. I braced my arms against the doorframe of my bedroom.

I already knew I was going to see her.

I was going to see her tonight.

And even as I paced and agonized, some part of me remained paralyzed on the lawn across from Lot 49. God only knows what I was doing out there in the dead of night with my rabbit. I thought I had hours to kill before Hannah called.

I had strapped on Laurence's little harness and leash, carried him down to the nearest green space, plopped him into the grass for a bit of exercise—and then I saw her.

She was dancing.

Through the glass front of Lot 49, she appeared and disappeared in the crowd on the dance floor. Her hands were in the air. Her unmistakable brown curls fanned across her back and a small skirt spun around her hips. Her beautiful face was tilted up, eyes closed. Was that how she looked when she came for me?

Hannah.

I couldn't make myself walk away.

I couldn't make myself look away.

I drank in the sight of her strong, full thighs, her tiny waist, and her round ass.

What were the odds she would end up in this bar, now, steps from my apartment?

I lost sight of her in the dim building. Hannah in her satin thong, just steps away from me. I needed to feel that garment between my fingers. I needed to touch her intimately. The thought had me shivering in the summer night.

I lapsed into a fantasy, and the next thing I knew, Hannah's kind, familiar voice was addressing me.

I didn't dare speak; she would know my voice.

I hardly dared to look at her. My eyes would scream who I was.

We were so close. Her knees bumped mine. I felt the pulse in her wrist. I saw her chest rising and falling under a loose beaded tank top.

Everything else disappeared.

The world was me and Hannah and the electricity between us. I saw when she felt it, her brow knitting in confusion. It took all of my strength not to speak her name—and not to pull her against me as she leaned in.

God, what was happening to me?

I was wound tight enough to punch a hole through the drywall. Instead, I smoked a cigarette and studied the picture of myself and Bethany in Miami Beach. I made myself stare at it. I made no excuses.

After all, I could tell myself whatever I wanted about Bethany—that she was suffocating, that she was like a second mother, that she harassed me about my writing more than ten Pams put together—and it would never make what I was going to do okay.

I had wanted Bethany once. I wanted her enough to move her into my apartment and live with her for two years. But I wanted Hannah more, and there was nothing else to say.

I showered slowly, suffering through a hellacious case of blue balls. I didn't put on any cologne. I brushed my teeth, toweled my hair semidry, and took my time dressing, choosing dark jeans and a black V-neck T-shirt.

At every opportunity, I met my eyes in the mirror.

You are doing this. You want her. You're taking her.

I paced to calm my nerves.

More than anything, I wanted to be that calm, confident man Hannah had met on the phone, back when this was a silly game. Yeah, back one day ago. Fuck. How did things escalate so quickly?

By the time I drove out of the parking garage, an hour and a half had passed. Hannah had called twice and texted once.

I miss you, Matt.

I couldn't find a damn song I wanted to listen to. I drove in silence, killing another half hour on Denver's familiar streets. Maybe I was giving myself time to change my mind. If I did this, I didn't want it to be a mistake.

I didn't want Hannah to be a mistake.

At half past midnight, I put Hannah's address in my GPS and drove out of the city. I was sorry to leave it behind. Denver's chill vibe might have been all that was keeping my emotions from spinning out of control.

Desire.

Anger.

Confusion.

Fear.

I found the house easily. The street was dark. From what I could make out, the house was old and sprawling, set far back on a big lawn and surrounded by trees. I killed the ignition.

God, now I felt super creepy, parked uninvited outside Hannah's house.

But she wanted to meet me. And she missed me. And she did say they have an open-door policy, which hopefully didn't expire at midnight.

Only then did it occur to me that Hannah might be asleep. The house was dark. So were most of the other homes on the street. Plus, she'd had a long day.

I thought about Hannah in her bed. Hannah stretched out on her back, sleeping in a cami and thong, her beautiful breasts heaving slowly and her legs crooked apart. Or Hannah on her stomach, her heart-shaped rump in the air.

I could climb over her, wake her with a kiss. Brush my body along hers.

I felt a throb between my legs. I glared down at my cock.

"Hold your fucking horses," I muttered.

God, fuck . . . was this seriously my life? Stalking a girl I'd met online, parked outside her house at midnight, speaking to my dick?

I flipped down the visor and checked myself in the mirror. I laughed at what I saw.

Though I was freaking out on the inside, on the outside I looked typical: bored, annoyed, and severely impatient. And one hundred percent asshole.

I smirked at my reflection.

"Right," I said. "Got it."

I pulled out my phone and sent Hannah a text.

Chapter 8

HANNAH

I couldn't sleep.

I was tired and wired.

How does that work?

I got up at the butt crack of dawn, took out Wyoming in a marathon drive, and capped the night with a super-strong Long Island. I should have been asleep before my head hit the pillow.

But Matt wasn't answering my calls. And then there was the weird encounter outside the bar. Call me crazy, but as I tossed and turned in bed I began to feel like I had broken my Matt spell with that intense jolt of attraction.

Like I said, call me crazy.

Still, it kept bothering me. There were plenty of good-looking guys at the bar, more than one of them eyeing me, and I wanted nothing to do with them. I wanted to dance and think about Matt. Matt watching me, Matt touching me, Matt whispering in my ear.

Fuck.

No one ever made me shiver with desire the way Matt did with his voice alone—until a stranger outside a bar made me feel the exact same thing.

So it wasn't something special about Matt. It wasn't Matt and I together, insane chemistry. It was just me being horny. God, I couldn't stand to cheapen that feeling . . . that feeling I got when Matt's voice faltered with need . . .

I have to. I can't help it. Hannah . . . God, do it. Come with me.

I sat up in bed and checked my e-mail. Nothing. I opened Safari. What was that weird phrase Matt said on the phone? *Optima* . . . something. He said it was Latin.

I Googled "optima latin phrases."

There it was: *Optima dies. Optima dies, prima fugit.* The best days are the first to flee.

My eyes began to sting.

Why would he say that? Was it some kind of hint? Had he intended all along to drop me like a bad habit when I reached Colorado? The best days . . . the first to flee.

Matt said he was scared to have me close. He told me not to make plans. Suddenly, I knew it was over. Whatever *it* was—our silly flirtation—was over.

I looked at the Web page again. The quote was from Virgil, popularized as an epigraph in *My Ántonia* by Willa Cather.

Huh. Cather. Why did that name sound familiar?

After racking my brain for a few minutes, I Googled "M. Pierce epigraphs."

I knew it. The epigraph to *The Silver Cord* was a Willa Cather quote: "Whatever we had missed, we possessed together the precious, the incommunicable past." And it was from the novel *My Ántonia*. What a weird coincidence.

Did Matt read Virgil or Willa Cather? Or both? He obviously read quite a bit. And given our collaborative story, I knew he liked to write.

I jumped when my phone chimed.

Who the fuck was texting me at 1 A.M.?

That was my first thought.

My second thought: Please let it be Matt.

Come outside.

I swallowed thickly. I couldn't move. Come outside . . . ? Oh . . . my God.

Matt was outside. Either Matt was outside, or he was weirdly ordering me to have an orgasm on the lawn. Fuck. Obviously Matt was outside. *Oh fuck oh fuck oh fuck.* Brain, work!

I scrambled out of bed and stumbled toward the door. I was wearing Aerie boxers that barely covered my ass and a lacy white cami with a shelf bra. Oh, and the blue satin thong, because on some pathetic level I still wanted to be wearing it when Matt called.

I grabbed one of Dad's old coats and threw it on before going out by the sliding door to the patio.

Fuck fuck fuck. Matt had come over. He was here. I was about to see him. If he was ugly as sin, what would I say? *Um . . . hi . . . yeah . . . I need to sleep.*

Awesome plan. And way to have the shallowest thoughts ever, Hannah.

I was on autopilot as I padded around the side of the house. I wanted to see Matt before he saw me. That turned out to be easy, because Matt had his back to the house and his hands braced against a black Lexus. Holy fuck.

This was textbook sketchy. Black car, strange man, middle of the night. Maybe I was about to be abducted. Maybe I was about to become one of those news stories that make people say, "I feel bad for the girl, but she was asking for trouble."

Was I asking for trouble?

Tonight, trouble was a beautiful body standing next to a beautiful car right outside my house, waiting for me.

I didn't feel a single twinge of fear.

I felt raw elation.

I hadn't broken the spell. Screw the hottie outside the bar. Matt was here and I hadn't even seen his face and I was already wet.

I jogged across the lawn, unable to compel my feet to walk. My breasts bounced as I moved. The joys of being a double D.

"Matt!" I called.

He turned. I'm a little blind without my glasses, but I knew immediately what I was looking at. The rabbit guy. The young god. The dude outside the bar.

My steps faltered.

I couldn't process this revelation.

Had he . . . followed me home?

He came to me, pushing away from the car, and his dark eyes were hungry. He closed the space between us in a stride.

The rabbit guy. Was Matt. Was the young god. Was the man I wanted.

"Yes," he said as if reading my thoughts. "That was me outside the bar. It was an accident. A coincidence."

Somehow, improbably, Matt's real voice was sexier than his phone voice.

He pulled me into his arms, shoving the coat from my shoulders. It fell to the grass. Oh, God. Oh, God, this was happening.

"Matt," I whispered.

He crushed my body to his. I was hyperaware of my hard nipples pressing into his chest. He stood a head taller than me and nestled his chin into my hair easily. I wrapped my arms around his waist. He was all lean muscle, heat, and a racing heart. I thought I might faint if I didn't cling to him.

"Hannah," he growled. He explored my body roughly, an arm keeping me pinned to him. I couldn't have escaped if I wanted to. That realization—and Matt's force and strength—made me tremble with excitement.

He wasn't shy.

I wouldn't be gentle, he'd told me on the phone.

He wasn't lying.

He raked his hand over my side and down to my ass, which he

squeezed and rubbed. I could hear his breathing grow ragged as he touched me. Abruptly, he yanked my tiny boxers into my crack—worst wedgie *ever*—and slapped my bare ass.

"Uhn!" I gasped. I rocked into him. Holy shit, was he already hard?

Move, hands, move! I wanted to meet his hunger; I wanted to tease him with my fingertips, to have the courage to feel his erection.

Instead, I was mewling like a kitten and clinging to him.

"My f-family," I bleated, my mouth leaving a wet spot on his chest. His T-shirt was so soft, his chest so firm. But God, if someone in the house happened to look out a front window, they were going to get an eyeful of my mostly bare ass (and a stranger fondling me).

"Oh, yeah?" Matt whispered into my ear. There it was—the cruel, sweet voice. The devil would have a voice like Matt's. My legs turned to jelly. "You think they might be watching? How about your neighbors?"

As he spoke, Matt tugged my little boxers tighter and tighter into the cleft of my bottom. He wanted me to be uncomfortable. And I was enjoying it.

"God, I hope they are," he said. "You deserve it, Hannah. You deserve to be humiliated for driving me so insane. Do you have any idea?" Again, the flat of his hand came down hard against my backside.

"Oh!" I lurched against him and he groaned.

"Fuck," he rasped. "Show me everything. God, show me."

Without waiting for my participation—which was just as well, since I couldn't seem to move—Matt yanked my cami up until my heavy breasts popped out of the shelf bra. I felt my skin glowing. I knew I was a violent shade of red.

Matt twisted me around, trapping my back to his chest and my ass to his groin.

Yes, he was definitely rock hard in his jeans. I felt my ass gripping the shape of him.

I wriggled as he began to grope my breasts, and he moaned softly.

"Now anyone can see," he whispered, his breath fanning over my ear. "Anyone in any of these houses. What would they say?" He chuckled. " 'Look at that slut,' they'd say, 'letting that man do those things to her right outside.' "

I moaned. Feebly, I lifted my arms to try to cover my breasts. Matt brushed my hands away. He cupped my breast and pinched my nipple, twisting it between his fingers. I gasped. My head rolled back onto his shoulder; my arms fell slack at my sides.

"That's it, baby, give in to it. You like it. I know you do."

He rubbed his hands over my breasts, his palm and fingers grazing my nipples. I twitched each time he touched the sensitive buds.

He was right, fuck, he was right. The thought that any one of my neighbors could be watching Matt manhandle me thrilled me darkly.

I licked my lips. My mouth felt like it had been stuffed with sawdust. I had to do something, at least let him know what I was thinking.

"I do," I whispered. The words came hoarsely from my throat. "I like it, I . . . please, Matt . . . please."

Matt relented suddenly. His iron arm loosened and his possessive touch turned gentle, caressing my belly. He leaned down and kissed the corner of my mouth.

A crackle of pure need shook me at the touch of his mouth. My tongue slipped out and flickered over his lips. God, give me more . . .

"I know," he said. "I know what you want, and I don't want to share you with the neighborhood."

Could have fooled me. The comeback died on my lips.

"Another time I'll make you ask. I'll make you say it and beg for it. But Hannah . . ." His voice faltered. Fuck, I loved that. "I need this, too."

Matt reached past me smoothly and opened the back door of his car.

"In you go, little bird. Get on your hands and knees. I'm going to take you from behind."

I swallowed. Why were those frank words so hot?

I didn't hesitate—but I could have. I could have turned and walked back to the house. Matt wasn't pushing me. He wasn't touching me at all.

Despite his strength and insistence, he was leaving this decision entirely up to me.

I brushed past him and climbed into the cool leather interior, struggling to master my shaking. Matt was right behind me. I could practically feel his eyes on my ass.

The car smelled brand-new and was ridiculously spacious. Matt pulled the door closed behind us. I knelt over the large center console, knees on one side, hands on the other, and glanced sheepishly over my shoulder. My mouth fell open.

Matt was shoving down his jeans enough to free his cock. I strained to see as my eyes adjusted to the darkness. He got it out and I must have made some noise, because his eyes snapped up to mine. He smirked at me.

"Like what you see?" he murmured.

My eyes strayed helplessly back to his cock. Yes . . . please. I could only nod as I watched Matt stroke himself, his hand traveling lazily up and down that thick, intimidatingly long organ. His burning gaze was glued to my expression.

"Stare all you want," he said softly. "I'm hard for you. I saw you dancing, Hannah. At the bar. When will you dance for me? When will you put on a show for me?"

I hung my head and exhaled. My long curls spilled over the seat.

"I want you," I breathed.

He slid my tiny shorts down my ass and left them around my thighs. I heard him inhale sharply. Of course, I was still wearing the thong.

"Oh, you're bad, you're wicked." He groaned, spreading my cheeks and massaging my ass. "God, you're perfect. Look at you."

I parted my knees farther and was satisfied to hear the gesture drag another groan out of Matt. He was crumbling.

He pressed a finger to my sex, digging the satin thong into it and making me roll my hips back helplessly.

"Fuck, Hannah, fuck."

Note to self: Wear thong, render Matt speechless.

He began fumbling for something in his pocket. A condom, I realized.

"No, I—" I stammered. "I have an IUD, I . . ."

I wanted it skin to skin. I wanted Matt to give it to me, now, hard. I wanted to be able to say these things, but all I could do was struggle not to drool.

Matt's eyes flickered to mine. In one motion, he pulled down my thong and climbed over me. My only warning that he was about to enter me came when I felt his plump head against my lips, his hand hastily positioning it.

"Ah, God!" I cried out as he slammed into me, burying himself to the hilt. I was so tight around him, or he was so big, or both—I felt like he might split me apart.

Matt gave a jagged moan as he entered me.

"Hannah! Ah, fuck, Hannah."

My name fell from his lips endlessly, mixed with strings of expletives. He planted a hand against the seat and held one of my breasts as he fucked me. Every time he slid into me, his fingers squeezed at my breast.

He talked dirty the whole time. Each stroke of his cock drove me higher. He told me I was wet and tight for him. He told me it almost hurt. He told me I needed a good long fucking and that I was his—his slut, his baby—that I made him so hard, that he was going to fuck me again and again and again.

I wanted to meet Matt's thrusts, but our close quarters and the pressure of his hips kept me jammed against the console. My clit pressed into the blunt edge of it.

I started to writhe—back onto Matt's cock, down against the console.

"Oh, God, Matt, I . . ."

Later there would be time to feel mortified about humping a piece of Matt's one-hundred-thousand-dollar car.

At the moment, Matt wasn't in much better shape.

"I need to come," he moaned. "Baby, I need to come."

"Do it," I panted. His simple admission sent me over the edge. My body squeezed and soaked his sex. He shuddered against me, crawling close to come deep inside.

Reality floated away.

Sweat dripped from my chin to the seat.

When the pleasure released me, I sagged against the console and lay there gathering my breath. Matt's strong hands dragged me onto his lap.

His arms enfolded me. I nuzzled into him, heedless of my tangled clothes.

"Little bird." He kissed the top of my head. "My little bird."

My motor skills had finally returned, though my powers of speech were still at large. I brushed my fingers over his chest and kissed his neck. I breathed in the clean scent of him.

Little bird, he called me. *His* little bird. And somehow, it made me feel like the most precious thing in the world.

Chapter 9

MATT

Hannah tugged at her shorts as we waited for the AC to clear the fogged windows.

My bravado aside, I hoped to hell that none of Hannah's neighbors saw our performance. We could be hauled off for indecent exposure. How awkward. And more: The thought of another man actually seeing Hannah's body made my blood boil.

I don't share well.

I just loved humiliating Hannah. I loved the way she squirmed when I exposed her.

"I hate to tell you this," I said, glancing over as she picked at her boxers, "but no possible arrangement of those shorts will bring them into the realm of modesty. Give up."

I reached over and pushed the tiny shorts up her thighs. My hand drifted between her legs. I could feel how swollen her pussy was in the wake of our exercise.

Hannah parted her legs as I touched her. Fuck. I could go again, right now. And again, and again, and again. Anything to get this fever out of my body.

"I thought that fucking you would clear my head a little," I admitted. I stared through the windshield as I rubbed Hannah through her shorts. "No such luck. Also, will you be communicating with me anytime soon? I'm aware of my capacity to leave women speechless, but this is somewhat extreme."

I grinned over at Hannah. She was staring down at my hand. Tentatively, she began to run her fingertips up and down my forearm. I clenched my teeth.

She had no idea what her touch did to me.

"It . . . it's hard." She sighed. *No kidding, love.* "Hard to speak with you . . . doing this."

"Sorry." I withdrew my hand, planting it firmly on the wheel. "There."

Out of the corner of my eye, I could see Hannah watching me.

"Okay." She laughed breathlessly. "Okay, maybe it's hard to speak near you, period."

"Try. I can't read your mind."

"Okay. Um." She poked the Enform display in the dash. "Fancy. I guess you can fly to the moon in this car, huh?"

"Not quite." I chuckled. "But you can get a massage, adjust the temperature of every seat, order movie tickets or make dinner reservations, get directions, and"—I opened Pandora and "10 Mile Stereo" by Beach House filled the car—"listen to music, of course."

"I like it." Hannah hunkered down in her seat and smiled, which made me smile. "A boy and his toys."

"Yup. I almost brought the LFA tonight, it's my baby. Not enough room, though."

Hannah giggled. "Why, Matt, what ever do you mean, not enough room?"

I smirked and shook my head. Sure, I was getting a little overexcited about my cars, but the small talk was bringing Hannah back to earth.

"Oh, by the way. Matt, seriously, a *rabbit*? Please tell me that sweet creature is more than your late-night chick magnet."

"He serves many functions."

I revved the engine and ran a hand through my hair. I wanted to fuck Hannah or drive. Or both. I couldn't sit here burning up in her atmosphere.

"You want to go for a drive?" I said. "I know you must be tired, but . . ."

"Could we? Yeah, let—" Hannah glanced out the window. I saw what she saw: the world still sleeping, pretty lawns and dark houses, and her borrowed coat crumpled in the grass. Our night. "Let's go," she said.

I pulled away from the curb and drove east, leaving the lights of the city farther behind. The smooth speed of the car relaxed me. Fuck, I had been so tense until then—even after I came. I was holding back. I wanted everything more: to pinch Hannah harder, squeeze her harder, spank her harder, fuck her harder—but I didn't want to scare her off.

"His name is Laurence," I said. "I named him after Laurence Sterne. Geniuses, both of them. Anyway, he's a dapper guy, very intellectual. And no, he's not my female bait. Clearly I need no assistance luring females into the night."

I flashed a grin at Hannah, who laughed and rolled her eyes.

I needed to see her in the daylight. I needed to be naked with her.

"I got him when I first moved out here. I was lonely, I don't know. Someone said they're quiet, clean pets. And that's the story of Laurence." I turned up the music. "Billie Holiday" by Warpaint was playing. Perfect: mellow music, the night stretching ahead of me, and Hannah in my car. I let myself really smile. "Surprised you don't own a rabbit, Hannah."

She caught my double entendre; I could tell by the way she laughed.

"I wish. I only had two toys, and . . . I don't know. Too many memories attached to them. Besides, one was half broken. I tossed them before the move."

"That's a pity. But now you have me."

"Yeah . . ." Hannah's voice was soft.

Now you have me. Fuck, I hadn't meant to say that.

We drove through the prairie for two hours, talking and listening to music and sometimes sitting in silence. We spoke about nothing important. It was nice not to have to dodge questions.

Every half hour, I asked if Hannah was tired. No, she insisted, no way, and she smiled at me in a way that made me ache.

We stopped by a walking trail that ran out through the scruffy grass.

"Let's go," Hannah said. "The stars will be crazy."

I got a blanket from the trunk and we walked down the trail, Hannah's eyes on the sky, my eyes on Hannah. She was beautiful.

After a while, she reached for my hand.

I found a soft spot off the trail—no easy task in the Colorado prairie—and spread out the blanket. Hannah sprawled across it. She grinned up at me.

"Hog." I chuckled.

"There's space," she said, "on top of me."

While I gazed down at her, Hannah wriggled out of her shorts and thong and tugged her cami up enough to bare her breasts to the night air. I was drunk looking at her. She parted her legs and held my gaze.

"Beautiful man. I wish you could see yourself. You look lost."

"I feel lost," I whispered.

Our pace was more sedate the second time. Hannah grasped my hair and guided my face to her breasts. I kissed them, sucked them, licked and bit them. She moaned as I fingered her. When I nuzzled my mouth into her pussy, she began to whimper.

"Touch your breasts," I ordered softly. I glanced up her body to see her hands move obediently to her breasts. I licked my lips. She smelled musky. She tasted fiery and sweet. I went back to work as Hannah kneaded her breasts and issued wild, indecent noises into the night.

Soon I was too hard to think. I fumbled with my jeans and freed my cock. As I crouched over Hannah's sex, three fingers inside of her and my lips, tongue, and teeth toying with her clit, I pumped my shaft.

She came moments before I did. She was still rigid with ecstasy when I climbed over her and milked my cum onto her sex.

"Perfect," I whispered.

Hannah reached for me.

I rolled her panting body onto mine and we laughed and held one another in the dark.

The sun was out when I pulled up to Hannah's house. It was near 6:00 A.M.

Hannah and I sat in the car trying to say good-bye. A black cloud settled over me at the thought of my empty apartment and a day apart from her.

When could I see her again? Would it be weird to ask?

"Well, it was nice to finally meet you," Hannah said, laughing halfheartedly.

I frowned at my phone. When all else fails, stare mopily at technology.

"Mm."

"Oh, okay." She nudged my shoulder. "What's up?"

"Nothing."

"Matt. I have no job and no obligations besides maybe driving my sister to work and walking the dog. We can hang out again, like, as soon as I wake up."

I glanced at her sharply. Was my neediness that transparent?

"Fine," I said. "Good. I'll call."

"After you get out of work?" she hedged.

Damn, *work.* Obviously Hannah was laboring under the impression that I had a day job. I had no desire to lie to Hannah more than I already was, but I definitely didn't need her to know about my career as a writer and my huge inheritance to boot.

I didn't want Hannah to see dollar signs when she looked at me.

I didn't want Hannah to see M. Pierce when she looked at me.

I wanted Hannah to see *me,* whoever I really was.

"Yeah," I said carefully. "I'll call you after work."

She beamed and leaned in to kiss my cheek. I turned and caught her face between my hands, bringing our lips together.

Despite last night and the best sex of my life, Hannah and I hadn't truly kissed yet.

She inhaled sharply and then melted against me. I moaned into her mouth. Her warm arms wound around my neck.

Finally, we drew apart and Hannah searched my eyes.

"No way," she mumbled. "Your eyes are green."

"Mm. My name is Matthew Sky. Matthew Robert Sky Jr."

Introductions, first kisses, even a good look at one another—Hannah and I had steamrolled over all of it in our frenzy.

"Sky," she repeated. Her dark eyes glittered. "Matthew Robert Sky Jr. I like it."

"That's convenient." I smirked. "Oh, and . . . it was nice to meet you, too, Hannah. More than nice." I trailed my hand down her chest. I felt her heart rate accelerating. I knew I needed to maintain the illusion that I had a job to get to, but at the moment I was more interested in where Hannah and I could have a morning quickie.

I looked toward the house just in time to see someone flouncing across the lawn.

"What the—"

"Oh, God," Hannah groaned. She stumbled out of the car and tried to intercept the girl. It must have been Hannah's sister. Same dark hair, same pretty eyes and expressive mouth, but where Hannah had soft curves and flawless skin, this girl had tight muscle and tattoos. Oh, and one too many piercings.

The girl blew by Hannah and thrust her head in the open passenger-side window.

"Hey! Oh wow. *Wow.* Very nice . . ."

I glared ahead. I couldn't tell if she meant me or my car or both.

"Hi," I muttered.

"Ha! You must be Mr. Frostypants."

"And you must be the stripper."

"Damn straight. I'm Christine. Chrissy, if you like." She slapped the side of my car. "I'm a Dyno Girl. You know, the Dynamite Club. Ever been? It's downtown Boulder. Oh, my God, you and Hannah should *so* come sometime."

I glanced at Hannah, who was hovering behind her sister and wringing her hands.

"Did you hear that, Hannah? Apparently we should come."

Hannah blanched, then blushed furiously. Adorable. She glared at me and began to tug on Chrissy's hand.

"Let's go," she hissed.

"I'm serious!" Chrissy insisted.

"I can tell," I said, grinning helplessly, "but I think the last thing your sister and I want to see is you shaking your tits, no offense, hon."

"Oh, my God, not when *I'm* working, you doofus. Seriously, though, couples have a lot of fun. Think about it!"

"Okay, going now, bye!" Hannah waved frantically at me and hauled her sister back toward the house.

I waved and then sat motionless behind the wheel.

What the hell . . .

The night had been surreal, but Hannah's crazy sister beat all. I was laughing as I pulled away from the curb. In a way, I was grateful for Chrissy's interruption. I didn't know if anything else could have pulled me from Hannah.

When I got home, I refreshed Laurence's water and went straight to my desk.

Sleep could wait.

My latest project was open on the computer screen—a pseudo-dystopian novel titled *The Surrogate.* Until Hannah, the writing was going really well. Even though I had never written science fiction (in fact I hated the genre until this story got hold of me), I knew *The Surrogate* could turn out to be my most important work.

But the novel could wait.

I minimized Word, opened Firefox, and navigated to lelo.com.

I had some shopping to do.

Chapter 10

HANNAH

I frowned at the list I was supposed to be preparing for my mother.

Jeez, she hadn't been kidding about delegating some of her work, but did I have any say in *when* I started? Evidently not, because I could have picked a better day.

I'd slept in until 2 P.M. and woke up horny. I remembered dream fragments—Matt's strong arms pinning me to him, the urgent press of his head to my slit—and for a panicked moment I thought I might have dreamed the whole night.

But I hadn't. I felt the ache in my back and limbs thanks to sex in Matt's car and sex in a lumpy field. Plus, when I staggered into the main area of the basement, Chrissy immediately assaulted me.

"Morning, sunshine!" Chrissy and Jay were playing the PS3. She tossed her controller. "Are you going to tell me if you banged that babe yet? Because if he's just a friend, I would *reallllly* like his number."

I glared at her. The thought of Matt with my sister—the thought of Matt with anyone else, actually—made my hands tighten into fists. Still, I knew Chrissy wasn't Matt's type. Chrissy was too abrasive; Matt was too bossy. Watching their interaction that morning was like watching a cage fight, and given enough time, I think they'd go Highlander on each other.

"He's mine," I announced. "Um, sort of. He's also seven years older than you."

"Hey, there's a manther in every guy!" Chrissy called as I left the basement.

Okay, I had forgotten the PS3 and Xbox 360 in the basement. So much for privacy. Then again, I didn't plan on bringing Matt into my room. Not for . . . not for sex, at least.

My skin tingled pleasantly and I hummed as I made my coffee. Not for sex, who was I kidding? I'd fuck that guy in a coat closet.

My thoughts drifted back over all the ways he'd touched me. My ass, my breasts, my sex. God, I loved the way he handled me, like he had a right to my body. Like I was his. I loved his voice, demanding, dictating, demeaning, and, in the end, desperate.

That had to be my favorite part—hearing Matt go crazy.

I need to come. Baby, I need to come.

I wished I could wield a little feminine power over him.

Too bad I turned into a total ditz in his presence. I had to work on that.

I shuffled into the office.

Dad must have unpacked and set up my desktop before leaving for work. I frowned when I saw it. First my bed, now the computer. I had to do some unpacking before Dad did everything for me. I felt like enough of a mooch just moving home.

I had to show my parents that I was going to be productive. In other words, I had to be useful around the house, start looking for a job, and not lunge into the first shitty relationship that came my way.

So . . . going out for drinks, staying out all night, getting laid, and sleeping in until 2 P.M. was an awesome start to my bum summer. Ugh.

Guiltily, I picked at the work Mom had e-mailed. She needed

every bit of this. She worked part-time as a nurse, part-time from home doing transcription, and she was still paying off loans for her nursing degree.

Maybe when she tried to pay me I would refuse the money.

I wondered how long I could gas my car and pay for food with the seven hundred dollars in my checking account. And what was I going to do about insurance?

It took me two hours to complete the simple tasks Mom had given me.

Too much daydreaming.

I opened my e-mail and cracked my knuckles, grinning like an idiot. Now I could write the next installment of my collaborative story with Matt. God, I missed this.

Lana and Cal were making camp by a river in the middle of nowhere. Maybe it was wishful thinking, but I thought I could feel the sexual tension building between our characters. Would it weird Matt out if this turned into smut?

Well, if it did, he was tactful enough to segue to the fluttering curtains—or the fluttering field grass, in this case.

Mm, the field. I spaced out for a moment as I remembered the way Matt stared at me when I sprawled on his blanket and bared myself to him. With looks like his, he couldn't possibly be sex starved—but he'd looked starved. Starved for me.

Suddenly the office felt hot. Damn.

I began to write.

I moved Lana and Cal summarily through a campsite routine—hitching the horses, building a fire, spreading the bedrolls—and then I focused on Lana. She was sore from riding and grimy with the dust of the road. The river looked cool and dark, swirling gently in a deep pool. She unpacked a lump of soap and began to undress as discreetly as possible.

After she slipped into the river and cast a glance back at Cal, I sent the paragraphs to Matt. An e-mail from Matt appeared almost simultaneously. I couldn't help but smile as I noticed he'd used a different e-mail account. His main account, by the look of it.

Subject: Frostypants
Sender: Matthew R. Sky Jr.
Date: Monday, July 1, 2013
Time: 5:32 PM
Hi, Hannah,
We'll do dinner at 8ish. I'll pick you up at 7. I need to be inside of you.
Matt

I wilted in the office chair. Fuck. There it was again, that crazy sexy candor.

Get on your hands and knees. I'm going to take you from behind.

Not to mention the bossiness. It should have annoyed me—this wasn't a gentlemanly invitation, it was an order—and yet I felt giddy. I could see Matt again. I could make sure he was real and that this was actually happening to me.

And maybe this time I could act like the smart, confident woman I was, not the blushing brainless mush of last night.

I spent the next hour and a half prepping. I unpacked a few boxes of clothes, showered and shaved, borrowed some of my sister's perfume and makeup, and dressed in a short strapless blue dress. Underneath, I wore a strapless gray push-up with creamy trim and a matching thong. At the last minute I threw on dangly earrings and a silver bracelet.

Matt arrived promptly at seven. I peeked at him from a front window. He stood leaning against his car, looking bored.

Holy. Fuck.

He wore pale gray slacks and a crisp white dress shirt. His wild hair was wet and pushed back. As I studied him, he glanced at his watch, then smirked toward the house.

Fuck, he looked right at me! I lurched away from the blinds. So uncool right now.

When I went out to meet him, I thought I saw his cocky smirk falter. Success! Maybe. It was hard to tell. Matt's smirks came in flavors—two parts kindness, one part wicked amusement, a little lust in the mix. Oh, and one hundred percent smug bastard.

Matt moved to meet me, and I thought he might grab me and start groping my ass again. I wanted him to, even if Chrissy was watching from her window.

Matt looked edible in dress clothes.

Instead, he hugged me gently and kissed my cheek. The air went out of my lungs. Oh, Lord, the way that shirt tucked into his slacks, showing off his trim hips. I got a whiff of cologne.

When he opened the door for me, I nearly fell into his car. Déjà vu.

"There's a place in Boulder I like," Matt said as he drove. He stared ahead, serious and unsmiling. Totally unlike the man who'd driven me for hours through the nighttime prairie. "The Number Nine. Great food. I hate formal stuff, but what the hell."

I frowned at him.

"So what, you're just doing this for me?"

"Sure." He glanced at his iPhone. "I figured you'd like a meal."

"Well, that's kind of shitty, Matt," I snapped.

"Excuse me?" He was scrolling through his Pandora stations and driving too fast, with an unnerving amount of inattention. He didn't even look at me.

"I'm not some idiot girl you have to wine and dine before fucking. God, I'm sorry you feel the need to endure a nice dinner with me."

Matt chuckled. What a prick!

"Hannah, I enjoy eating." He'd settled on music. I recognized the Lumineers. Of course this jackass had great taste in music. "And I'll enjoy eating with you. I only meant that formal things . . . make me uneasy, okay? Don't worry, we'll do something I really enjoy afterward."

He reached for my hand. I held it stiff on my lap for all of three seconds.

"I love when you're feisty," Matt murmured. He pulled my

hand onto his lap and pressed it against his thigh. Oh, God, oh, God, not again. I felt my ability to articulate gliding away. "You look amazing, Hannah. I know you want to get fucked, wearing a dress like that. I'll deliver, don't worry. I held back last night, but not this time. You're bad to wear that. I love it."

Matt slid my hand a little closer to his cock and left it there. He was watching the road with a stony expression. He reached over and squeezed one of my breasts, slipping a few fingers into my cleavage. I heated from head to toe.

"Matt," I squeaked. Cars were passing us and we were passing them, and I knew people must have seen Matt with his hand on my breast.

"What? This is what you want, Hannah. Don't try to deny it. You want to be used. I'm enjoying you, little bird. God, I love your body . . ." He shifted in his seat. The music seemed to dissatisfy him and his hand left my breast to switch to a dubstep station. Then, as if it were nothing, he retook my breast and wriggled his fingers into my cleavage again.

We rode most of the way to Boulder like that. When I tried to inch my fingers closer to his cock, he brushed my hand away and started to tease me. He said he wasn't surprised I wanted to touch his cock. He pushed his fingers into the cup of my bra, pinched my nipple, twisted it, and held it that way.

"Nn . . . no," I gasped, but I didn't try to stop him. Why? I was getting so turned on I'd started to worry about leaving a wet spot on my dress.

"It's okay, baby, it's okay," he soothed. "Don't fight it. I'm going to fuck you so hard tonight. Just think about that."

I closed my eyes. My nipple was quickly going numb, but Matt kept readjusting his fingers, twisting it tighter and pinching it to keep stimulating the nerves.

I was in a daze by the time we parked and walked to the restaurant. I couldn't understand how Matt kept his cool. Fuck, I wanted to drive him insane tonight. What happened to my feminine power?

At least he couldn't tease me in the restaurant. I would use the time to refocus.

The No. 9 was small and dimly lit, and I could tell right away that it was crazy expensive. Matt had made reservations.

When we were seated, I smirked and nudged his foot under the table.

"You're so cocky. How did you know I'd agree to go out with you?"

"Oh, I didn't," he said. His serious eyes skimmed the menu. I loved the way he looked at things—with withering dismissal or raw hunger.

I wanted to be the center of his attention.

Shit. Was I falling for a stranger? This was not in line with my productive summer plans.

He sighed and closed the menu.

"If you'd said no, I would have had to bring Laurence, I suppose."

I snickered. "What, don't you have any friends?"

"Not many," he said. He leveled me with a stare, and suddenly I felt so . . . sorry for him. My heart knotted up. Who the hell was this amazing-looking guy who lived alone with a rabbit and wrote stories with strangers online?

The restaurant's cheapest plate was thirty dollars and I had my eye on it. Matt had other plans. The waiter arrived and Matt fired our order at him before I could open my mouth.

"She'll have the seared scallops and a glass of your best white; I'll have the steak roulade and a Coke." He smiled at me. "We'll trade if you don't like seafood. The white will go well with the scallops, trust me."

"I love seafood. You don't want a drink?"

"Quit five years ago," he said negligently.

Sexy god is also sober. I tucked that information into my Matt file.

Our plates arrived and they were works of art, mine an arrangement of fat scallops with shallots and a buttery sauce swirled over the plate, Matt's a cascade of rolled spinach-stuffed steak. We shared. The flavors were exquisite and Matt was right, the white wine complemented my meal perfectly.

The wine got me buzzed and I fell under Matt's spell, talking and laughing with him like we had on our nighttime drive.

Matt got me chatting about the work I'd done that afternoon.

Yeesh, for someone who felt uneasy in formal environments, Matt carried conversation effortlessly—and he looked like he belonged in this restaurant, whereas I felt out of place.

The waiter returned to check on us.

I planned to insist on paying for my part of the meal, though I had a dreadful feeling about the cost, but Matt only smirked when I mentioned it.

"Another time, Hannah. I already paid."

How the hell had I missed that? Ugh, drowning in Matt's sexy smile, that's how.

He took my hand as we left the restaurant and strolled up Pearl Street.

If he was in a rush to get inside me, he gave no indication. His eyes trailed over the shops. Sometimes he smiled down at me. Holy height discrepancy. Good thing I love tall men.

I caught people watching us. Oh . . . we obviously looked like a couple. A good-looking couple, I hoped. I felt eclipsed by the elegant man at my side.

Matt stopped.

I followed his gaze to a neon sign at the entrance of an alley. It read DYNAMITE.

"You've got to be kidding me," he said drily.

"Ha. Wow." I shook my head. "I guess it's good I know where the place is. My sister's going to be begging rides off me, I know it."

"Kind of a long haul from Denver." Matt's tone was inscrutable. His eyes were trained on the glowing orange letters. What was he thinking, looking so somber? "Mm. Let's go in."

"Wait, what?" I laughed.

Matt tugged me down the alley and I traipsed after him,

struggling on my heels. I'd never been inside a strip club. This was about to get interesting.

"You're crazy," I said as he paid our cover.

He smirked down at me. Uh-oh. I recognized that smirk.

One hundred percent trouble.

The club was surprisingly busy. I couldn't think over the music. The lighting was garish, red and yellow. A beaded curtain hung in front of some booths, and there were red velvet chairs arranged beside a stage.

Three topless girls were strutting along the stage, floating toward men with bills. Everyone I saw had a drink.

I got on my tiptoes to whisper in Matt's ear. "I think we probably have to buy drinks."

Matt glanced at the girls, then smiled down at me.

"Now *this* is seedy as fuck," he whispered back.

"I'm glad you think so! It really is. What are we doing here?"

"Having some fun," he said. He pulled out his wallet and headed for the stage. He'd caught the eye of an attractive dancer with chin-length blond hair. They leaned together to chat briefly, and I saw Matt pass the woman a bill. Her eyes widened and she smiled. Shit, how much money did he just give her?

Matt made his way back to me and took my hand. We followed the blond stripper toward the back of the club and down a hall. It got dramatically quiet when we stepped into a midsize room with mirrors on every wall. There were a few ottomans, a black velvet couch, a simple armless chair, and a table. I edged closer to Matt.

"Hi, hon," said the stripper. "I'm Kelly. Don't be nervous, darlings."

Darlings? The girl looked maybe twenty-five. She was pretty, though, and amazingly calm for someone wearing only a G-string and stilettos.

"Your boyfriend said you two wanted to have a little fun," she said, looking meaningfully between Matt and me.

Boyfriend? I glared at Matt. My glare dissolved as soon as I met his eyes. Oh . . . no. There it was—that starved, absorbing look that made me wild to please him. My heart went double time. I smiled faintly.

"Yeah," I said quietly.

Matt squeezed my hand, then prowled over to lean against a wall and watch us. Typical, he couldn't even sit. Restless . . . controlling. Intoxicating.

"Sit," he ordered, nodding at the chair. "Give her a lap dance," he said to the stripper.

I sank onto the chair. I was agonizingly aware of Matt staring at me, but I couldn't meet his gaze. I knew I was beet red.

The stripper straddled me and began to dance. She ignored Matt. She winked at me, ran her tongue along her lips, and brought her breasts close to my body as she ground her ass against my thighs.

I realized with a jolt that I was getting wet.

I wasn't into girls, not really, so what gave?

It had to be Matt. Matt watching me, enjoying my discomfort. Probably getting hard.

"Touch her," he said softly.

When I gave the stripper a questioning look, she took my hands and brought them to her breasts. I squeezed and she moaned.

Okay, I thought, I got this—but Matt's next order brought me up short.

"Show her yours, Hannah."

The stripper went right on grinding into my lap.

Show her mine? He wanted me to . . .

"Do it," Matt growled, leaning forward. "Show her your nice big tits, Hannah."

With shaking hands, I unzipped my dress enough to peel it down. Thank God I'd chosen a strapless dress. I rolled down my bra without unclasping it. My nipples were hard. I heard Matt exhale roughly.

"Good," he said.

The stripper lifted my heavy breasts and pressed them to hers. I moaned. Fuck, there was definitely a wet spot on my dress.

Matt stalked toward us suddenly.

"Get out," he snarled at the stripper.

Unfazed, the stripper accepted another bill from Matt, smiled at us both, and breezed out. The door clicked closed behind her. Matt stared down at me, tilting up my chin as if I were a disobedient child. My legs trembled.

"God, Hannah," he whispered, "you're perfect. Did you like that? Did you like making me hard like that? Look at my cock."

My eyes traveled down the buttons of Matt's shirt to the tent in his slacks. I swallowed.

"Looks good, right?"

I nodded.

"Did you enjoy showing your tits to that woman?" He chuckled and reached for my breasts, squeezing them mercilessly. "You're a slut for me, aren't you, Hannah?"

"Yes," I gasped. I covered his hands with mine. My brain screamed: *Feminine power, feminine power*! It was *my* turn to drive Matt crazy, goddamn it.

I slid off the chair and fell to my knees at Matt's feet.

Before he could react, I yanked down his slacks and boxers, grabbed his cock—damn, I'd forgotten how huge it was—and began to suck hard on his head.

"Mm!" Matt groaned. "Ohhh . . . fuck . . ."

Success! His noises spurred me on. I swirled my tongue around his head and stroked his shaft with one hand, fondling his balls with the other.

"H-Hannah," he stammered. "Oh, God . . . what . . . are you doing . . ."

I looked up at him. His eyes sent a shiver through me. He was gone, totally gone. A soft shock of hair swept across his brow. His head was lowered, his lips parted slightly. He watched in a stupor as my tongue and mouth made his cock glisten.

"Mm," he moaned again. He clenched his teeth. Fuck, he was fighting it—fighting his pleasure, fighting for control. So hot.

I worked faster. With long, deep sucks I drew his head into

the back of my throat. I ignored my own little gagging sounds as his huge member filled my mouth. I could never have taken the whole thing, but I did the best I could with my hand and the seal of my lips.

Soon I tasted cum. I moaned onto his cock.

Matt staggered back. He pressed himself against one of the mirrors. I eyed his shaft.

"Hannah," he growled.

I crawled forward, smiling up at him. My breasts swayed pendulously.

"It's okay, Matt," I whispered, licking my lips. Oh, it felt good to have control this time. "I know you need this. Come on. I bet you're already about to explode."

I was teasing him, but when I took him back into my mouth, I realized with surprise that I was right. After just minutes, Matt was close to coming. His balls were tight in my hand. His shaft throbbed in my mouth.

I saw him glance aside and then I saw what he saw: us, reflected in a mirror.

His chest rose and fell fiercely. He looked stricken and delirious. God, I loved it.

"My cock, God, my cock Hannah," he pleaded.

I began to bob my head on it, looking up at him.

"A-ah, yes . . . fuck . . . no . . . not yet, f . . . fuck not yet, Hannah, don't."

I would have crowed in triumph if I could.

His protests notwithstanding, Matt was giving tiny, helpless thrusts into my wet mouth. I squeezed his shaft harder and picked up the pace. He arched away from the wall, tugged at my hair, and came hard, coating the back of my throat with cum.

"Fuck!" he rasped.

I had no doubt Matt's moan was heard beyond the door.

I swallowed and sat back on my heels.

"You taste amazing," I murmured.

Matt swayed against the wall.

Before he could turn the tables on me, I yanked up my bra and dress, gave Matt's tight ass a squeeze, and scrambled for the door. To be honest, I was afraid to linger in the room with him. He was watching me with his steady green eyes, though he had yet to do up his slacks, and I felt precisely like I was standing in a cage watching a tranquilized tiger wake.

I blew him a kiss at the door.

"I'll meet you outside," I said, and then I got the hell out of there.

Chapter 11

MATT

HANNAH-PROOF THE APARTMENT

1. Buy time (a day)
2. Frozen food (Pam?)
3. Pictures, photo albums
4. Bethany's clothes & shower stuff
5. Girly things (esp. in bathroom)
6. My books
7. My writing

I reread my list.

I glanced at the TV.

How disturbing. My list seemed infinitely more important than the coverage of the riots in Brazil, where my girlfriend happened to be traveling.

I knew Bethany was safe, though. She'd sent me an e-mail that morning.

> In case you were wondering, which I'm sure you were since I can feel your concern all the way in South America (sarcasm), my parents and I are safe. We narrowly missed some rioting in Florianopolis but now we're far from any of it. I'll start calling if you don't write. How are the meals? Kisses, Bethany

Her threat to start calling felt very real—and very menacing.

I couldn't deal with Bethany calling while I was with Hannah, and I wanted to be with Hannah all the time. Dropping her off last night had been hell.

I had driven Hannah home in stunned silence—no girl had ever made me come that fast and that hard with her mouth. Maybe her boldness angered me, but I liked it, too. I liked being caught off guard. I liked being provoked. I wanted nothing more than to blow by Hannah's house, drive her to my apartment, bend her over the kitchen counter, and spank her until she cried. And fuck her hard and make her come, too.

Damn. This girl was getting under my skin.

The worst part was, I could see Hannah's disappointment when I pulled up to her house. She tried to play it off, but she was a shit actress. She'd just given me the blow job of my young life and I must have seemed annoyed about it.

Why else would I end the night so abruptly? Why else wouldn't I take her to my place?

The questions were plain in her eyes, and the hurt.

She thanked me for dinner.

I barely replied.

My mind was already churning.

How could I have Hannah over when every corner of my apartment screamed, "I have a girlfriend! A female resides here! Look, tampons!"

Step 1: Buy time

Subject: Dynamite
Sender: Matthew R. Sky Jr.
Date: Tuesday, July 2, 2013
Time: 8:15 AM
Morning, Hannah,
I have plans after work that will go on indefinitely, so if you don't hear from me tonight you know the reason.
Matt

I sent the e-mail and called Pam.

Step 2: Get rid of the suspicious labeled food in my freezer

It would be a shame to throw out the food, and anyway, I'm not that coldhearted. I felt a stab of guilt as I thought about Bethany cooking and labeling the meals.

My behavior was starting to beg the question: Why not just break up with her? Call her and do the deed. Make this right. It had to happen.

But not yet.

Dumping my girlfriend over the phone while she was on vacation felt about as wrong as cheating on her under the same circumstances, and two wrongs . . .

Shit, think about this later.

"Matthew?" Pam's clipped voice came on the line.

"Hey, Pam." I paced through the kitchen. "Look, I need a favor. I need you to swing by and pick something up."

"You have new pages for me?"

Poor Pam, she sounded ridiculously excited. I smirked at the gridlock of Tupperware in my freezer. Pam was the only person I knew who would store and return these without asking any questions. To her, I was simply M. Pierce, eccentric writer extraordinaire.

"New pages?" I said, closing the freezer. "Mm . . . not quite . . ."

After Pam left with three grocery bags of frozen meals (and assurances to restore them when I asked), I began to comb my apartment and remove all traces of Bethany.

I thought listening to hip-hop would help distract me from the scumbagginess of my task, but after "99 Problems" and "Heartless," I flung my iPod away.

Everything went into duffel bags: pictures of Bethany and me, all my photo albums, her razors, makeup, shampoo, and other toiletries, her jewelry and clothes, my books, manuscripts, files with documents pertaining to royalties and film deals—shit, I even threw my tax stuff in the bag. Yeah, like Hannah would look in my file cabinet. I was getting paranoid.

I locked the stuff in the trunk of my Lincoln.

Damn, I felt like a gangster closing a trunk on a body. This was getting seriously fucked-up. Another surge of guilt went through me as I made my way back up to my apartment.

I felt like I'd taken a ten-mile run, minus the stress relief. I also didn't have a thing left to eat besides a few cans of soup, pasta, and cereal. Awesome.

It was 7 P.M.

It took me all day to transform my apartment into a bachelor pad, and the exercise left me feeling dirty and hollow. Plus, I missed Hannah. I missed her voice and the candied scent of her shampoo. I missed her open thighs. I missed her furious blushing, her wet cunt . . .

I checked my e-mail.

She sent a post for our story yesterday, nothing else.

I added a couple paragraphs to *The Surrogate.* They were dry and plodding compared to my racing fantasies of Hannah.

I could call her, but I'd already blown her off for the day. Besides, I didn't want to come off as some loser with no life.

Was I a loser with no life? I needed to schedule an appointment with my psychiatrist. He always helped me think my way out of corners, and he was one of a handful of people who knew that Matthew Sky was M. Pierce.

He didn't spare me hard truths, either. I just wasn't sure I wanted to hear the hard truths about Hannah.

I already knew that the price of great pleasure is great pain.

I also knew that this thing with Hannah would hit the ground sooner or later and she would be hurt, God help me, and I wouldn't be able to protect her—to protect her from my own stupid, selfish choices.

Finally these thoughts became too much. I showered and resigned myself to a date with my hand and my poor sketch of Hannah (and the memory of her hot mouth making me come against my will), but when I got out of the shower I saw I'd missed two calls.

Both from Hannah.

I pulled on a pair of boxers and called her back.

"Matt?"

"Hey." I smiled compulsively at the sound of her voice. My cock perked up, too. Perfect, just call me Pavlov's dog. "You called?"

"Yeah. Matt, I . . ."

Maybe it was because I'd just been knee-deep in my girlfriend's stuff, but I had a sudden gaping sense of dread.

"Go on," I said quietly.

"Well, first off, are you busy? I know you said you'd be busy. I don't want to—"

"No! No." I ruffled my damp hair. "I got done with my obligations sooner than expected. I'm home, just kind of dicking around."

Okay, could have phrased that better.

"Oh." Hannah sounded distant. "If you were bored, you could have called me."

"Hm? No, um . . . I do have stuff to do."

"So do you need to go?"

"No!" Jeez, I was starting to feel exasperated. Lies on top of lies on top of lies. "Please, just . . . talk," I stammered.

"Okay. Okay. So." Hannah gathered a shaky breath. "Did I make some epic mistake last night? At the club?"

"What?" I flopped onto the couch in shock. "God, no. No."

"No?"

"No! No no no. I loved it, Hannah. Fuck, I've thought about little else besides repaying you for that sassy display." I chuckled. "Mm, I almost invited you over last night, except my apartment . . . was wicked dirty." Another lie on the heap. I probably owned the cleanest apartment in Denver. "I didn't want you to see the sloppy side of Matt."

"I think I've already seen the sloppy side of Matt." Hannah giggled. Her relief was palpable. I laughed with her. Maybe my relief was palpable, too.

"God, little bird. Trust me, your mouth on my cock, goddamn . . ." I trailed off. My dick was already far too interested in this conversation.

"Okay," Hannah said, "so the next thing. Matt, I can't . . . accept these." She cleared her throat. I heard a door close. "I mean, my God. I went online, so I *know* how much they cost. And you obviously had them overnighted. Are you insane? We're going to have to figure out . . ." Hannah rambled on about returns and money and paying me back.

For a beat, I was in the dark. Accept these? How much they cost?

Then I remembered. The LELO toys. I jumped up and began pacing around my living room excitedly. Laurence pricked an ear in my direction.

"They arrived? Excellent."

"Yeah, like I said. And I can't—"

"Good, good. I had a hell of a time getting them overnighted, that required a little finessing. You opened them?"

"Yes. Are you not hearing me?"

"Hm?" It was true, I wasn't hearing Hannah. The toys had arrived and my gutter-dwelling mind was whirring. "You have a laptop? With a webcam?"

"Yes, uh, why? If—"

"Good. Okay. Get on your laptop, Hannah, let's Skype."

"Matt—"

I ended the call. I may very well have skipped into the office.

Hannah was already on Skype when I logged on. I started a video call.

She was sitting in bed with her back to the headboard and wearing a gray camisole, no bra by the look of it. She grinned when she saw me.

"Are you naked?" She laughed.

"What? No. Shirtless." I frowned down at myself.

"I demand proof."

I rolled my eyes. I also started VodBurner to record our call.

"I think you called enough of the shots last night, Hannah. But so you don't think I'm a total perv"—I aimed the webcam down at my lap; I was wearing pale Etiquette Clothiers boxers—"there you go. Would you like me to keep the camera at this angle? Clearly you were making a play to see my junk, so . . ."

"Matt!" Hannah turned red. I smirked and fixed the camera.

I could have grabbed my laptop and gotten more comfortable, but my desktop was already on—and I was feeling impatient.

"Lemme see your room," I said.

Hannah turned her laptop, giving me a quick view of the room. I saw a bed, bookshelves, boxes, and . . . not much else.

"I like what you've done with the place."

"I just got here," she grumbled, twisting the laptop back around, "and I've had zero time to unpack. Some guy keeps distracting me."

"What a wanker," I said. "He should really give you some time to turn that den into a cute little nest. Maybe he should help you pimp out your nest . . ."

"No, he shouldn't!" Hannah glowered at the screen and I laughed. God, it felt good to be talking to her again. And she definitely wasn't wearing a bra. When she leaned closer, I could see her nipples.

My cock stirred.

"You might want headphones if anyone's in hearing distance," I said. "I'm about to start talking about those beautiful tits of yours."

"Oh, yeah . . . be right back." Hannah slipped away.

I dashed to the bathroom, found my lube, and beat her back. She reappeared with a bulky headset. Her blush was still firmly in place.

"Don't judge me," she said as she plugged in the jack and fit the earphones on. They engulfed her ears. Noise-canceling, by the look. "I used to be a gamer."

"Nah, they're perfect," I said.

They *were* perfect, even if they looked a little silly. With the mike right by her mouth, I would be able to hear every noise she made, and she would be able to hear only me. "You're not wearing a bra, are you, Hannah? I can see your nipples. They're hard. Is your door locked? Show me a breast, just one. Keep it out."

"It's locked," Hannah whispered.

"Your breast," I demanded.

I heard her breath quicken.

"Right, sorry." She slid off the thin straps of her cami and stretched the neckline below one of her breasts. It spilled down and I heard her sigh.

"Mm, is that nice for you?" I began to rub my cock through my boxers. "To let it out? I know they're heavy. You love it when I lift and squeeze them, don't you? Show me the other one. Shake them for me."

Hannah's blush extended down her neck to her chest. She rolled down the other half of her cami, and I clenched my teeth against a moan. Her dark curls fell softly around her, framing her chest. She twisted from side to side. The motion made her breasts bounce and sway.

"Mm, fuck," I hissed. "Good, baby, fuck. That's exactly how they bounce and shake when I fuck you. It makes me want to fuck you harder. Are you getting wet showing off for me?"

"Yes," she whispered. Her eyelids fluttered.

"Let me see the toys."

Hannah pulled two black boxes onto her lap and fumbled with the lids. She displayed the toys one at a time.

I had gotten her a large plum-colored waterproof vibrator, the largest one LELO sold, and a small high-powered clitoral stimulator. As Hannah handled the larger vibrator, she stroked her fingers over it.

"You like it?" I said.

"Matt, it feels so incredibly silky. I don't even know how they can make something feel this luxurious. Oh, and it has a ridiculous number of speeds and settings. And this little one? The vibrations are so strong!"

Hannah's blush darkened. I reached into my boxers, glad she couldn't see me doing it.

"So, you already played with them?"

"No! Er, not like that. I tested the speeds."

"Good. You'll use them for the first time now, with me watching. You're keeping them, Hannah. They're yours, but I'm going to get a lot of pleasure out of them. Position your laptop so I can see your pussy. Get out of your shorts and panties. Let me watch."

While Hannah was busy positioning the laptop and shimmying out of her shorts and thong, I pushed off my boxers and squirted lube into my palm. I glanced at my cock. It stood stiffly from me, nine thick, smooth inches for which I didn't thank God often enough. I tensed as I began to spread the cold lube along my shaft.

On the screen, I watched Hannah struggling to position her laptop. She spread her legs and I got a beautiful shot of her pussy, open like a rose and glistening.

"Damn it," I whispered. "Look how wet you are, you gorgeous slut. I love the color of your cunt."

I heard Hannah moan softly. She closed her legs a little.

"Spread them," I snapped. "Spread your legs for me. Are you embarrassed? Are you embarrassed to know I'm staring at the most private part of your body? God, look at it, Hannah."

"Yes," she admitted quietly.

"And you like it, too. You like how filthy I am. You like it when I embarrass you."

"Yes."

I laughed. Hannah's vocab dropped radically when we got intimate. I loved it. She turned from my silver-tongued sparring partner into my docile minx.

With a shudder, I remembered that I was recording this video call.

"Slip that vibrator into your tight body, Hannah. Work it in. Don't use any lube. You shouldn't need any, you're so wet. Turn it on."

I stroked my cock and massaged my sac as Hannah tried to maneuver the phallic toy into her sex. I watched her lips spread around it.

"Nn . . . too big," she murmured.

"Get it in," I snarled. "I'm bigger than that, and I'll be fucking you tomorrow. Do it."

"Oh, Matt, Matt . . ."

I forced myself to jerk off slowly. I could have come then and there, watching Hannah wriggle the vibrator into herself. She kept pulling it out and then pushing it deeper.

"Look at you, fucking yourself with it already. A girl and her toys . . ." I smirked. It felt good to be cruel, to mock her at moments like this. "Faster, Hannah. What do you need to get off, hm? Something inside or just something on your clit?"

She shoved the vibrator in deeper, turned it on, and began to fuck herself with it.

"Ohhh," she groaned. "B-b . . . both, I . . . I need both."

"Ah, God." I let myself moan. "You're making this so good for me, Hannah. It feels so good. I knew you needed both. You love to have my dick inside of you, don't you? You need it."

"Yes, God, yes," she panted.

"Hannah, baby, you make it easy for me to come. Use the other toy on your clit. I'm going to watch you come. Make it good, make a big mess and I'll go easier on you tomorrow. Tomorrow I'm going to teach you a lesson. I wanted to fuck you in the Dynamite Club and you sucked me off, you filthy girl. Couldn't wait to get your mouth on my cock, could you?"

I couldn't stop the dirty talk spilling out of me. Damn, I really was depraved. All I knew was that arousal worked on me like a drug. It took my mind and body to another plane.

"Let me see it," Hannah pleaded as she sped up the vibrator inside her. She added the smaller toy, fitting it against the hood of her clit and dialing up the speed.

She began to gasp and writhe. I couldn't tear my eyes off her tight sex clamped around the vibrator.

"Please," she rasped. She fiddled with the setting on the toy inside. I heard its two motors firing in a fast alternating rhythm.

"You want to see my cock, Hannah? Look at you, playing with your toys. How's that setting, are you making it pulse? You want me inside, don't you?"

"Oh, yes, please, yes."

My hand worked furiously. I wanted to wait for Hannah, but I didn't know how much longer I would last.

"Look what you do to me," I gasped. As I angled the webcam down at my lap, I felt a twinge of the shame Hannah must have been feeling. It was so intimate, to let her see me pleasuring myself.

"Matt, fuck," Hannah moaned. "I'm coming, God . . . oh, God."

At that, I stiffened in my office chair and grabbed a tissue just in time to come into it. Holy fuck, had seeing my cock pushed Hannah over the edge? As pleasure tore through me, I watched Hannah squirm and clutch her toys, fluid spurting around her fingers.

What an incredible orgasm.

We laughed as we cleaned up and came down.

I stopped recording the video call and pulled on my boxers. Hannah lounged on her belly, propped up on her elbows. She hadn't bothered to fix her cami. Her bust rested on the quilt. It was beautiful to see her looking so relaxed; I only wished she were in my bed.

"Hey," I said, smiling and sinking into my office chair.

"Hi." Hannah smiled. She was a goddess wearing nothing but her glasses. "So Matt, where are you going to have your way with me tomorrow?"

"At my place," I said, "if you'd like to see it."

"I'd love to."

"Good. You going to be busy at all?"

"Not by the time you get off work," she said. "I'm sure I'll have some work from Mom. It won't take me long. I should probably spend some time looking for a real job."

"I'll take a day. I'll pick you up around noon. Will you be free then?"

"I should be, yeah."

"Good. Hannah, have you ever thought about a career in publishing?"

"Seriously?" Hannah laughed and tousled her hair. The longest pieces reached to the middle of her back. I wanted to yank on those dark curls while I spanked her. "That would be my dream job, hence the English and business double major. It's so tough to break into, though. I can't afford to do an unpaid internship right now."

I paused before speaking.

"Mm. I'll keep that in mind. I have a few connections in the city."

"Matt, if you don't stop doing me favors, I'm going to start feeling like a kept woman."

"Hey, I like the sound of that. I'll keep you tied to my bed and let you suck on me when you're hungry. What do you think?"

Hannah giggled and bunched up a pillow beneath her chest.

"I'd smack you with this if I could," she said. She stifled a yawn. Fuck, she was precious. "Oh, hey. Will you do me a favor, Matt?"

"Anything."

"This is easy. Just repeat after me. 'It was nice talking to you, Hannah. I'll see you tomorrow. Good night.'"

I gave her an incredulous look.

"Don't give me that look. I'm trying to teach you this mysterious skill, one that you seem to lack. It's called 'How to say good-bye.'"

I smiled and rubbed the back of my neck.

"What are you grinning at?" she said.

"I never want to," I said.

"What? Never want to what?"

"I never want to learn how to say good-bye."

I closed Skype and then closed my eyes, laughing into the silence of my apartment.

Chapter 12

HANNAH

"You have plans for the Fourth?" Matt asked as we drove through the city. He'd arrived at my house at noon sharp and stood by his car waiting for me. I got the definite impression that he was avoiding my family—or humanity in general.

He looked edible, as usual.

He wore charcoal gray slacks and a pale dress shirt with the sleeves rolled up. I felt reasonably sure his shoes were Ferragamos, though I wasn't about to ask, and the timepiece on his wrist could have doubled as an anchor.

I, on the other hand, was wearing a tiny yellow sundress from Macy's. Excellent, I probably looked like Matt's niece.

I was carrying my big slouchy purse because Matt had insisted I bring the sex toys. God, I had to find out what this guy did for a living. He dressed like sex, drove the sexiest car I'd ever been in, and bought me the Cadillac of sex toys without blinking.

Besides, it was starting to feel weird to have these repeated intimate encounters with a man who was still so much of a stranger.

"The Fourth?" I said, trying to peel my eyes off his bare forearms. "I don't think so. We can see one of the shows decently well from our deck. I guess we'll do brats and hamburgers, that's all we usually do." I had honestly forgotten about the Fourth of July, along with everything else in the world, thanks to Matt. "What about you?"

"No plans."

"You have any family around here?" I said, watching his face.

Matt kept his eyes on the road. Nothing changed in his expression.

"No, not around here. Two brothers on the East Coast."

"Brothers? That's cool. You guys get along? Are they older or younger?"

I wanted to fire a zillion questions at him.

"This place is good," Matt said. We had pulled up near a Mediterranean deli. Conversation over.

After lunch, Matt took my hand and began dragging me along the sidewalks of Denver with trademark impatience.

"Matt," I huffed. "Short legs over here."

"Don't I know it." He winked at me.

We stopped suddenly outside a midsize corner building. Stylish landscaping drew my eyes toward a statue near the stairs. It was a stone wing jutting up from a small fountain.

No. Way.

I looked to the lettering engraved above the doors: THE GRANITE WING AGENCY.

"Matt, what are we—"

He didn't hear me. He'd moved off a few feet and was on his phone. I heard him laugh.

"Yes," he said. Then, "Right, right. I didn't want to deal with your secretary. Oh, moving down in the world?"

After some more banter and a terse laugh, Matt dropped the phone into his pocket. He took my hand and led me into the building.

I was babbling wildly. I don't think Matt was listening, though he smiled down at me from time to time. Was it his smile making my knees weak, or being inside the agency rumored to represent M. Pierce?

And the M. Pierce rumor was only a footnote to the agency's reputation. Pamela Wing and her partner, Laura Granite, represented some of the biggest names in literary fiction. They were notorious for spotting talent and for being cutthroat in their negotiations. Oh, and they ruthlessly poached writers from other agencies, all from their humble Denver hub.

"Matt, what are we doing here?" I demanded.

My voice echoed around the lobby. Matt frowned at me.

"I told you I had some connections in the city."

I felt the color draining from my face.

Connections? Employment connections? Here, now?

"No, no no. I am not dressed for this moment," I said. "Please, let me just—"

I rummaged in my bag. Did I have anything that could lend me a shred of professionalism right now? Or maybe a weapon with which to dispatch myself? My hand closed around the purple vibrator and I nearly yanked it out for the world to see. Shit! Shit shit shit!

"Relax," Matt murmured.

"Matt, fuck, how can I—"

I heard heels clicking through the marble lobby and looked up to see a blond woman approaching. She and Matt shook hands briskly.

"Matthew," she said. She glanced at me and I shrank. I was an eyesore next to Matt and this fierce-looking lady, and again I had the distinct impression of being in a tiger enclosure.

I thrust out my hand. "Hannah Ca—"

"This is Hannah." Matt spoke over me. "Good friend of mine, new to the city. Look Pam, I don't have a world of time and I'm sorry to spring this on you—"

Oh, my God. He said Pam. Pamela. This was Pamela Wing, in the flesh.

"It's so unlike you to spring strange requests on me," Pamela said. She gave Matt an iron smile and he returned it. They seemed so familiar with one another and yet so restrained. A horrible thought jabbed at me. Were they ex-lovers?

"Long story short, Pam, Hannah's looking for work. I'm not asking you to move mountains or do me any favors. She's a smart girl, though. MA from Kenyon College, business and English major. You can read the rest in her résumé." He waved a hand. My God, he was practically talking down to Pamela Wing, a literary agent who ate souls for breakfast. "Do you get what I'm saying? That is, keep her in mind, would you? I wanted you two to meet."

My hand had been hanging limply in the air the whole time.

Pamela finally grasped and shook it. My fingers crumpled in her grip.

"Hi, Hannah," she said. "Pam Wing. It's great to meet you. As I was just telling Matt on the phone, my secretary, in her infinite wisdom, recently eloped in Vegas and telephoned informing me of her immediate resignation."

Pam's eyes glittered. I would *not* want to be that former secretary.

"No promises, but if you're not opposed to secretarial work and shadowing me a bit, and if you're as capable as Matthew suggests, the job is yours. I'm a firm believer in providence. Drop off your résumé as soon as you can. We'll be in touch. Matthew." Pam gave Matt a curt nod and breezed out of the building. Her perfume bit at my nostrils.

What the fuck . . . had just happened?

I hadn't said a single coherent word in the whole encounter, and I had basically just been offered a job. That, or I had been brushed off in the most diplomatic fashion. I blinked and shifted my purse on my shoulder.

Matt was watching me.

"Don't overthink this," he said softly. "She won't care if you never drop off your résumé, but the job will be gone in days. And don't thank me, either. That woman is a shark. You'll be out on your ass if you cross her once. There is no margin of error."

Matt ruffled my hair, a sweet gesture that unfortunately emphasized my feeling of childishness, and strolled toward the exit.

I rushed after him, my flip-flops slapping the floor.

"Who *are* you?" I said as we headed back to the car. "What do you do? What *was* that?"

Matt didn't answer until he was comfortably ensconced in his car.

"I'm a businessman." He sighed. "Can we leave it at that?"

"Do I have any choice?"

I didn't know what to feel. I was angry—angry at Matt for ambushing me with that impromptu interview, angry at myself for going mute—and elated at the job prospect and quietly in awe of the man beside me. Ugh, he was so fucking infuriating. And he was so fucking delicious, and mysterious, and impatient.

At the moment, Matt was driving like the grim reaper.

"My place next," he said as he glared ahead.

"That itinerary update would have been nice before you hauled me in front of one of my literary heroes."

"Mm, I take it you believe the gossip about that agency?"

"What, that they represent M. Pierce? I don't know."

Matt smirked.

"I wouldn't have pegged you for a fan girl, Hannah. Don't believe every tale you read. I'm sure that hack has some glitzy New York agent licking his boots."

"I'm not a fan girl, unless appreciating the books makes me one. And I happen to think the author is entitled to privacy. What makes you say *his* boots anyway?"

Matt went quiet for a moment.

"His or her," he said. "Probably her, come to think. So sentimental."

"So sexist!"

Matt flashed one of his sense-melting smiles at me.

God, was I in over my head with this guy?

Matt had a sprawling, high-rise apartment in downtown Denver. I probably should have guessed. The rooms were clean and modern, harshly white, with light hardwood floors and gorgeous area rugs. The fixtures were all of matching brushed metal and the décor was spare but tasteful. I recognized a framed John Singer Sargent print on the wall.

Matt loomed as I padded through the neat, quiet rooms. Each time I smiled at him, I thought I caught a glimmer of anxiety in his expression. Why would he be nervous? Was my opinion really that important to him?

"This place is lovely," I said. "It's amazing. I can't believe it was ever messy."

"Oh, I had a maid come through," he said.

"Laurence!" I squealed when I saw the rabbit's hutch in the living room. The hutch was as swanky as Matt's apartment, made of beautiful varnished wood with little gold knobs.

"Your lady love is back," Matt said to the rabbit.

We watched Laurence hop around his hutch for a while. Matt's hovering was making me uneasy—and strangely aroused. He hadn't touched me yet, but I knew he planned to. I assumed his bedroom was down the hall.

Was something wrong? Tension and desire made my stomach clench.

We drifted into the kitchen, Matt right at my back.

"Nice." I swallowed and brushed my hand over the granite countertop. Even the kitchen was immaculate.

I could feel Matt behind me. I thought I heard him take a soft breath. My skin prickled. God, if he didn't touch me soon—

I exhaled in a rush as Matt brought his chest flush against my back. He pinned me to the edge of the island and cupped my breasts from behind. I moaned.

"Are you ready?" he whispered in my ear.

"Yes," I said immediately, willing volume into my voice.

I had been ready since I woke up that morning. Ready and apprehensive.

"Then bend over the counter."

I did as Matt ordered, though the angle was uncomfortable.

The counter dug into my belly, and Matt pushed me down against it so that my breasts were squashed.

He was silent as he flipped up my sundress and tucked it around my waist. I thought my exposed ass and pink thong would pull some comment from him, but he remained quiet.

He jerked the string of my thong between my cheeks. A gasp escaped me. Fuck, I was getting nervous.

Matt smoothed a hand into my hair. The thick curls stopped his fingers. He got a handful of hair and yanked, and at once he began to spank my ass hard and fast.

"Matt!" I shrieked. The strands tugging at my tender scalp and the stinging pain on my bottom made me convulse against the counter. Instinctively, I tried to push away from the hard surface, but with Matt's hand in my hair and his strong arm against my back, I couldn't move.

God, I couldn't get away! And God, it was such a turn-on. I remembered Matt's words about teaching me a lesson—about not being gentle.

I had no choice but to take it.

"Ah! Ah! Ah!" I cried out in time with each firm slap to my bottom.

"Hannah," Matt finally growled. "Listen to yourself. God, you're perfect."

He slid his hand under my thong and began to finger me forcefully. I was soaked.

My exes had never humiliated me like this, much less been this rough with me, so I could never have known . . . how much I loved it.

"Ohhh, God," I breathed.

No sooner had Matt begun to finger me than he was spanking me again. One minute I was trying to wriggle closer to his fingers, the next I was trying to squirm away from his ruthless hand. My ass was hot.

"You're my slut," Matt told me over the slapping sounds and my own degrading cries. "You're mine, Hannah. You were bad to suck me off that night when I wanted to fuck you, and that's why you're getting punished."

He was fingering me again. I twisted and panted. Tears rimmed my eyelids.

"I know you love to suck my dick, Hannah, but I'll put it in your mouth when I want it there. You don't give me pleasure, do you understand? I take it from you."

I lost track of time between the pleasure and pain and Matt's moans and teasing. I was dimly aware of his soft slacks pushing against my leg, and his hard cock. He laughed and told me my ass was glowing. He asked how my breasts felt and whether I'd had enough. He told me my pussy was tight and needed fucking.

It ended abruptly. Matt pulled me into his arms, both of us breathless, and began to kiss me. His hands roved my body, squeezing any ample flesh.

"God," he gasped through the kiss. "Hannah, God. Do you want this? Feel what you're doing to me." He seized my wrist and pressed my hand to his cock. I curled my fingers around it.

Too many times I'd lost my nerve around Matt. I wanted this, whatever the hell it was. I trusted him. And if I didn't answer unequivocally, I knew he wouldn't force me into it.

Into *what*?

I shoved the anxiety out of my mind.

"Do it," I whispered. "Do it, Matt, I'm yours."

Chapter 13

MATT

Playing with Hannah had a beautiful way of simplifying things.

Worries plagued me as she inspected my apartment. Was I moving too fast? Would today frighten her? What if she found something of Bethany's? Was she angry about the meeting with Pam? And was that a stupid idea on my part, a major conflict of interests?

Then I got Hannah bent over the kitchen counter and I had no worries.

The world condensed to us. Hannah's ass. My hand. Hannah's pussy. My fingers.

I should have known she could handle anything I threw down.

She was fearless.

When I led her to my bedroom and showed her the items on the bed, I asked if she saw any problems.

She didn't run screaming. She didn't throw herself at my feet, either.

She carefully studied the things—a collar with attached nipple clamps, black tape, four silk cords, a blindfold, and a simple cloth gag—and gave me a small smile.

Just seeing Hannah handle the items made my cock throb. I had purchased them that morning before picking her up. Not only didn't I play with Bethany like this, but I had no desire to see Hannah in the context of Bethany's stuff, especially in bed.

Even my assholery had limits.

"This is fine," Hannah whispered. "Do it." She came closer and I trembled. She wrapped her arms around my neck and brought her mouth to my ear. "Do it to me, Matt."

She was pliant as I prepared her.

I blindfolded her and stripped her down to her thong. Before I gagged her, I pressed a large marble into her palm.

"If you want me to stop," I told her, "you drop this, and I'll stop. Do you understand?"

She nodded and opened her mouth for the gag.

I guess I started to lose it then. Something about Hannah's lovely lips parting and her pink tongue, her obedient mouth. Her submission. It drove me mad.

"You really like this," I murmured, "don't you?"

Before she could answer, I fit the gag into her mouth and tied it tight at the back of her head. I laughed and gave her a push that sent her tumbling onto the bed.

She fell across the quilt with a muffled cry.

"You asked for this, you slut," I snarled. I couldn't help myself; I shucked off my shoes and shirt and crawled over Hannah's quivering form. I ground my arousal against her sex, her thighs, her stomach, her breasts, her face. My slacks were getting painfully tight.

She tried feebly to participate, reaching for me, but I shoved her back and began tying her to the bed.

"You won't have the use of your limbs today, Hannah. I'm going to use you. All you're going to be is a body for me to play with. A cunt, a mouth, and a beautiful pair of tits."

I tethered Hannah spread-eagle to my bed, the silk cords

bound to her wrists and ankles and extending to the four bedposts.

I smiled down at my handiwork. I sat beside her and lazily pulled on her nipples.

"Hnnn! Nnnn!" She made glorious noises against her gag.

"Good girl," I soothed. "I'm testing your bonds. They're nice and tight, I see. You can barely move. Does this hurt?"

I began to twist and yank on her nipples and squeeze and slap her breasts. She jerked on the bed. My cock was already wet at the tip, I could feel it. My gaze flickered to the hand that held the marble. Her fingers were secure around it.

"Time for your collar, Hannah. We'll get pictures after this."

She groaned.

I fit the leather collar around Hannah's neck, securing the buckle. I tightened the clamps and fastened them onto her nipples. Hannah started to breathe in short, tiny bursts through her nostrils. At that, I had to undo my slacks and slide them off, along with my boxers.

I climbed over her as I worked, my heavy cock resting against her stomach.

"You're keeping me nice and hard," I told her. "I know your nipples hurt. This is a special collar, just for you. When I adjust these chains like so"—I shortened the chains extending from the collar to the clamps; they grew taut between Hannah's nipples and her neck—"the slightest movement of your neck is going to pull on your nipples. I know how you love to have your most sensitive spots abused, Hannah. And just so these don't slip off when you thrash . . ."

I tore away two pieces of black tape and pressed them over Hannah's nipples and the clamps, deliberately squeezing her nipples as I secured the tape.

"Mmmnnn," Hannah moaned.

I could tell she was trying to keep her head still.

I rubbed my cock against her belly and smirked down at her. "Why, Hannah, I believe you're drooling a bit."

I touched the saliva leaking from her gagged mouth.

I fetched my phone from my slacks and snapped a few pictures of Hannah. I got a nice shot of her thong, the pink fabric soaked through, and her beautiful face blindfolded and gagged.

Her toys were on the bed. I turned on the smaller egg-shaped vibrator, set it to the highest speed, and fit it into Hannah's thong.

"Try to stay still while I position this," I told her. I gazed over Hannah's body, knowing that stillness would be impossible. As soon as the first vibrations tickled her sex, she began to squirm. Her head twisted on the pillow and the chains and clamps tugged so hard on her nipples that her breasts trembled.

She yelped around the gag.

Fuck, I wouldn't last long with Hannah like this. Then again, I didn't plan to.

"I'm going to leave this in your thong, Hannah, just like this." I positioned the vibrator against her clit, the soft electric hum of the motor drowned out by Hannah's groans. "And I'll give you a little time to think about your silly play for control at the club."

I grabbed my lube and flopped into an armchair with a view of the bed. Perfect.

Hannah's moans came at irregular intervals. Sometimes she grew still and quiet, fighting the sensations overpowering her body, but soon she resumed shaking and struggling. Her moans became desperate squeals. Her thighs twisted and her back arched. The little lump in her panties kept buzzing away, driving her insane.

I let Hannah suffer for nearly twenty minutes. I lubed my cock and stroked it as I watched her. When I couldn't take any more, I climbed back onto the bed. She twisted her head to and fro as if she could see what I was doing.

"That's it." I panted. "Look around. Pull on your nipples. Can you feel what I'm doing? I'm right on top of you."

I straddled Hannah's chest. I was jerking off above her face. A drop of lube hit her chin and we moaned together.

"Oh, God, Hannah, God," I whispered. "I'm going to come, baby, fuck, I'm—"

I gasped and gripped the headboard, coming spontaneously. Pleasure bowed my back. I fought to keep my eyes open as I milked my cum onto Hannah's face.

I had played this way with other lovers in the past, but the memories were like ashes. No fire. Not even a spark. No other sex in my life had touched this level of eroticism.

Hannah began to shudder in her bonds, fighting and making obscene sounds. I checked her hand. She held the marble fast. I felt a surge of admiration for her, and dark gratitude.

"I know," I whispered into her ear. "You wish you weren't gagged so you could lick up all that cum, don't you? Or maybe you'd like to come as well. I told you last night that I would go easy on you if you made a mess for me, and you did. You squirted for me like a bitch in heat."

Hannah's cheeks flushed. I jostled her nipple clamps.

"I recorded that little show last night. I thought about making you watch it today, but I couldn't wait to get you blindfolded. I love you like this. You love it, too. If I wanted to be cruel, I would make you wait for release until I'm hard again. But you've been perfect, Hannah. Now beg to come. Beg for something inside. Do your best, lover."

With a few deft tugs, I loosened her gag and tossed it away.

Hannah sucked in air like she'd been drowning.

"Please!" She sobbed. The word sent shivers through me. I grabbed her long purple vibrator and dialed it up to the highest speed.

"Ins-inside! Inside me, God! Let me come, M-Matt, let me, in . . . please, I—"

I allowed myself one last look at Hannah bound, Hannah in the throes of desperation, and then I slid her thong aside and plunged the vibrator into her sex. I didn't even need to move it. As soon as I pressed the curve of it up into her G-spot, she began to come.

Pleasure gripped Hannah the way it gripped me—first in a powerful paroxysm, then in rolling waves of bliss.

I watched her face as she came. No wonder they called it the little death. Her pain sounded so much like her pleasure, or her pleasure like her pain, and the ecstasy on her face could have been agony.

She moaned and wet my hand with her desire, and I held the toys against her until her struggling ceased.

We slept in a sweaty tangle. The ties and toys lay strewn around the edges of my bed. For the first time, I held Hannah's naked body as she held mine. Our hearts slowed together. Our breaths grew even and deep.

When I woke, Hannah was exploring my body with her small hands. I realized I had been feeling her touch as I dozed, like the touch of some curious animal, on my face, my hair and neck, my shoulders, my back. I sighed and she paused.

"Keep going," I whispered.

Her feathery touches grew urgent. She pawed at my ass; she squeezed the lean contours of my torso and smoothed her hands over the hard planes.

When she scooted down to hold my thighs, she began to lap at my cock.

We made love as the evening sun burned away.

We touched all of one another, tasted everything. We were slow, gentle, and quiet. We took what we wanted. We gave it up. Hannah rode my face, I wriggled my tongue into her ass, she pinched and licked my nipples. My eyes watered with the force of my climax. We drowsed and woke again. I mounted her. She mounted me. Our skin glistened.

Again and again we went there together—tumbling over the raw edge, touching the live wire, collapsing, exploding, dissolving like dead stars.

Chapter 14

HANNAH

I watched Matt sleep in the morning sunlight. He lay sprawled on his stomach with his head beneath a pillow and an arm around my middle.

He was beautiful.

He was more beautiful now than I had ever seen him. My gaze lingered over his long body, the line of his spine, his thighs and calves. I felt the wildest urge to roll him over and kiss my way down his golden treasure trail.

God, I felt amazing. I felt tattered in the best possible way, like our violent passion had blasted me clean. When I eased off Matt's arm and climbed out of his bed, I knew that I was leaving something behind. It was my old skin. He'd taken me for all I was worth.

I pulled on Matt's dress shirt and buttoned it once. I crept down the hall and guzzled water from the tap, then wandered into the library.

Wow, had I ever been right about this guy's reading habits. The room looked like the inside of a professor's office, only larger. The wall-to-wall shelves held reference books, fiction and nonfiction, translations, titles in foreign languages, books on CD, poetry, plays, maps—in short, an abridged library.

I trailed my fingers over the book spines, some so old they were flaking.

I found a large Willa Cather section. I grinned as I plucked *My Ántonia* off the shelf. Ha! I felt like a detective.

There was the Virgil epigraph, which Matt had circled. I flipped to the end of the book. He had highlighted the whole last paragraph and then, in pen, underlined the last sentence: "Whatever we had missed, we possessed together the precious, the incommunicable past."

In the margin he'd scribbled "epi?"

I frowned.

Epi? Epigraph? This was, I knew, the epigraph to *The Silver Cord* by M. Pierce.

My frown shifted to a smirk. Was Matt a secret M. Pierce fan? That might explain why he kept hassling me for liking the author—because he was a fan boy and too much of a literary snob to admit it.

I scanned the fiction, my eyes zipping toward the *P* section. Walker Percy, Sylvia Plath, Thomas Pynchon, Puzo, Proust—huh, no Pierce . . .

"Hannah."

I jumped.

Matt stood in the doorway. His face was pale and his hair was crazy. Black lounge pants clung to his hips.

"Matt, hey." I gave a shaky laugh. "You scared me . . ."

Fuck, his eyes were so deadly serious. Girl in a tiger cage. Girl about to be devoured. He looked between the shelf and the book in my hands.

"Your um—" I cleared my throat. "Your hair is awesome right now."

Matt eyed me a moment longer, then reached to touch his hair. A few pieces stuck straight up. The rest was matted.

"This is the new style," he murmured.

A cautious smile spread on his lips. I laughed too readily. Jeez, what was *that* all about? Mr. Frostypants in the morning? Or did he think I was snooping?

I glanced guiltily at the book in my hand. Okay, maybe I was snooping.

Matt slipped the book from my hand and returned it to the shelf.

"Mm, Willa Cather. A brilliant author. And this is her best, hands down. It's the one she was meant to write."

Matt smiled as he studied the shelf. I stared at his handsome profile. Now he was warm and enthusiastic; a moment ago he'd looked ill and nearly violent. I had to admit, his changeable moods excited me, but they worried me, too.

"Do you know what I mean?" he said. "Authors write book after book, throwing darts at the board. Many stick, but one hits the bull's-eye. The one they were meant to write. Nice shirt." He squeezed my ass as his eyes traveled the shelves. "I read to find the bull's-eye. *The Sound and the Fury, Never Cry Wolf, Franny and Zooey, Four Quartets—*"

"*The Silver Cord,*" I blurted.

Matt snorted. "Oh, please, not again with the M. Pierce fan girl routine."

"Okay, if I'm such a fan girl, then why do you—" My voice quavered. I was staring at Matt's copy of *My Ántonia* and debating the wisdom of calling him out. Calling him out for what, though? He obviously despised M. Pierce. My evidence to the contrary was convoluted and conspiratorial, and it made me look Matt obsessed more than anything, like I memorized and picked over his every word.

"Why do I *what*?" Matt demanded.

"Why do you . . . know . . . about the Granite Wing rumor?" I cringed. Lame.

Matt's eyes were hard as emeralds.

"As you can see," he said, gesturing to his books, "I'm decently well-read. I like to stay abreast of literary trends. That means I may read shitty online zines like *Fit to Print* once in a blue moon, and I can't really be blamed for their chronic hard-on for that second-rate author. I happened to glimpse their article with all the alleged Pierce facts, including that Granite Wing gossip. *Fit to Print* indeed." Matt scoffed. "In a tabloid."

I flattened my hands against Matt's chest. His expression softened.

"It's like you have an axe to grind with that poor author," I said. I nuzzled my face into his skin and he folded his arms around me.

"I doubt she's poor. And I don't have an axe to grind, all right? I just don't think she's any Cather. Not even close."

"Well, I do." I kissed his nipple and he twitched. God, I loved that. "And I studied literature, so that's that, Mr. Businessman."

Matt gave me a swift smack on the ass.

We showered together and had a morning quickie, which involved Matt rubbing my clit with a soapy finger until it stung. Maybe he was depraved, after all. And damn, did I enjoy it.

We took our time getting dressed. Matt watched everything I did with those smoldering green eyes of his, and when I caught him staring, he didn't look away. God, he looked delicious with a towel around his hips.

I didn't think I could ever get tired of his body.

When he pulled off my towel in the living room, I bent and gripped the arm of his couch. I smiled over my shoulder at him. The hunger in his eyes thrilled and frightened me, and I yelped as he entered me all at once. His powerful thrusts slapped our bodies together. I felt his balls hitting my sex.

Like I said, we took our time getting dressed.

Finally, around noon, we got into our clothes and kept them on. Unhappiness settled over me as we stood together in the kitchen. Matt would drive me home soon, and I hadn't gotten enough of him.

I picked at his shirt. It was a soft white T-shirt that he'd paired with loose brown linen shorts. I was in my wrinkled sundress.

I had an internal debate going over whether Matt looked better in formal dress or casual dress. I also had an internal debate going over whether Matt was real. He didn't add up. Sexy well-read guy with a god's body, the cutest pet ever, ridiculous influence, lots of spare change, and an interest in me? No way.

"Happy Fourth," he said quietly, breaking into my thoughts.

"Oh, yeah. I totally forgot." I frowned and tousled my wet curls. Right, it was a Thursday and Matt wasn't working. He was here fucking me all over his apartment. Thank you, America. "Yeah, happy Fourth, Matt."

I smiled up at him. He grinned back at me.

"Can't imagine why you might have forgotten."

"Pfft. It's not a big-deal holiday anyway. You've been weirdly aware of it, though." I squinted at him. "Maybe you're like special ops. Or a CIA agent."

Matt smirked.

"Do I strike you as a patriot?"

"You don't strike me as anything yet."

He leaned down and his husky voice tickled my ear.

"Oh, but I do strike you, Hannah."

I shivered. He pulled back. Good on him, because I was about to provoke him into bending me over the counter again.

"No, but seriously," he said, "if I seem very aware of the holiday, it's only because it'll take you away from me."

My heart fluttered. Okay, add obscenely charming to his assets.

I remembered Matt asking me if I had any plans for the Fourth. Was he worrying about this yesterday?

"Hey," I said, "crazy idea, but you mentioned you didn't have plans. Why don't you come over? My family won't care at all, and I promise they're not as crazy as my sis—"

"Yes, fine."

Matt stared at a wall.

Again, I felt that unexpected, fierce pity.

Matt had been waiting for me to ask, I realized, but he would never have imposed.

I remembered him admitting that he didn't have many friends. If I hadn't invited him, what would he do?

I pictured Matt sitting alone on his balcony.

"Matt, God." I hugged him. He lifted me off my feet and I squeaked. "You should have asked. I don't want to be apart from you, believe me."

"Hannah . . . there are so many things I want to tell you." He crushed me to his chest. He kissed my temple. I would have given anything for a look at his expression—why did he sound so distraught?—but my feet were dangling and my face was pressed into his neck.

We got lunch in the city. Matt stopped at a florist and bought two lily bouquets. He shoved one at me.

"Flowers," he muttered.

"I see that." I gave him a peck on the cheek. "You're so adorable. So sweet and strange. Thank you, Matt."

"Mm. Do you think I should bring anything? Food? Potato salad? Buns?" I recognized the restless look in his eyes. It was the same look I'd seen when he drove me to dinner in Boulder, the same look I'd seen when I was inspecting his apartment. Matt in anxious mode.

I was starting to learn some things about Matt, even if I didn't understand them. For one, he was most comfortable in his car. Given any remotely social setting, his confidence did a carriage-to-pumpkin transformation and he became this endearingly awkward no-eye-contact guy staring at his phone and jangling the keys in his pocket.

I hauled him back to his car.

"No, no buying food, relax. This isn't a formal thing, Matt. We'll just chill."

"Chill," he repeated.

"Yeah, chill. If you're uncomfortable, we can hide in my room."

handsome stranger at my side with three bags of chips, two jars of salsa, and a bouquet of lilies, which he had the good grace not to thrust into my mom's chest.

I'd never brought home a guy who gave my mom flowers.

Matt just about charmed her pants off. As she thanked him profusely for the flowers and food, she kept shooting these intense, meaningful looks at me.

Ugh, I knew exactly what she was getting at. Mom harangued me and my sister on a regular basis about "not making the same mistakes she made" and being sure to "marry a rich man." Matt reeked of wealth, even in casual clothes. His shorts? Boss Black. I'd snuck a peek during one of our abortive efforts to dress.

Chrissy came bounding into the kitchen. Matt was petting Daisy, who had her head on his knee and was whining and swishing her tail a mile a minute. It was surreal to watch Matt's magnetism work on my family, even the damn dog. At least it wasn't just me.

"Hey, kids!" Chrissy grinned at us.

"Hey." I gave her a flat look. "Thanks for texting to check up on me."

"I . . . didn't text."

"Exactly."

"Aw, come on." She bumped my hip. "I didn't want to interrupt your afternoon delight."

Matt made a choking sound that might have been a laugh.

Mom's eyes lit up.

I dragged Chrissy into the backyard, my face on fire.

"How about let's not make sexual innuendos in front of Mom?" I rolled my eyes. "And for the record, that's nighttime delight, morning delight, *and* afternoon delight."

Chrissy's jaw dropped.

Worth it.

Watching Matt with my family that day was pure pleasure, and I'm not exactly sure why. He shook hands with my dad and they quickly fell into conversation about the stock market. Even I

A little smile played on his lips.

"Hide," I repeated, emphasizing the word, "not bang and p tentially embarrass me in front of my family."

"I can be quiet."

I tried not to think about the litany of dirty talk that poure out of Matt every time we fooled around.

You're a slut for me, aren't you Hannah?

I love the color of your cunt.

Faster, Hannah.

I'm hard for you.

Fuck. I was not going to arrive home with my thong soaked.

"I'm not so sure about that," I said.

"Then I view today as an opportunity to prove it." Safe in the fortress of his car, Matt was all smirks. "Anyway, I'm capable o exchanging pleasantries. I won't be bunkering in your room. I *am* relaxed. This is me relaxed."

Relaxed, my ass. Matt became increasingly agitated as we neared the house. He sneered and adjusted the rearview mirror. He drummed his long fingers on the wheel.

And he sped past my house.

"My . . . house is back there," I said, peering at him.

"Mm."

Matt drove like a bat out of hell to the nearest King Soopers and proceeded to buy an embarrassing amount of potato salad and chips.

"Stop buying things!" I wailed as he dragged me down the aisles.

"It makes me feel better," he snapped.

In the end, all I could do was laugh as Matt glared at the various brands of chips and muttered to himself, the pile in his arms growing.

My mother was speechless when we finally arrived. I couldn't blame her. Daisy was barking and making a puddle in her excitement, and I had four tubs of potato salad in my arms and a tall couldn't get Matt's attention at that point. Dad offered him a beer and he politely declined, though later Matt brought a bottle to me.

"I should have brought a six-pack," he whispered. He wrinkled his nose as he handed me the Coors. Our fingers brushed and a jolt went through me. Our eyes met. Had he felt that?

"Sorry my family's beer doesn't meet with your approval."

"Mm, no help for it. At least I'm not drinking it."

"Ooh, the snob emerges."

"No help for that, either."

I laughed and shoved him. I could feel Mom, Dad, and Chrissy staring at us. When I looked up, they all jumped back to their tasks, Mom setting the table and Dad grilling, Chrissy messing with an extension cord so she could get her CD player outside.

Mom had to forcefully extract my brother from the basement. Jay came sulking out with a Frisbee. Matt grinned when he saw it.

"Oh, a Frisbee," he said, sidling up to my brother. I could tell he was trying to sound nonchalant. So fucking cute. "Nice . . ."

Matt plucked the Frisbee from my brother's hand, kicked off his flip-flops, and jogged across the lawn. Jay looked forever grateful for the absence of introductions.

The table was set and Dad was grilling and Chrissy was dancing scandalously on the lawn. Mom went in and out, lighting citronella candles. I leaned against the deck railing and watched Matt and my brother throw the Frisbee.

It seriously wasn't right, especially when Matt decided to follow Jay's lead and shucked off his T-shirt. Holy Adonis in motion. He moved with effortless grace, his long limbs flexing as he tore after the Frisbee, and every time he leapt to catch it I would swear his shorts slipped lower on his hips. Was he doing this on purpose?

I couldn't wring a glance out of him—even when I tried. I tossed my hair and cocked out my hip. I leaned forward, making my cleavage swell. I tried a little wave. Nothing.

The boy was as bad as Daisy, speeding single-mindedly after the Frisbee.

Hmph. Two could play at this game.

I went inside and changed into tiny torn-up jean shorts and a blue bikini top.

Back outside, I leaned into the rail again and pretended to be enjoying the sun.

Nothing.

Matt laughed as Jay and Daisy collided.

What the hell! Show the man a Frisbee and I no longer exist?

Chrissy tugged on my arm.

"Dance lesson time," she said. "Don't fight it, Hannah. I told you this was coming, and the time is now."

I resisted for a moment. I was so not about to make a fool out of myself in front of Matt. But who said I'd make a fool out of myself?

"Yeah." I smiled hesitantly. "Okay, let's do it. Teach me how to twerk."

Chrissy squeed and pulled me onto the grass by her CD player. Hip-hop throbbed out of the speakers. First she demonstrated, her hands on her knees and her booty popping to the rhythm, then she arranged my arms and legs and started coaching me through the motions. It was surprisingly easy. Once I got the basics down, she showed me how to throw in body rolls and make my ass jiggle like Jell-O. I could feel my jean shorts riding up.

"This feels *amazing*!" I shouted way louder than necessary.

I glanced over my shoulder just in time to see Matt gaping at me. The Frisbee sailed past his head, narrowly missing it.

Success.

My parents aren't priers, thank God, so no one pestered Matt about his work or life as we ate. My twerking lesson also had more than the desired effect. I caught Matt watching me every time I looked at him. He slid his bare foot over mine. Fuck, I'd done this to myself.

When Mom and Chrissy started to clear the table, Jay darted back inside. Dad went to fiddle with the grill and avoid cleanup.

Fuck, fuck, fuck. Matt was gazing at my little blue bikini top.

"Why don't you show me around?" he said quietly.

Another thing I was learning about Matt: This guarded, dark look in his eyes meant only one thing. I was about to get fucked.

I took him on a tour of the house. I lingered upstairs, around people, and Matt followed me patiently. In fact, he seemed unusually interested in everything. He smiled at a picture of five-year-old me with curling pigtails.

"The little bird," he said, touching the frame.

We were in the living room. I shoved my hands into my back pockets.

"Yup. And that's really about it. Home sweet home."

Matt smirked at me.

"Show me your room," he said. He closed the distance between us and seized my breast. I gasped. My hand flew to my mouth. In the next room, I could hear Mom humming as she loaded the dishwasher. "Or I'll do this right here."

Matt wasn't bluffing. He slid the little triangle of fabric off my breast and started to rub his thumb over my nipple. I staggered back.

"Okay, okay!" I whispered. I adjusted my bikini top. "God, down, boy."

Matt laughed and I fake glared.

Bossing me around in my own house! He had no limits, a fact I should have known by then. I also should have known better than to tease him with the dance, but maybe I did. Maybe knowing better was exactly why I did it.

I wanted him in my house.

I wanted him in my room, wanting me.

I wanted him everywhere, more and more.

Chapter 15

MATT

Hannah's ass twitched as she led me down to the basement.

I felt my pulse accelerating. Too bad we needed to be quiet. After her show outside, I wanted to tie her up and give her the spanking of her life.

Jay was in the main area of the basement, installed in front of a computer. There were two other computers, three gaming consoles, controllers, remotes, two old TV sets, and wires everywhere, not to mention empty soda cans and bags of chips.

How depressing.

Jay was smashing keys and leaning toward the screen, shouting into a headset like the one Hannah had. He didn't even look up as Hannah led me to her room.

"Some view in there," I said as she closed and locked her door.

I wanted to look around, but I couldn't tear my eyes off of Hannah. The little bikini top she wore barely covered her breasts and her jean shorts were like denim panties. I pulled her to me.

Hannah threw her arms around my shoulders and began to kiss my neck.

"Hannah, never deny me," I whispered. My hands traveled over her, squeezing and pulling. "Never deny me your beautiful body."

"Never," she promised.

"Seeing you in this . . ." I slowly untied her bikini and let the long strings dangle down her back. Seeing her in this had nearly given me a heart attack. I let the bikini fall. I undid her shorts and pushed them down her legs.

"I wanted your attention," Hannah whispered.

On my knees before her, I bit her sex through the fabric of a pale purple thong. I squeezed her ass. Hannah covered her mouth with both hands.

"You got it," I said.

I rose and brushed past her, glancing around her room. It looked much the same as it had during our video chat. Damn, the room was small, made smaller by Hannah's queen-size bed and piles of boxes. The only window was high and narrow.

She'd hung a paper lantern from the ceiling. The sight of it tugged at my heart.

Why wouldn't she let me buy her things? I could get her an apartment—a nest where I could visit and play with her. I could get her any clothes she wanted, any books, any furniture.

I closed my eyes and ran my fingers through my hair. This would all be right if I were single. Instead, it was all wrong, and I was dragging Hannah into the wrongness of it, making her a party to my cruelty.

"Matt?"

I turned, and I was back in the dream. The risk and the wrongness were worth it. Hannah stood before me in nothing but her thong, her heavy tits peaked with hard nipples. I sat on the edge of her bed and smiled at her.

"You wanted to dance for me? You wanted my attention? So dance. Let's see those moves again, Hannah."

My cock was already semihard. Giving Hannah orders turned me on. Fuck, being around Hannah turned me on. She was a regular exercise in self-control (or my lack thereof).

Hannah balked.

"Now?" she said.

"Mm, now." I stretched out on her bed, propping my head on her pillow. I undid my shorts and slid my hand into my boxers. "What you did outside. You wanted me to see. You wanted to make me stare. So make me stare, show me. All I could think about was this—us."

I could practically see Hannah kicking herself for teasing me with the dance. I knew she was congratulating herself, too. The girl was one sexy heap of contradictions. She took pleasure in pain. She was exultant in debasement.

Hannah moved to the center of the room and turned her back to me. She held her knees and stuck out her ass. My cock stirred under my hand. Nothing but her tiny thong concealed her sex from my view.

"You're making me ready," I whispered, careful to keep my voice low.

Hannah started dancing, making the cheeks of her ass pop and jiggle. She bent so low that I could see her breasts hanging down. I slid my cock out of my shorts.

"Mm, Hannah . . ."

She peeked back at me and her mouth fell open. I smirked. Damn, I loved when she had that reaction to my cock. I'd seen it first in the back of my Lexus—her eyes widening, her lips parted in shock. It would never get old.

"You're blushing," I informed her. "Don't stop."

Hannah bit her lip and looked away. She kept shaking her ass for me and I kept stroking my cock until I thought I would go mad with wanting to touch her.

"Lose the thong."

Obediently, Hannah wriggled out of her thong and went on dancing. Now I could see her plump pussy between her legs. I pulled out my phone and shot a quick video.

The videos, the pictures, the sketch. Would they be all I had one day? Fuck, I needed to stop worrying about this shit—at least for now.

Fuck now, worry later.

I slid off the bed and went to Hannah. I pushed her smooth body into the wall.

"You want it?" My cock touched her ass, and she began to pant. The exertion of dancing heated her skin.

"Yes," she whispered.

"I'm going to finger your ass first, Hannah. Where's your lube?"

She gestured to a box. Near the top, I found a small black tube of water-based lubricant. I squirted it onto my hand and lubed up my pointer finger, which I slid along Hannah's crack and poised at her puckered entrance. I wasn't planning to try to get my dick in there. Hell, I hadn't been planning on putting my finger in there. Hannah made me crazy.

She pressed her hands to the wall and stuck out her ass. I felt a tremor pass through her and I smiled.

"Nervous?" I murmured. "This is your fault, Hannah. You just had to dance out there and make me look at your ass. Now I have to play with it. Did your other boyfriends like to play with your ass?"

"No," she whispered.

"Good. It's mine. You've got a nice round ass. Can you feel your little anus twitching? Trying to squeeze my finger out, trying to deny me."

I gazed down at my slick digit and the tight ring of muscle contracting against it. I hadn't even started to push. When I did, applying a slow pressure, Hannah jerked and tried to move away.

I chuckled. "Uncomfortable, right?"

"Nn . . . Matt."

"You're a good girl," I whispered. "Relax your ass, darling. Or don't. Stay nice and tight and nervous. Either way, I'm doing this."

My finger popped in suddenly and Hannah yelped. I clamped a hand over her mouth. Through the door, I heard Jay yelling into his headset.

Hannah's body clenched at my knuckle. Holy hell, she was tight.

"You're all right, baby," I spoke into her ear. Her nostrils flared and her dark eyes rolled toward me. "I know, I know, you want to see my finger in your ass, but you can't. It's only halfway in, Hannah. You like it? I know you want to moan and beg for my cock, but it seems like one of us has trouble being quiet." My soft laughter stirred her curls. "I'll have to keep your mouth covered. Do you feel your ass trying to get used to my finger?"

I wiggled my finger in Hannah's bottom. The muscles fluttered and tightened. Hannah grunted against my palm.

"That's nice, baby, I like that noise. I like those embarrassing noises. You yowl like a cat when I fuck you hard, and you whine and beg like a dog. This might be my favorite, though. You're grunting like a pig. Does that mean you like this?"

I shoved my finger in another centimeter. Hannah shuddered.

"Where's my noise? Come on, baby, start grunting. If you don't make this good for me, I won't fuck you."

As usual, I couldn't keep my mouth in check. At least I was still whispering.

I pushed my finger in all the way, and Hannah released another low, involuntary grunt against my palm. Fuck, I had her right where I wanted her. I started to finger her ass hard and fast, forcing my knuckles in against her body's resistance. Hannah jerked against the wall and the noises kept coming, snorts and grunts and snuffles that were driving me wild.

"That's nice, Hannah, God, that's nice." My cock throbbed and I rubbed it against her skin. "When you stop snorting and grunting, I can hear your ass kind of squelching with my finger in there.

I'm getting a lot of lube inside you. I bet you can't wait to be back upstairs, walking around with that lube in your ass, maybe feeling a little sore. This is what you wanted when you shook your ass for me, right?"

Hannah gave a low, humiliated moan.

I stopped fingering her and she tensed.

"More?" I chuckled. "It's your turn now, lover. You need to show me how much you like this. Ride my finger. I'm going to uncover your mouth. Think you can keep your voice down?"

Hannah nodded frantically.

"All right. You stay quiet and ride my finger good with your ass. Make sure you're rubbing your breasts against the wall. You're making me feel perfect."

I lowered my hand from Hannah's mouth, and she took a careful breath. Her eyes slipped closed. With her hands pressed to the wall and her chest thrust into it, she began to bounce her ass on my finger.

"Nnnn . . ." A low, trembling hum sounded in her throat.

"Oh, darling," I breathed. I didn't dare take hold of my cock as Hannah forced her ass onto my finger. I would come. It was too sexy, the sight of Hannah's ass like that.

God, I had to get inside of her. It was hell to delay. It was heaven, too.

"Good girl, Hannah, good girl. Too bad you locked that door, huh? I know what you really want is for someone to come in here and see you riding my finger with your ass."

"Oh," she gasped.

I moved my other hand between Hannah's legs so that her next motion forced three of my fingers into her pussy.

She made a strangled noise.

"Shhh, shhh. Keep going. Now you're nice and full, aren't you?"

"Yes . . . yes."

"Good. This is how you like it, right? Something in your ass, something in your pussy. All you need is something in your mouth."

The possibility excited me as I considered it. A cute little plug for Hannah's butt, her purple vibrator deep in her cunt, and my cock in her mouth. We'd both come so hard. I shivered.

"God damn, Hannah, let's go." I slid my fingers out of her body and grasped her hips. She knew what was coming. She positioned her body so sweetly; I was wrapped around her finger. She gazed over her shoulder with half-lidded eyes and whispered my name. Why did I think I had any power over Hannah? I was hers.

I impaled her slowly. The cushioned walls of her sex gripped my cock, and when I slid back they sucked at me greedily. Mesmerized, I watched my shaft dip in and out of her, the smooth organ coated with her wetness.

"You . . . hold me so tight," I whispered. My voice was strained.

Usually I wanted to pound my way toward climax, at least for the first round, and especially with Hannah. She made me desperate.

But it was different this time. This time it felt profoundly personal—what Hannah's body was doing to me, what mine was doing to her.

When I glanced up, I found her watching me with hazy eyes. She smiled. I returned a shaky smile.

"Hey," I murmured. So much for my dirty talk. Hannah smiled and my brain melted.

We were silent as I picked up the pace. Hannah spread her legs and jutted her ass toward me. Her instincts were perfect; she did exactly what I needed. She didn't try to meet my thrusts with clumsy motions, she simply stood firm and let me beat into her from behind.

I was swelling or she was getting tighter, or both. The stimulation was exquisite.

Even as I neared climax and reached around to start rubbing Hannah's clit, we kept quiet. I think we were both straining to hear the sound: the squishing and slapping of our bodies coming together desperately. We had no shame in our pleasure. We were perfect partners.

Hannah's orgasm brought on mine. Her cunt squeezed and I exploded.

"Come inside me," she panted. "Oh, God . . ."

I told her that I was coming. I told her to come on my dick. I almost told her I loved her.

Sex is the damnedest thing.

Chapter 16

HANNAH

Matt started to cry after we had sex in my room.

This was a day of firsts.

A guy giving my mother flowers. A guy crying after sex with me.

I always thought if a guy cried after sex, I would forever see him as a milquetoast. I'm not heartless; the idea just seems sappy.

That was before I met Matt. Matt crying, and trying to hide his tears, was the saddest, sweetest thing I had seen in a long time. And it was deeply affecting. I felt my own eyes watering as he shuffled away and swiped his forearm across his face.

"Sorry, fuck." He fumbled with his shorts.

"Hey, come here."

Another first: not feeling hella awkward comforting someone. I had never been good at this kind of thing. With Matt, it came naturally. I went to him and pulled him into a warm hug. I stroked my fingers through his hair and rubbed his back.

"It was just a really intense orgasm," he mumbled.

Just a really intense orgasm? Matt wasn't sobbing, but I had seen the tears rolling down his cheeks. They weren't happy tears. He was sad, and he looked shaken.

Where did this grief come from?

"Matt, let me in," I said. "Let me into your life a little bit."

When we pulled apart, there was no trace of his tears except for the faintest redness to his eyes. He smiled and ruffled my hair.

"I am," he said. "I will."

I sent Matt upstairs before me so that we wouldn't stumble into the kitchen together, suspiciously flushed. Matt's hair looked a little wild, but I let that go. Only Chrissy might notice and know what it meant, and the thought made me wickedly gleeful.

I pulled on my bikini top and shorts, throwing on a long T-shirt overtop.

We strolled through the yard as night came on. Matt took my hand.

I couldn't shake the feeling that something was troubling him, though other times he looked so content that my worries seemed silly.

Whatever the case, we gave up trying to avoid public displays of affection. In plain view of Dad on the deck and Mom in the kitchen (and Chrissy potentially spying from her room), Matt pressed me against an old cottonwood and kissed me longingly.

We lay together in the hammock, cackling and nearly pitching out of it until we got settled. I told him how much his library impressed me. We chatted about the authors we both liked—Frost, Chandler, Kerouac—and Matt quoted a poem to me, "The Fire of Drift-wood."

"That's one of my favorites," he said.

He'd recited the lines with feeling and then flashed a small, self-deprecating smirk, as if I might mock him.

"It's beautiful," I said, "and sad. Do you like sad things?"

I ran my fingers along the neckline of his shirt. I had finally relaxed enough to stop worrying that I was crushing the breath out of him. The only hammock arrangement that didn't end with us in the dirt was me stretched out on top of Matt.

He feathered his fingers through my hair and gazed up into the sky.

"I guess so. At least, sad things seem truest to me."

"Truest? Happiness isn't true?"

"It's true." He smiled. "But sadness is truer. Whatever else life contains, it's sad because it has to end."

"But life would be hell if it went on forever."

"Or heaven," he murmured.

I traced my fingers down Matt's side. I could feel a few ribs. God, he was all muscle and taut skin. I'd watched him pick at his lunch earlier while leering at me like I was the most appetizing thing at the table.

I wanted to feed him. I wanted to comfort and take care of him.

And I never wanted to let him go, which would be unavoidable tonight. He probably had work tomorrow, and I absolutely had to start pulling my weight at home—unpacking, making a more serious effort to help with Mom's work, and brushing up my résumé for Pamela Wing. Which reminded me.

"Matt, do you know the fax number at Pamela Wing's office?"

"Actually, I do," he said. "I'll give it to you before I go."

Before I go. My chest tightened.

I heard a distant pop.

"The fireworks are starting," I said. Thank God. I couldn't lie there thinking about Matt driving off tonight. "We better get up on the deck."

"Yeah." He sounded as subdued as I felt.

It was a hot night, but Mom lit a fire and we all sat on the deck watching three distant displays. Matt shoved his chair laughably close to mine and still looked unhappy about the arrangement. I think he would have preferred me on his lap.

He checked his phone neurotically. I had to nudge him a few times to show him the prettiest fireworks, the ones that fell like gold dust and lingered in the sky.

When the finale went off, Matt helped put away the folding

chairs and clear the citronella candles. Daisy whined and followed him. I wanted to whine and follow him, too.

He shook hands with Dad. He hugged Mom. Jay and Chrissy were already downstairs on the PS3, where they'd be until two in the morning.

I trailed Matt to his car.

I could get in and go home with him. Would he want that? Tonight had been magical for me, but maybe Matt was putting on a show. Maybe he couldn't wait to be alone. He was a puzzle, and the more I opened up to him, the more closed he seemed to me.

"I know I can't steal you away tonight," he said. "Would you come?"

"In a heartbeat, Matt. But—"

"I know. Life."

"Yeah." I held his hips. "Tomorrow's Friday, though."

"Can I see you?"

"Of course! There's no one I'd rather see, and it's not like I have any other friends."

"What about the high school friend?"

"Evan?" I laughed. "Doesn't count. He's trying to get in my pants."

For a moment, Matt looked frankly homicidal. I swallowed and tried to hug him. His body was unyielding.

"Hey, hey," I said. "You're my only friend here. You're my only lover."

Lover. Fuck, that word sounded strange. What were Matt and I, anyway? Were we dating, or just fuck buddies?

"Lover," Matt murmured. He must have been pondering similar questions.

He hugged me at last and kissed me, telling me with his body that he didn't want to say good-bye. He deepened the kiss. He moaned softly into my mouth and began to pull my body against his. God, he wanted me again. And I wanted him again. I wanted him until we were both too exhausted to move.

I hooked a leg around him and squeezed his ass.

He tugged at my earlobe.

"If you get me hard," he growled, "you have to deal with it."

"Yes, sir." I began to tug on his shorts.

We laughed and broke away from one another.

"Tomorrow," he said. He texted me Pamela Wing's fax number as we stood together by his car, and then he got in and drove away slower than I thought he was capable of driving. I watched his taillights disappear around the corner.

I was starting to understand his aversion to good-byes.

I revised my résumé and faxed it to Pamela Wing's office that night, along with a cover letter reintroducing myself, apologizing for my ill-prepared state at our first meeting and expressing my enthusiasm about working under her.

Writing the letter and retooling my résumé took my mind off Matt for an hour. As soon as the fax machine spit out the pages, I felt his absence. It expanded inside my chest until it hurt. Why was this happening?

Maybe I was seeing too much of Matt.

Maybe I wasn't seeing enough of him.

I drifted around the house. He'd been everywhere, and he made everything beautiful. He made my kitchen beautiful. He made my backyard radiant. He even made our hideous gaming room funny. Now the same rooms were dark and lonely.

I checked my e-mail as I lay in bed. I was surprised to see a story installment from Matt, sent about five minutes earlier. I checked the time: 12:50 A.M. My night owl. I smiled and snuggled down to read his paragraphs.

In the whirlwind of the last two days, I had forgotten about our story. Suddenly I couldn't wait to see Cal's response to Lana bathing. My eyes skimmed over the text.

Oh, this was good.

A familiar heat spread through me as I read.

Cal stared at Lana's naked body, making no effort to conceal his interest. "He was no gentleman," Matt wrote, "and enjoyed the luxury of knowing it."

Matt wrote without reference to the setting, which worked. Cal was oblivious of his surroundings. There was only the human bathing with her back to him. I knew things were going to get good when Cal glimpsed the rounded sides of her breasts.

Cal wasn't without complexity, though. As he undressed and approached the dark river, he considered what it would mean for him and Lana to be together. He was a demon, after all, and she was mortal. Matt made his plight sincere—and aching.

Cal walked the world in the skin of another.

He could have Lana, but he couldn't keep her. He couldn't love her.

I projected myself shamelessly onto Lana as that dangerous creature prowled toward her and slipped into the river like a snake. He extracted the soap from her hands. He began to wash her body. The roiling undercurrent bumped them together.

Hot damn.

I texted Matt.

Nice post. Thanks.

He replied instantly.

Yw. Writing it beat lying here missing you, which I'm doing now. Good night, little bird.

Matt was lying in bed missing me. And I was lying in bed missing Matt. Okay, we were in the same boat. Now where was this boat going?

My cell woke me at 7:15 A.M.

I groped for my glasses and took the call, though I didn't recognize the number.

"H—" I coughed. Crap, morning voice. "Excuse me. Hello?"

"Hi, Hannah, Pam Wing. Impressive résumé. Matt neglected

to mention your US-UK Fulbright. Very nice. I need you in here today."

I threw off my sheets. Pamela freaking Wing needed me today. I was not about to go starry-eyed and speechless for the second time.

"That sounds great," I said. "I'm excited to get started. I'll be there within the hour."

"Perfect."

Click.

Within the hour. Within forty-five minutes. Maybe I should have given myself a little latitude, but I had to make up ground with Pamela Wing.

I showered and shaved in fifteen minutes and took more time with my outfit. I wanted to look professional, and I wanted to be comfortable. I wore nude nylons, a gray pencil skirt, a white blouse, and black pumps.

I forced my mind to stay on track. That meant no thinking about Matt, because thinking about Matt meant drooly daydreaming.

I flew through the doors of the Granite Wing Agency at 7:55 A.M. Score.

The building was empty. After some cautious wandering, I found my way to Pamela Wing's office. Her door was open and she was seated at her desk, flipping through a sheaf of papers and frowning. She didn't look up when I knocked.

"Not quite within the hour, Hannah, but close enough."

Not quite within the hour? I glanced at my watch, my cheeks burning. Okay, so ten minutes of searching the building put me in Pam's doorway at 8:05 A.M., but seriously?

I remembered Matt's words. *There is no margin of error.* He wasn't kidding. And fuck, now was *not* the time to start thinking of Matt with his sly smile and hard torso and huge—

"You're in there." Pam pointed with her pen to a door off her office, still not looking up from her paperwork. "I've laid out some documents for you to go over. You won't find any errors; these

are finalized documents pertaining to electronic rights for one of our authors. I need you to get familiar with them today. I also need to get a feel for your ability as a reader. You'll find five partial manuscripts on your desk; read them and write up your impressions. E-mail those to me by the end of the day. I've already been over the samples. If we're on the same page, you'll be helping me cull the slush pile. Finally, I need you to . . ."

Pam went on for about five minutes, piling on tasks.

I refused to feel intimidated. (Or rather, I refused to let how intimidated I felt show on my face.) She was probably trying to see if I scared easily, and I don't. I listened to her instructions, made mental notes, thanked her, and got started.

Well, first I texted Matt.

Working for the shark. Lunch break at 1. Meet me?

Then I got started.

Chapter 17

MATT

I called Pam on Friday morning.

I had to cover my bases about Hannah.

To be honest, I was starting to crack.

I met Hannah's family. I cried after we fucked. Oh, and Bethany texted once and called twice while I was at Hannah's house. Fuck.

Lists. Look at the lists. Get control. Make an appointment with Mike. Call Pam. Fuck, I fucked up. I fucked up with my overblown reaction to M. Pierce. Hannah noticed. *It's like you have an axe to grind with that poor author.*

That poor author. Me. I was overdoing it. My anger looked suspicious, the way I mocked Hannah for liking my books, the way I put down Pierce. Should have played it differently. Should have feigned indifference.

Now I had Hannah shadowing my fucking agent. Fuck. Brilliant move, Matt. You just couldn't resist the opportunity to throw your weight around.

No, that wasn't it. I couldn't resist the opportunity to help Hannah get a job.

But I wasn't a businessman. I didn't have dozens of connections in Denver. I had one connection and I used it for Hannah, and now I was losing sleep over it.

Losing sleep? That implied I had sleep to lose, and I didn't sleep a wink last night. I tossed and turned in my net of lies.

"Pick up, pick up," I muttered as I paced through my apartment.

"Morning." Pam sounded harassed. "How's the writing going?"

"It's not. We have to talk."

"You have a therapist. I'll give you five minutes."

"I'm fucking serious, Pam. It's about Hannah. You know, that—"

"Yes, I know. She faxed her résumé—on the Fourth, no less. I hope she works out."

"What? Are you taking her on?"

"Trying. She's on her way here now. I'll think about thanking you if she doesn't have a breakdown by the end of next week."

"Go easy on her," I snarled. Fuck! I pulled at my hair. Why did I say that?

"Is there a point to this call? I appreciate the secretary. I don't appreciate being told how to run my business. I assume when you recommended Hannah you felt she was capable of—"

"Pam, sorry. Listen. Forget that. She's a friend. That's why I'm calling. This goes almost without saying, but it's imperative that . . ."

I stopped pacing. I rubbed my neck as I searched for words.

For once in her life, Pam didn't seize my silence as an opportunity to interject. Even that unnerved me. Was she curious about my relation to Hannah? Pam did a good job of disguising any interest in me and my life, but she was also one of the most cunning people I knew. She had probably figured out a lot about me over the years.

God, now I was analyzing Pam. Was Pam analyzing me? Fuck, I just needed to eat. My morning coffee on an empty stomach was giving me the shakes.

"Imperative that she . . . not know who I am," I stumbled. Awesome phrasing. Way to go, bestselling author. "Ah, that is, documents and . . . things you might have with my name . . . in connection with . . ."

Pam let me flounder. I despised her for it.

"Pam, I know you take my privacy as seriously as I do, but in this circumstance I . . ."

Finally, the steely bitch spoke up. Goddamn, I was glad to have Pam Wing as a friend and not an enemy.

"There is nothing in this office," she said, "on paper or otherwise, in that connection. It's all at my home office, and even there, the computers have passwords and the file cabinet is locked. I'm surprised you've never asked about this before."

Pam was right. Until now, I never cared to know how Pam safeguarded my identity, I only cared that she did it. She had to be wondering what about Hannah inspired my paranoia. Fuck, fuck. This call was another mistake.

"You say you know I take your privacy seriously," she went on, "but maybe you don't know. Your publishers and I cannot publicize you—more's the pity. All we *can* publicize is your mystery. I trust this makes sense to you. I have a vested interest in your anonymity. Now, rather than insulting me with insinuations that I am careless, why don't you join the working world and do some writing. Your five minutes are up."

Pam hung up.

I sank into my office chair.

Fuck, I felt like puking.

Normally, Pam's zingers delighted me. Not today.

I opened my lists. I'm a list maker. Mike says I need to break away from the lists; he says that I need to feel comfortable with the conditions of life, which are often out of my control.

I say fuck that.

Just opening the documents made my hands stop shaking.

I could cover all my bases. I wasn't living a double life. I was protecting the integrity of my prose. I could be with Hannah. I could keep her from getting hurt. I could do it all.

I zoned out as I scanned my lists.

First, I had a list of people who knew I was M. Pierce (and their nondisclosure agreements on file): Bethany, one of my exes, my brothers Nate and Seth, my uncle, one friend, Pam and her partner Laura, my psychiatrist Mike, and a select group at Knopf.

I also had lists of important dates. I had lists of precautions to take in protecting my identity. I had to-do lists. Lists of things that frightened me. Lists of unhealthy thought patterns. Lists of ideas for my novels. People to call in emergencies. Reasons to stay sober. Good restaurants. Movies. Songs and artists. Books. Adjectives. Web sites. Colors. Critics. Blogs. Bookshops. Streets. Cars. Quotes. Prizewinners. Magazines. Clubs.

It was all there. It was all organized. I lost nothing.

I opened a new document and typed THINGS I WANT TO DO WITH HANNAH.

I smiled and brooded while the churning in my stomach ceased.

Things I want to do with Hannah: dance, watch a movie, camp, swim, hike, bike, take a trip, build something, have a food fight, write more, do Christmas—

My phone chimed. It was a text from Hannah.

Working for the shark. Lunch break at 1. Meet me?

My carefully collected calm scattered. Hannah. Working for Pam. Wanting to meet me. In five hours. My hands started to shake again.

I didn't need food in five hours. I needed food now. Too bad anxiety kills my appetite.

I texted Hannah.

In spite of the minimeltdown I had going, I jumped at the thought of seeing her. I missed her like hell.

Sounds great. I'd say my place but neither of us will get back to work. The med. deli.

I tried to write over the next two hours. No dice. I tried to eat some cereal. It was like chewing on glue. Finally, I tried to sleep.

I must have drowsed, because I woke with a jolt at 12:50 P.M. Shit, I had to go. Now.

I was in the parking garage when I realized my attire was definitely not "businessman." Not even "casual Friday businessman." More like "I walk dogs for a living."

Fuck. I dashed back to the elevator.

Upstairs, I scrambled to dress.

At 1 P.M. on any Friday in the past, I would have been lounging in front of my computer, sipping coffee, and adding sentences to my latest novel. Now I was putting on a Brooks Brothers suit for the purposes of meeting a girl who thought I was a businessman.

Not even removing Bethany's stuff from the apartment had felt this vile.

I was beginning to really hate myself.

Twenty minutes late, with my jacket slung over my shoulder, I jogged up the sidewalk to the Mediterranean deli. I was sweating profusely and I couldn't stop the tremor in my hands.

I spotted Hannah at one of the tables outside. She beamed when she saw me. When I got closer, her smile faltered.

"Hey," she said uncertainly.

"Hey, bird. Looking sharp."

We hugged and she held onto me. I'll admit, the sight of Hannah in an ass-hugging pencil skirt went a long way toward distracting me, but I couldn't suppress my panic. I felt so damn sleazy, and seeing Hannah tore at my heart.

"Matt, you're shaking."

I pulled away from her.

"Yeah. Yeah, I—" I collapsed into the chair across from Hannah. No way could I eat right now. I held my head in my hands. I knew how I looked: glassy-eyed and ashen, with dark sleepless bags. "I'm hot as hell, too." Better to point that out before Hannah noticed the sweat beading on my brow. Too bad it was another lie. I was in a cold sweat; my skin felt clammy. I draped my jacket around my shoulders.

"Matt . . ."

I glanced up. I met Hannah's big brown eyes, full of concern.

"Work is stressful," I mumbled. "Really stressful. It's a rough day. I'm fine. I couldn't park for shit, I . . ."

At least I was saying a few true things.

Hannah reached for my hand and squeezed it. Such unconditional affection came across from her. And I was trash. I was filthier than trash.

I slid my hand out of hers.

"Hey," she said, "let's get something to eat, yeah?"

"I'm not hungry." I pulled a fifty from my wallet and tossed it across the table. "Get whatever you want."

"Matt, I am not taking—"

"Just take it!" I slammed the table. The umbrella shook above us.

Hannah clutched the bill and shrank in her chair. A few people paused to look at us. God, I was losing it.

"Sorry. Hannah, sorry. It's work." I gestured vaguely. "How's . . . how's work for you, by the way? Pam being a monster?"

"No." Hannah gazed at her lap. "Um . . . she's fine. Impressed, I think."

"Has she asked about me?" I leaned forward. Trying to appear offhanded was never going to work right now. "How we know one another or anything?"

"No, Matt. And don't worry, I didn't ask her about you either. I'm—" Hannah stood. "I'm going to get my lunch. I'll be right back."

I watched her walk into the deli.

When I saw her ordering, I gathered my jacket and bolted.

I couldn't do this anymore.

I had to make it right.

I had to call Bethany.

And maybe I wouldn't tell Bethany the whole truth, and maybe I wouldn't tell Hannah the whole truth, but I had to tell one it was over, and I had to tell the other it was starting.

When I got to my car, I texted Hannah.

I'm so sorry. I got called away. I'm sorry I yelled at you. I'll be better tomorrow. I have an obligation tonight. I'd rather be with you but I have to do this. Let me take you camping this weekend. Tomorrow. We'll go into the mountains. Say yes.

Chapter 18

HANNAH

"You're home early . . ."

Chrissy raised her eyebrows and watched me expectantly.

Chrissy just happened to be in the kitchen when I got home from work. Mom, too. Maybe it was a coincidence, but it felt like they were lurking, waiting to see whether I came home after work or went to Matt's place.

At least Mom didn't beat around the bush.

"You haven't already lost that sweet boy, have you?"

"He's twenty-eight. Not cxactly a boy." I rummaged through the pantry, hiding from Mom's prying eyes and looking for comfort food. "Also, he's not that sweet. He's kind of a douche bag sometimes."

Chrissy clicked her tongue.

Mom made one of her know-it-ally *mhmm* sounds.

I emerged with a bag of cheese puffs and found them nodding at one another.

"Yup, they had a fight," Chrissy said as if I weren't standing right there. "Which works out for me. Can you drive me to work, Hannah?"

"Drive your own ass to work."

I slammed the pantry door and stormed down to the basement.

I couldn't think straight. Was my fairy tale romance crumbling? Was Matt wonderful up until the parental introductions, after which he turned into a snarly, strung-out ogre?

He seriously looked like he was on drugs today, and he acted like it, too. I followed that unsettling line of thought.

He said he quit drinking five years ago. What about drugs?

He had the crazy mood swings. He had the appetite of a bird. Today he was late (he was *never* late) and sweating and shivering in ninety-degree heat. Oh, and then there was the suspicious apartment deep clean before having me over. Fuck.

I unpacked like a hurricane to distract myself.

For the first time since I met Matt, I was starting to feel like he might be too good to be true. Too perfect, too right for me, too interested in me. There had to be a catch.

I was sweating by the time I finished emptying all the boxes in my room. The physical labor felt good. My arms burned and my knees ached.

Never mind the fact that I checked my phone every ten minutes.

I put all my books on the shelves and my one stuffed animal on the bed. I remembered Matt sitting on my bed, smiling at me.

He wanted to go camping tomorrow. Overnight, I assumed. I hadn't given him an answer yet. Yes, I wanted to go camping with the guy who came over on the Fourth of July. No, I didn't want to go camping with the guy I met for lunch today.

Beautiful Matt. Scary Matt.

But in spite of scary Matt's pasty skin and irrational rage, I felt this weird urge to protect him. Maybe he *was* on drugs. Or maybe he was telling the truth. He had money; he could have the high-stress job to go with it.

Whatever Matt's problem was, I wanted to wrap my arms around him and snarl at the world until everything left him alone.

Everything but me.

I put my clothes on hangers and organized the closet. A wardrobe update was in order as soon as I got paid. I needed more work clothes. I needed more thongs. I also needed more clothes that made me feel like I belonged next to Matt.

I frowned as I hung up the blouse and skirt I wore to work.

I wanted to watch Matt trip over himself when he saw me in that skirt. Before I met him for lunch, I undid the top three buttons of my blouse. My platform pumps accentuated my shapely calves. I was even wearing makeup.

Matt's jaw should have hit the sidewalk.

Instead?

Looking sharp. That was all I got.

Meanwhile, albeit sweating and stammering, Matt looked like a male model in an elegant slate gray suit and white shirt.

I strung Christmas lights around the top edges of my room. I hung my posters, calendar, and art. I arranged the knickknacks on my desk and bedside table.

After piling the empty boxes in the garage, I threw myself onto my bed and fiddled with my phone.

Camping. I hadn't been camping in years.

Mick's idea of camping was getting rowdy at an overcrowded campsite.

Matt's idea of camping probably involved little-known uses for stakes and rope.

I smirked and sighed. Why was I pretending I had a choice? The moment Matt asked, I knew my answer. I craved his company. I couldn't wait to be alone with him.

I texted Matt around 7 P.M.

At least I kept him waiting for my answer.

Camping sounds good. No problem about lunch, you were stressed. I was pretty worried. I still am. How's the "obligation" going?

I bit my lip and waited for a reply.

Nothing.

I curled up on my quilt and fought the urge to call.

I wanted to know what Matt's "obligation" was and what he did for a living and a dozen other things he seemed hell-bent on keeping from me. God, he was putting his dick in me multiple times a day. Didn't that entitle me to some illusion of closeness?

Two hours later, my phone chimed.

Birdy bird. Rough day for me. It's over now. I want to be with you. Want to tell you so many things. I'll pick you up early. 9ish.

My body warmed. *I want to be with you.* What did he mean by that?

And why did he keep saying he wanted to tell me things? Why couldn't he just tell me?

More questions, no answers.

God, but I loved when he called me bird.

I pictured his green eyes, sad and serious—or dark with desire, lit with amusement. I fell asleep smiling.

Matt arrived at nine sharp. Right, *9ish.*

He came to the door and Mom answered before I could get upstairs.

As I rounded the corner, I braced myself to see Mr. Frostypants barking at my mother and shivering, and I may have breathed a too-loud sigh of relief when I saw him.

Beautiful Matt was back.

He was smiling and conversing easily with my mother.

He wore a black jersey with three-quarter sleeves and black zip-offs. I wanted to jump him. Matt looked fucking gorgeous in black. I was beginning to grasp that Matt would look fucking gorgeous in a paper bag, but goddamn, every outfit he wore was sexier than the one before.

When he saw me, his smile brightened. He came to me and hugged me; his lips brushed my cheek.

"Hannah," he whispered.

I clung to him.

"Hey. Hi." I ran my fingers through his hair and held his face.

Mom took a hint and wandered off.

"Hey." Matt stroked my cheek. He kissed my jaw, then my mouth. He let me get a good look at him, as if he knew I needed it.

He was clean shaven and freshly showered. There were no signs of the haggard Matt I'd seen yesterday, except for a little darkness beneath his eyes. I traced the shadowy smudges.

"Night owl," I murmured.

"Hannah, I'm—"

I could see the apology forming on his lips and I kissed him, hard. He squeezed my waist. Oh, that felt good.

"It's okay," I said, pulling back. "It's over now, right? We're going camping. We're going to have a blast."

"Yeah . . ."

Matt tugged on my ponytail. He was different today, different in the best possible way, and I found myself watching him as he loaded my stuff into his Jeep. Car number four. Jeez.

"Cute." He smirked as he wedged my puffy blue sleeping bag in beside his tent.

Did the weekend always have this effect on Matt? For once, his smiles weren't edged with unease. There was no distantly troubled look on his face, and not once did I catch him frowning at me like I was the biggest mistake in his universe.

Even his body language was more relaxed. He helped me into the Jeep, then lingered at my side for a slow, maddening kiss.

The drive up to Rocky Mountain National Park was breathtaking. As we neared the mountains, the road wound alongside gushing rivers, sheer walls of rock, and towering stone formations that looked like faces.

Matt asked about my first day of work. He was smiling and curious, not gruff and paranoid. Thank God.

I had barely considered my first whirlwind workday as Pam's secretary; I'd been too worried about Matt. It was a relief to describe the work and make Matt laugh with anecdotes about Pam.

"But I love the job," I told him. "I wish I could describe the feeling that came over me as I read manuscripts. It was like . . . I was meant for this. Like I was finally doing a job I could see myself making into a career."

When I looked at Matt, he was glowing.

He was surprisingly chaste on the drive up to the park. Sometimes he took my hand, and once he ran his fingers from my knee to the top of my thigh.

We stopped in Estes Park, a quaint town on the front range, and waded through crowds of tourists for a lunch of the best fudge I ever tasted.

Matt made me try each flavor he bought—vanilla, maple, amaretto, chocolate cream. That I had never been to the park flabbergasted him. He dragged me into the shops and bought me a beaded bracelet, a little bird figurine, and a tiny bronze padlock on a chain.

"I'll get it engraved," he said, fastening the chain behind my neck.

Engraved with what? I smiled and touched the lock. *HM,* I thought. Hannah & Matt. Maybe I would surprise him and get the engraving done myself.

It was near 2 P.M. when we finally drove into the park proper.

We left everything in the car and hiked out to a glacial lake. I took pictures of Matt when he wasn't looking. His athletic body was beautiful in motion, and his dark shirt and shorts emphasized the gold tone of his skin and the natural highlights in his hair.

The air was thin and cool and smelled of pine. I felt giddy.

"Exhilarating, right?" Matt caught my hand as we looked across a vista.

"God, I feel like Wordsworth in the Alps!" I laughed.

Evening's shadows fall suddenly in the mountains. One minute Matt and I were sweating on the trail, the next I was shivering and squished to his side.

"I packed an extra fleece," he told me as we headed back to the Jeep.

The hike and altitude sapped me. My sugar rush was crashing. Still, as we set out on the trail toward our campsite, I began to feel a very different kind of energy—the rising anticipation of Matt's touch.

Our site was a secluded clearing surrounded by pines. I heard water rushing in the distance. Matt built a fire in the metal ring and hurried through pitching the tent. We spread foam mats under our sleeping bags.

I don't know if I could have felt less sexy. I was sticky with sweat and bug spray, and wearing old sneakers, jeans, and a T-shirt—and now an oversized black fleece.

I perched on a rock by the fire pit. Matt stood nearby, staring into the woods. In the half-light, he looked wild—an animal that would melt into the shadows if I snapped a twig.

Sparks whirled upward. Beyond the light of our fire, the night was cool and silent.

"I brought food," Matt murmured. He turned his gaze down at me. His dark, hungry eyes flashed with reflected flames. "Are you hungry?"

I shook my head.

I didn't want to speak. I didn't want to shatter the magic of the night. My eyes traveled down Matt's body. I knew he was watching me and I looked boldly at his groin.

"Yeah?" he whispered. He stepped closer and reached for my hair, winding my ponytail around his hand. "Suck on me, Hannah."

I undid Matt's shorts and slid his semierect cock from his boxers. It swelled in my hands. I began to lick and suckle at it, taking as much as I could. I fondled Matt's balls as I sucked.

"Oh, Hannah . . . baby."

Matt was fully hard in moments. He pulled me to my feet and we undressed one another. Talk about exhilarating; standing naked in the woods with Matt made my heart rush and skip.

The heat of the fire baked my legs. The chill of the evening hardened my nipples.

I knew we were alone, and yet I felt like we were on a stage. I felt as if the impenetrable darkness were filled with eyes.

Matt kissed me, trapping his cock between us. I stroked his muscled body and rocked into the hard organ, making him moan.

"Hannah," he sighed. "Hannah . . ."

I loved the way he said my name. I loved the hundreds of flavors of his voice.

I hooked my hands over his shoulders and climbed onto him. He lifted me easily, gripping my thighs. He lowered me onto his cock.

We locked eyes as he penetrated me. The pleasure of the invasion made me wriggle against his body. God, he was letting me down so slowly. I felt each inch stretching me open.

"Tell me about my cock," Matt whispered.

As always, I felt disturbingly eager to please him.

"Matt . . ." I wet my lips. "It . . . it fills me. It almost hurts, but I always want it. The whole thing. I want it inside of me."

Matt lowered me another inch and I gasped. He had all the power in this position. I had no leverage to force myself onto his shaft.

"Go on," he said, his voice low in deference to the night.

"I love the taste of it," I whispered, "and the taste of your cum. When you ride me hard, I—" I moaned as Matt let me down all the way, his cock pressed up into me deeply. "Ah, God . . . Matt, God, I lose my mind."

"Tell me, Hannah. Do you like it deep?"

"Yes." I rolled my head back. I felt secure clinging to Matt. He would never let me fall.

I wished suddenly, desperately, to be both myself and a spectator. I wanted to see Matt holding me in the firelight, his feet planted firmly on the earth, his strong thighs and buttocks tensed. And myself, wound around him, our bodies locked together intimately.

We were night and day. Gold-skinned and pale. Fair-haired

and dark. Tall and short. Lean and lush. And Matt was so ample between his legs, where I was so small.

"You almost hurt me, too," Matt whispered. "So tight, Hannah. But you get so wet and let me in. My body—"

Matt lifted and lowered me minutely and bucked his hips as he did, bouncing me on an inch of his cock. I groaned and bit his shoulder. He breathed raggedly into my hair.

"T-tell me," I stammered.

"My body . . . craves your body." Matt bounced me again and we moaned together. "It f-feels the distance . . . when we're apart. Hannah, I can't be apart from you."

"You never have to be," I said.

I shifted to get a look at Matt. Each motion of my thighs and spine made the muscles of my sex clamp at Matt's shaft. Pleasure trilled through me. God, I could come like this, but I needed Matt to see my sincerity.

Matt caught my gaze and searched it.

"Hannah, God," he whispered. He began to bounce me steadily on his cock, his fingers digging into my bottom. He thrust from deep to deeper, again and again, and my clit ground into his pubic bone. My breasts rubbed along his chest. My hard nipples bent against his skin.

When I came, I gasped in shock and pleasure. My sex pulled and pressed, and Matt growled in my ear.

"There's my little slut," he hissed. "Come on me, come on my cock."

Oh, and there was the dirty boy I loved.

Matt lifted me off his cock and set me on my feet. My legs felt watery. Moisture trickled down my inner thigh.

He led me into the tent and I stretched out on my back. Matt climbed over me. He dragged his wet tip along my belly and smirked.

"Still hard," he murmured. "Now you have to help me, Hannah."

I thought Matt was moving toward my mouth, but he stopped

with his shaft between my breasts. I knew what he wanted then. I clasped my breasts and forced them together, sandwiching Matt's throbbing member. God, he was huge. I glanced down to see his head squeezed out of my cleavage.

Matt moaned. "Mm, that's it, baby, keep looking. You're going to make me come hard. Oh—fuck, you're going to lick it all up when I'm done."

Matt thrust through the seal of my breasts, his sex slick with my desire. The moans falling from his lips made me tremble. I watched his abs flexing. God, he moved beautifully. When his head plunged toward my neck, I licked and sucked at it.

"Hannah!" His cry filled my ears.

He grasped his shaft and hot spurts hit my breasts. I licked at the milky fluid while Matt watched. I brought my nipples to my mouth and sucked them clean.

When I glanced up, Matt was smiling cagily at me.

"Perfect," he whispered.

Matt clambered out of the tent to douse the fire and fetch our clothes.

We fell asleep on top of our sleeping bags.

I awoke freezing in the night and climbed into my bag, but Matt remained slumbering on his stomach, sprawled out beside me. I inched closer to him, and he chuckled in his sleep. He threw an arm over my cocooned body.

Through my sleeping bag, I could feel the weight of his arm and the incredible heat of it. I peered at him in the darkness.

Half awake, halfway in the land of dreams, I imagined Matt was a tiger in a man's skin. He must have been extraordinary, though I knew so little about him. Some wild heat—some extravagance, some consuming ambition—must have kept him burning in the cold night.

Chapter 19

MATT

I woke too early on Monday. I didn't need to look at my clock to know it was early. The light coming through the window was pale and depressive.

No Hannah.

I didn't know how to be apart from Hannah anymore. I didn't know how to wake up without her. When I was with her, I felt right and the world felt full of possibility.

We'd spent all of Sunday driving and hiking around the park. We drove back late last night. When I dropped Hannah off and pulled away, a familiar desperation came over me.

Why the desperation, still?

Why did every small separation still seem to echo a future good-bye?

I had broken up with Bethany. I called her the same day I tried to meet Hannah for lunch. In vague terms, I told Bethany that I could no longer be with her. I apologized for the timing, the phone call, everything.

Bethany sobbed and swore. She was by turns accepting, then

venomous and threatening. She demanded to know if I was seeing someone else.

"There's no one," I lied.

I would protect Hannah no matter what. I wouldn't drag her deeper into my mess.

"I don't believe you!" Bethany's voice was shrill. "You lying, cheating fuck!"

"Bethany, please—"

"Don't say my name! You fucking asshole. I've always been able to do better. Like I need you and your ridiculous antisocial neurotic bullshit. Good riddance. You don't give a fuck about anyone or anything but your fucking writing."

I didn't hang up on Bethany. I smoked and let her rip into me; I watched the city darken and thought of Hannah. When this was over, I could really be with her.

Finally, Bethany wound down to tearful hiccups.

She said she couldn't wait to tell her father that he was right about me, that I was no good after all. He *was* right, I thought.

She said she would get her things when she returned and stay with a friend, and could I please not be around when she packed.

"Of course," I said, lighting my third cigarette. "I'll go out. I can gather up your things, if you want . . ."

I thought of Bethany's stuff crammed into the trunk of my car.

"Fuck you," she said, and she was gone.

That night, I didn't let myself reach out for Hannah. Bethany might call back for another round of cussing and questioning, and besides, I didn't deserve Hannah's comfort. I deserved a night alone.

I deserved worse.

Had I really made things right by breaking up with Bethany? I had no intention of telling Bethany about Hannah or Hannah about Bethany. Could I pull this off? Could I blithely begin a relationship with Hannah on this foundation of lies?

I peeled back the sheets and checked my phone: 8:45 A.M.

Hannah would be getting ready for work. More like on her way to work. I hoped she wasn't too wiped out from our weekend in the mountains.

Maybe today I could meet her for lunch—for real.

I frowned. Would I need to dress up like a "businessman" again? Sooner or later, and preferably sooner, I had to tell Hannah that I was M. Pierce. She would understand. She would see how I'd been cornered into the lie about my line of work. Wouldn't she?

I pulled on a T-shirt and flopped into my office chair. I opened my e-mail. An e-mail appeared as I was deleting spam. I smirked at the sender name: FIT TO PRINT.

That goddamn zine. I subscribed to their updates simply because they were openly obsessed with the mystery of me. They weren't idiots, either. Somehow they had uncovered my representation by Pam's agency. Keeping an eye on them couldn't hurt.

I skimmed over the subject line.

My body went cold.

My throat constricted.

It wasn't possible. I clicked the link to the story.

M. PIERCE'S IDENTITY UNVEILED; FIT TO PRINT FIRST TO PRINT

JULY 8, 2013

Author M. Pierce is Denver resident Matthew Robert Sky Jr., an anonymous source recently revealed.

Though Sky forced friends and family to sign nondisclosure agreements protecting his privacy, sources close to his girlfriend say they have long known she was protecting Sky's secret.

"She would never tell and always fudged about his work," said one friend, "but we had a bet going about it. There were a lot of small clues. He controlled and manipulated her with threats."

I tried to keep reading.

The words blurred on the screen.

I knew I was having a panic attack. I knew this. I knew the symptoms.

I couldn't get enough oxygen. The air in my apartment was suddenly frigid. I began to sweat. I needed to breathe. I had to breathe.

Sources close to his girlfriend.

Sky's secret.

She would never tell.

Bethany.

Bethany ratted me out.

I broke up with Bethany and she ratted me out.

My lists.

Hannah.

I thought I felt my heart stop.

Where was my pulse? I clutched at my chest.

I was still breathing, but I couldn't find my heartbeat.

My cell rang and rang and rang. How long had it been ringing? The tone was discordant.

I brought it to my ear with a shaking hand.

"Matthew?"

It was Pam.

"Matthew? Are you there? Are you seeing this?"

"Hannah," I managed.

"Excuse me?"

"Is . . ."

"Matthew, listen. I need a word. I don't care how this happened, it's out. I need to know how you want to spin it. There's a reporter here."

I tried to stand and found myself on the floor.

A reporter.

No, it didn't matter. Pam didn't matter. *Fit to Print* didn't matter. Bethany didn't matter. My secrets and books didn't matter.

Hannah.

usand Nights in 2007. The book was published to na-
d eventually global acclaim.
ched, dazed, as everything I wanted to know about Matt
nto the Internet.
The month of Matt.
month without Matt.
the big news stations and papers ran stories on M. Pierce's
g. No one could get an interview from him, not even a
t, but Pam quietly confirmed the author's identity and
several generic statements.
Sky's private life is very important to his writing," said
Wing of the Granite Wing Agency. "The media has re-
him as an artist; now they need to respect him as a human
splashing his life all over the Net."
reporter finally caught Matt outside his apartment. An
on ensued. The reporter was badly beaten. Charges were
en settled out of court.
local papers and news stations lost interest by the middle

Print got national attention for uncovering the story but
vealed its source. They continued to run a column on
fe and writing. Pictures appeared there regularly.
a nine-year-old Matt boating with his parents, his hair
ack.
e was Matt in his high school graduation gown.
on the rowing team at Cornell.
and his friends riding lunch trays down a snowy hill.
and his girlfriend, Bethany Meres.
t to tell you so many things.
as Bethany Meres, various articles speculated, who re-
e information that led to Matt's uncovering.
hany was crazy about Matt," said a close friend of Meres,
was crazy about her. She said more than once that she
a proposal was coming. Then he ended it out of the blue."
s three days before the story broke.

"Hannah," I said. "Where—"

"Matthew! For God's sake. I would happily throw Hannah at this reporter and make him schedule an appointment with me in 2016, but she's not here yet. Listen. I can call security and have him removed, or I can sit down with him and pretend ignorance. Or we can let the cat out of the bag. It's already basically out, so we—"

Not here yet. Hannah wasn't at work yet. The reporter. The e-mail. Did Hannah get that e-mail? Did she subscribe to *Fit to Print*?

I don't remember ending the call with Pam and calling Hannah. I only know that her voice was on the line.

"Hey you!" she said.

I could tell that she was moving. Wind rushed over the receiver. She sounded normal. She sounded cheerful.

"Hannah. Hannah, listen."

"Matt?"

I reached for my office chair and it swiveled out of my hand.

"Matt, what's going on?"

"Hannah." I swallowed. I tasted bile. "Where are you?"

"I'm . . . about five steps from the agency, and about ten minutes from getting growled at by Pam for being late. Look, are you—"

"Don't go," I said. "Hannah. I need you to come over. Don't go in. Don't go to work." My voice broke.

Hannah hadn't read the article yet, but she was about to collide with a reporter who had.

"Matt, you're scaring me. What's going on? Are you okay?"

"No, Hannah, I'm not. I need you, please. Come over. Now, please."

"I will. It's okay. Breathe. God, Matt, you make me so scared for you. I'm coming right now, okay? Let me—"

"Please just come, please Hannah . . ."

Hot tears spilled over my eyelids.

"Matt, I swear, I'll be there. I have to tell Pam I'll be late. I'll be there, though, just . . ."

My mouth worked speechlessly. I wanted to beg her not to talk to Pam. I wanted to threaten her. Come directly here, or else . . .

He controlled and manipulated her with threats.

"Please," I whispered.

"I'm coming. I'm going in, I'm telling Pam I'll be late, and no matter what, I'm coming over, Matt. Give me ten minutes. Five minutes."

"No matter what," I repeated.

"No matter what."

"Promise. Hannah, promise. Promise you'll be here no matter what."

"Matt, I promise. I'll be right there. No matter what."

Chapter 2

HANN

Matthew Robert Sky Jr. was born
His father, a renowned orthopedic han
a pediatrician, were killed in a bus a
when he was nine. They were doing
favelas of Rio.

Matthew and his brothers, Nathani
their uncle in New Jersey.

He graduated at the top of his high
Cornell University. He published his fi
twenty.

He left graduate school after a failed
in a psychiatric ward for over a month.
downward spiral into drug and alcoho
string of petty crimes and misdemeanc

Until getting sober at the age of tw
a playboy lifestyle on the East Coast, f
inheritance released to him on his eigh
stopped writing.

After over fifteen rejections, he qu

Ten Th
tional a
I wa
spilled
July.
The
Ever
unveilin
commer
released
"Mr
Pamela
spected
and sto
One
altercat
filed, th
The
of July.
Fit t
never r
Matt's
I sa
swept b
The
Mat
Mat
Mat
Wa
It w
leased
"Be
"and h
though
That w

Despite his nondisclosure agreement, Matt never pressed charges.

He kept his head down.

Bethany made no statements.

Pam fielded the occasional reporter.

Matt's family and friends maintained a stony silence.

As for me, I was nothing to no one in the story of Matt.

I ignored his calls. I didn't listen to his messages. I didn't read his e-mails. Eventually, I changed my cell phone number and made a new e-mail account.

With a loan from my mother and my first paycheck from the Granite Wing Agency, I got a small apartment in Denver.

I began my hollow life.

There was nowhere I could go and nothing I could do to escape memories of Matt. I accepted a perpetual feeling of nausea as a new condition of my existence.

I loved him—I realized this when it all collapsed—and I had never known him.

So it was possible to love a stranger.

I didn't allow myself to dwell on the extent of Matt's lies. Matt the businessman. Matt with the bachelor pad. Matt calling me his. Matt laughing and smirking as I enthused about M. Pierce. And worst of all, Matt making me an unwilling accomplice to his cheating.

How could he do it?

How could he smile and chat with my family while he used me like that?

The only people who knew I was suffering were my family members. I told Chrissy, Chrissy told Mom, and Mom told Dad. If Jay knew, he didn't care.

Matt didn't go to the house, but Mom thought she saw him drive by a few times.

He didn't come to the agency.

I probably should have quit the job on principle—after all, Matt helped me get it—but it was my dream job. I needed the money. Matt had his fun with me and I got the raw end of it. At least I had something to show for my pain.

Pam must have known I had some stake in the M. Pierce identity explosion, but we only had one conversation about it. It was the day after the news broke, the day after I walked into a reporter babbling about Matthew Sky being M. Pierce. The day after I read the infamous *Fit to Print* article.

The day after I promised to go see Matt *no matter what* and never showed.

I remember how I felt when I woke that day, as if someone had scraped out my insides. I was a walking shell of Hannah.

I had a job to get to. I had motions to go through.

I showered and dressed mechanically. I arrived at work ten minutes early. Pam was waiting for me, leaning against her desk.

"Hannah," she said, giving me one of her terse smiles.

"Morning." My voice didn't sound like mine. It was a croak coming out of my hollow body. I didn't bother to clear my throat.

"I'm glad to see you. I wasn't sure . . ."

I paused on my way to my office.

I had been worried Matt would be there, camping on the steps of the agency, waiting for me. It was a relief not to see him—and it hurt, too. By that point, he hadn't begun his barrage of phone calls, texts, and e-mails. I didn't know if he would even fight for me.

His secret was out. His fun was over. Maybe he would simply discard me, a casualty of his double life. I couldn't put anything past him.

I turned and took a shaky breath.

"I love this job," I said as calmly as possible. I forced myself to meet Pam's eyes. Worse than her usual steely stare was the concern I saw in her gaze. "I have no reason to miss a day."

"No?" She smiled at me. Fuck, I was ill equipped to deal with this friendly side of Pam. I needed Pam the bitch, not Pam the shoulder to cry on. And I *would* start blubbering if she didn't quit with the soft eyes and concerned smiles.

I cried myself ragged last night. I cried through my shower that morning. My reservoir of tears was by no means exhausted.

"No," I said.

"All right." Pam pursed her lips. "Matthew was asking about you yesterday. He sounded very concerned. In fact, he hung up on me."

I never want to learn how to say good-bye.

My eyes stung. I swallowed.

"We got in touch," I said.

Pam studied me a moment longer. I wondered how much she knew, how much she might have inferred. The big news to the literary world was that M. Pierce had a name, Matthew Sky. The big news to me was that Matthew Sky had a girlfriend.

I was reeling in my own private agony. Pam might have guessed as much.

"All right," she said again, this time with a finalizing tone. The all-business façade fell back over her face. "Today I need you to . . ."

I listened. I took notes. I did my job.

I went home, skipped dinner, and crashed.

I woke and repeated my hollow routine.

I won't say the pain inside of me dulled. Rather, I came to expect it. I even came to expect the fierce spikes of hurt I felt at random—when I saw my brother's Frisbee, when I saw a Lexus, when I heard a pop like fireworks.

Anything could bring it on. The smell of pine. A warm breeze. A certain sort of smile on a stranger's face.

Sometimes I thought I saw Matt in the city crowds.

I would look and find a tall stranger heading to work.

Chrissy tried to coerce me into vandalizing Matt's cars.

"You know what they look like, Hannah. You know where he parks them! Take a baseball bat to that motherfucker's windshield. He wouldn't do anything about it, the pussy."

I winced and walked away.

In spite of my anger and misery, and in spite of how idiotic and used I felt, the thought of hurting Matt galled me. I couldn't stop myself from watching the news and reading the articles about his life. I couldn't stop the surge of sorrow I felt when I learned about his parents and his botched suicide, his stay in the psych ward and his descent into addiction.

Matt. My Matt. I loved him, and I hated him.

My family watched helplessly as my appetite dwindled. I lost fifteen pounds. On the weekends, I went to bed at 10 P.M. and slept around the clock until 2 the following afternoon.

I couldn't stand to hear my own name. Hannah, Hannah, Hannah.

Matt used to say it constantly.

He growled it, he moaned it, he whispered it. He said it like a curse—like a plea.

Hannah, oh, fuck, Hannah.

Hannah, never deny me.

Hannah, I can't be apart from you.

Promise. Hannah, promise. Promise you'll be here no matter what.

I couldn't stand to see myself. I avoided mirrors. I dressed plainly. I got a severe A-line haircut and began to straighten my hair.

When my family's vigilant concern became too suffocating, I got the apartment in Denver and holed up. I had no friends to see and no desire to go out anyway. That bastard had been my life every day since I returned to Colorado.

And that bastard was still my life, even when August rolled around and I hadn't seen him in four weeks.

He was there because he wasn't there.

How could I make anyone understand?

He was still with me. He was the negative space.

"Hannah," I said. "Where—"

"Matthew! For God's sake. I would happily throw Hannah at this reporter and make him schedule an appointment with me in 2016, but she's not here yet. Listen. I can call security and have him removed, or I can sit down with him and pretend ignorance. Or we can let the cat out of the bag. It's already basically out, so we—"

Not here yet. Hannah wasn't at work yet. The reporter. The e-mail. Did Hannah get that e-mail? Did she subscribe to *Fit to Print*?

I don't remember ending the call with Pam and calling Hannah. I only know that her voice was on the line.

"Hey you!" she said.

I could tell that she was moving. Wind rushed over the receiver. She sounded normal. She sounded cheerful.

"Hannah. Hannah, listen."

"Matt?"

I reached for my office chair and it swiveled out of my hand.

"Matt, what's going on?"

"Hannah." I swallowed. I tasted bile. "Where are you?"

"I'm . . . about five steps from the agency, and about ten minutes from getting growled at by Pam for being late. Look, are you—"

"Don't go," I said. "Hannah. I need you to come over. Don't go in. Don't go to work." My voice broke.

Hannah hadn't read the article yet, but she was about to collide with a reporter who had.

"Matt, you're scaring me. What's going on? Are you okay?"

"No, Hannah, I'm not. I need you, please. Come over. Now, please."

"I will. It's okay. Breathe. God, Matt, you make me so scared for you. I'm coming right now, okay? Let me—"

"Please just come, please Hannah . . ."

Hot tears spilled over my eyelids.

"Matt, I swear, I'll be there. I have to tell Pam I'll be late. I'll be there, though, just . . ."

My mouth worked speechlessly. I wanted to beg her not to talk to Pam. I wanted to threaten her. Come directly here, or else . . .

He controlled and manipulated her with threats.

"Please," I whispered.

"I'm coming. I'm going in, I'm telling Pam I'll be late, and no matter what, I'm coming over, Matt. Give me ten minutes. Five minutes."

"No matter what," I repeated.

"No matter what."

"Promise. Hannah, promise. Promise you'll be here no matter what."

"Matt, I promise. I'll be right there. No matter what."

Chapter 20

HANNAH

Matthew Robert Sky Jr. was born on November 9, 1984. His father, a renowned orthopedic hand surgeon, and his mother, a pediatrician, were killed in a bus accident in South America when he was nine. They were doing philanthropic work in the favelas of Rio.

Matthew and his brothers, Nathaniel and Seth, were raised by their uncle in New Jersey.

He graduated at the top of his high school class and attended Cornell University. He published his first short story at the age of twenty.

He left graduate school after a failed suicide attempt and stayed in a psychiatric ward for over a month. Upon release, he began a downward spiral into drug and alcohol addiction, followed by a string of petty crimes and misdemeanors.

Until getting sober at the age of twenty-three, Matthew lived a playboy lifestyle on the East Coast, funded by the considerable inheritance released to him on his eighteenth birthday. He never stopped writing.

After over fifteen rejections, he queried Pamela Wing with

Ten Thousand Nights in 2007. The book was published to national and eventually global acclaim.

I watched, dazed, as everything I wanted to know about Matt spilled onto the Internet.

July. The month of Matt.

The month without Matt.

Even the big news stations and papers ran stories on M. Pierce's unveiling. No one could get an interview from him, not even a comment, but Pam quietly confirmed the author's identity and released several generic statements.

"Mr. Sky's private life is very important to his writing," said Pamela Wing of the Granite Wing Agency. "The media has respected him as an artist; now they need to respect him as a human and stop splashing his life all over the Net."

One reporter finally caught Matt outside his apartment. An altercation ensued. The reporter was badly beaten. Charges were filed, then settled out of court.

The local papers and news stations lost interest by the middle of July.

Fit to Print got national attention for uncovering the story but never revealed its source. They continued to run a column on Matt's life and writing. Pictures appeared there regularly.

I saw a nine-year-old Matt boating with his parents, his hair swept back.

There was Matt in his high school graduation gown.

Matt on the rowing team at Cornell.

Matt and his friends riding lunch trays down a snowy hill.

Matt and his girlfriend, Bethany Meres.

Want to tell you so many things.

It was Bethany Meres, various articles speculated, who released the information that led to Matt's uncovering.

"Bethany was crazy about Matt," said a close friend of Meres, "and he was crazy about her. She said more than once that she thought a proposal was coming. Then he ended it out of the blue." That was three days before the story broke.

Despite his nondisclosure agreement, Matt never pressed charges.

He kept his head down.

Bethany made no statements.

Pam fielded the occasional reporter.

Matt's family and friends maintained a stony silence.

As for me, I was nothing to no one in the story of Matt.

I ignored his calls. I didn't listen to his messages. I didn't read his e-mails. Eventually, I changed my cell phone number and made a new e-mail account.

With a loan from my mother and my first paycheck from the Granite Wing Agency, I got a small apartment in Denver.

I began my hollow life.

There was nowhere I could go and nothing I could do to escape memories of Matt. I accepted a perpetual feeling of nausea as a new condition of my existence.

I loved him—I realized this when it all collapsed—and I had never known him.

So it was possible to love a stranger.

I didn't allow myself to dwell on the extent of Matt's lies. Matt the businessman. Matt with the bachelor pad. Matt calling me his. Matt laughing and smirking as I enthused about M. Pierce. And worst of all, Matt making me an unwilling accomplice to his cheating.

How could he do it?

How could he smile and chat with my family while he used me like that?

The only people who knew I was suffering were my family members. I told Chrissy, Chrissy told Mom, and Mom told Dad. If Jay knew, he didn't care.

Matt didn't go to the house, but Mom thought she saw him drive by a few times.

He didn't come to the agency.

I probably should have quit the job on principle—after all, Matt helped me get it—but it was my dream job. I needed the money. Matt had his fun with me and I got the raw end of it. At least I had something to show for my pain.

Pam must have known I had some stake in the M. Pierce identity explosion, but we only had one conversation about it. It was the day after the news broke, the day after I walked into a reporter babbling about Matthew Sky being M. Pierce. The day after I read the infamous *Fit to Print* article.

The day after I promised to go see Matt *no matter what* and never showed.

I remember how I felt when I woke that day, as if someone had scraped out my insides. I was a walking shell of Hannah.

I had a job to get to. I had motions to go through.

I showered and dressed mechanically. I arrived at work ten minutes early. Pam was waiting for me, leaning against her desk.

"Hannah," she said, giving me one of her terse smiles.

"Morning." My voice didn't sound like mine. It was a croak coming out of my hollow body. I didn't bother to clear my throat.

"I'm glad to see you. I wasn't sure . . ."

I paused on my way to my office.

I had been worried Matt would be there, camping on the steps of the agency, waiting for me. It was a relief not to see him—and it hurt, too. By that point, he hadn't begun his barrage of phone calls, texts, and e-mails. I didn't know if he would even fight for me.

His secret was out. His fun was over. Maybe he would simply discard me, a casualty of his double life. I couldn't put anything past him.

I turned and took a shaky breath.

"I love this job," I said as calmly as possible. I forced myself to meet Pam's eyes. Worse than her usual steely stare was the concern I saw in her gaze. "I have no reason to miss a day."

"No?" She smiled at me. Fuck, I was ill equipped to deal with this friendly side of Pam. I needed Pam the bitch, not Pam the shoulder to cry on. And I *would* start blubbering if she didn't quit with the soft eyes and concerned smiles.

I cried myself ragged last night. I cried through my shower that morning. My reservoir of tears was by no means exhausted.

"No," I said.

"All right." Pam pursed her lips. "Matthew was asking about you yesterday. He sounded very concerned. In fact, he hung up on me."

I never want to learn how to say good-bye.

My eyes stung. I swallowed.

"We got in touch," I said.

Pam studied me a moment longer. I wondered how much she knew, how much she might have inferred. The big news to the literary world was that M. Pierce had a name, Matthew Sky. The big news to me was that Matthew Sky had a girlfriend.

I was reeling in my own private agony. Pam might have guessed as much.

"All right," she said again, this time with a finalizing tone. The all-business façade fell back over her face. "Today I need you to . . ."

I listened. I took notes. I did my job.

I went home, skipped dinner, and crashed.

I woke and repeated my hollow routine.

I won't say the pain inside of me dulled. Rather, I came to expect it. I even came to expect the fierce spikes of hurt I felt at random—when I saw my brother's Frisbee, when I saw a Lexus, when I heard a pop like fireworks.

Anything could bring it on. The smell of pine. A warm breeze. A certain sort of smile on a stranger's face.

Sometimes I thought I saw Matt in the city crowds.

I would look and find a tall stranger heading to work.

Chrissy tried to coerce me into vandalizing Matt's cars.

"You know what they look like, Hannah. You know where he parks them! Take a baseball bat to that motherfucker's windshield. He wouldn't do anything about it, the pussy."

I winced and walked away.

In spite of my anger and misery, and in spite of how idiotic and used I felt, the thought of hurting Matt galled me. I couldn't stop myself from watching the news and reading the articles about his life. I couldn't stop the surge of sorrow I felt when I learned about his parents and his botched suicide, his stay in the psych ward and his descent into addiction.

Matt. My Matt. I loved him, and I hated him.

My family watched helplessly as my appetite dwindled. I lost fifteen pounds. On the weekends, I went to bed at 10 P.M. and slept around the clock until 2 the following afternoon.

I couldn't stand to hear my own name. Hannah, Hannah, Hannah.

Matt used to say it constantly.

He growled it, he moaned it, he whispered it. He said it like a curse—like a plea.

Hannah, oh, fuck, Hannah.

Hannah, never deny me.

Hannah, I can't be apart from you.

Promise. Hannah, promise. Promise you'll be here no matter what.

I couldn't stand to see myself. I avoided mirrors. I dressed plainly. I got a severe A-line haircut and began to straighten my hair.

When my family's vigilant concern became too suffocating, I got the apartment in Denver and holed up. I had no friends to see and no desire to go out anyway. That bastard had been my life every day since I returned to Colorado.

And that bastard was still my life, even when August rolled around and I hadn't seen him in four weeks.

He was there because he wasn't there.

How could I make anyone understand?

He was still with me. He was the negative space.

Chapter 21

MATT

My life imploded on Monday.

Hannah e-mailed me on Wednesday.

To this day, I don't know what I did on Tuesday. It was the first of my lost days.

I reread Hannah's e-mail until I could recite it.

Subject: (no subject)
Sender: Hannah Catalano
Date: Wednesday, July 10, 2013
Time: 7:20 PM

Matthew,

I'll try to keep this brief.

You know I didn't come over on Monday, and you know why. By now you also know I won't answer your calls, texts, or e-mails.

Please stop trying to contact me. Please don't try to see me. I want to tell you "it's over," but it never started, did it?

Against my better judgment, I am keeping my job at the agency. The purpose of this e-mail is to ask you not to attempt to see me there. I love and need the job.

If you have any respect for me (do you?), show me by leaving me alone. If you harass me at work, I'll have no choice but to quit. Please don't make me do that.

Hannah Catalano

She signed the e-mail so formally: Hannah Catalano. I felt the cold anger stretching between us.

She was no longer my Hannah, my little bird, my slut.

She never had been.

I spent the rest of the week in my apartment. I made lists. I made a list of ways to get Hannah back. I made a list of ways to apologize. I even made a list of specious claims to catch her attention: I have cancer, I left something at your house, I lost Laurence.

Admittedly, these lies were petty and pathetic, but the key was to brainstorm. If I brainstormed enough, I would find the solution.

I e-mailed and called Hannah multiple times a day, despite her request for no contact. I had to fight. I knew she wanted me to fight. I would have wanted her to fight for me.

I also knew that the right combination of words, or the right call on the right day, would bring her back to me. I just needed to keep trying.

A deluge of calls and e-mails came my way—from Pam, my brothers, my uncle, my psychiatrist—but nothing more from Hannah. I ignored them.

I ventured out after a week.

I guess that was when I "assaulted" the reporter. The story was a gross exaggeration.

To be fair, I don't remember exactly what happened, but I find it hard to believe that I beat the man "within an inch of his life."

Fucking papers.

I know it happened around noon. I remember the dreamlike heat. I was starved, dizzy, headed to the corner store to buy a bag of litter for Laurence.

I remember a man calling out to me.

"Matthew Sky! Over here! M. Pierce!"

I tried to jog away.

"Matthew, hey, Matthew Sky, right here!"

He was chasing me, shouting at me.

I remember thinking that tenacious asshole could be the same reporter Hannah ran into at the agency.

He could be the reason she didn't come to me. The reason I didn't get to explain. I had things to explain. I needed that chance.

I needed to cry with her.

I needed to hold her.

That reporter, he got to her. He stopped her. He ruined it.

Then I remember sprinting along the sidewalk. My fists hurt and they were hot and wet.

I ran home and locked my door, washed my hands, and sat in the bathtub.

My uncle's lawyer handled the assault charges. Then, without any encouragement from me, he launched the libel suit that would ultimately shut down *Fit to Print*.

After that, I only went out at night. I wore a hoodie with the hood up, sunglasses, and sneakers. I could outrun anything. I ran everywhere I went.

I jogged to pay phones and tried Hannah's cell. I drove past her house.

I took cold showers and only ate when the hunger hurt. I did jumping jacks in the living room. I was fixing things with Hannah. I needed to keep up my energy.

Another week passed and I called Pam.

"Matthew! My God, check your e-mail. I've only sent about twenty."

I jogged through my apartment with my cell to my ear. I was always ready to run. When Hannah called, I would be ready to go to her, no matter what.

"Hey," I puffed. "I got your e-mails. I haven't had time to reply."

"Drowning in damage control?"

"I guess." I circled the kitchen island. "I'm calling to ask about Hannah."

"Hannah? What about her?"

"How is she?"

"How are you might be a better question." A hard edge came into Pam's voice. I stopped jogging. I braced myself against the counter. God, I was winded.

"Why won't you tell me about Hannah? What's going on?"

"Hannah is fine. She's a first-rate secretary. Are you writing? Not that I could blame—"

"Why are you lying?" I sat on the kitchen floor. Fuck, I had to get some water into my system. "How is she? Is she there?"

"Matthew. Whatever this is, I am not doing it. Hannah is your friend. If you need to talk to her, you talk to her. I'm your agent. I'm concerned for you. We have things to discuss and—"

"Are you talking to the reporter?"

"Excuse me?"

"Are you talking to him? The reporter. Is Hannah?"

"Look, I need you to—"

I ended the call.

Fuck.

I guzzled a bottle of water and started to laugh. I was thinking about how Hannah would laugh at me now if we were together. We laughed a lot. We had a good thing going. We laughed about Laurence. And that night when I got on the webcam and she asked if I was naked, we laughed pretty hard.

"You're a funny little bird," I said, smiling and shaking my head.

I started to read the news online.

The *Fit to Print* people still had a huge boner for me. Or rather, it was bigger than ever. They printed everything they could get their hands on.

I wrote long, meticulous e-mails to Hannah clarifying the facts.

Speaking of boners, I was blessedly free of them. I don't think I could have gotten it up if I tried. I didn't try. Arousal would only distract me.

I printed the e-mails I wrote to Hannah and filed them in a

manila envelope. I was beginning to think she had blocked my e-mails. If she were reading them, she would have called.

I typed and printed letters for her. I kept a daily diary addressed to Hannah. Sometimes I rambled for pages, describing the way she looked and laughed. I apologized. I revoked my apologies, saying I would do it again. I told her about Laurence. I described the reporter and warned her to steer clear.

I also one-sidedly continued the story of Cal and Lana. Nothing was over. Everything went into the manila envelope.

Three weeks had passed, and I felt a growing sense of urgency about getting the material to Hannah. I needed to see her.

My brothers and uncle called and e-mailed relentlessly. What the fuck did they want? I couldn't deal with them yet, and their barrage of attention was making me anxious.

I couldn't lose focus.

I hadn't seen Hannah, but I knew I was close to getting her back. If I could just get the envelope to her. The letters explained everything.

Bethany texted me on the 29th.

> *I'm in the city staying with a friend. I'll be over on Friday to get my stuff. Stay away from the apartment this weekend.*

Under different circumstances Bethany's tone would have pissed me off, but I wanted to see her about as much as she wanted to see me. Besides, I was on a mission. August was two days away, and I'd be damned if I started a new month without Hannah.

I gathered Bethany's stuff from the trunk of my car and piled it in the living room.

I never considered taking Bethany to court, though I could have. She was the source, I knew it, and we had a nondisclosure agreement—but the damage was already done, and the lawsuit would bring more publicity.

I packed a light bag and installed myself in a corner king room at the Brown Palace Hotel. I brought my manila envelope.

At the last minute, I slid my sketch of Hannah into the envelope.

I knew what I was going to do. I couldn't trust Pam and I didn't dare go to Hannah's house, where her father might greet me with a sawed-off shotgun.

If I mailed the envelope, Hannah might throw it away. Plus, I needed to talk to someone who could tell me the truth about how Hannah was doing.

On Friday night, I dressed casually in jeans, a T-shirt, and of course my sneakers. I jogged around the hotel room psyching myself up. I had a good plan. Finally, a good plan.

My phone rang.

For fuck's sake, it was my brother. Again.

"Nate," I grumbled. "Look, could you not call anymore ton—"

"Hey, buddy, there you are."

I paused.

I could picture Nate's face as he spoke. Warm, open, patient. Nate was my oldest brother, Seth was in the middle, and I was the youngest. Nate had always been the best of us. He had a family, a brilliant career, and a natural charisma that drew people to him.

When I had my breakdown in grad school—and all through my rough tumble down the rabbit hole—it was Nate who came alongside me, his presence so gentle and nonjudgmental. Seth and my uncle just wanted to smack some sense into me. (They tried.) It was Nate's kindness, though, that finally nudged me onto the path to sobriety—and sanity.

"Hey." I sat on the edge of the bed. "I'm kind of—"

"I know, you're kind of busy," Nate cut in smoothly. He laughed. His laughter was slow and easygoing. Listening to it, I realized how manic I sounded by comparison.

"Yeah, I kind of am. I've got something to do." I tapped the envelope on my knee.

"Well, I've got an idea for you, buddy."

"Have you talked to any reporters?"

"Nah. Now listen, Matt."

I rose and began to pace.

"They're telling everything about me. Have you seen it? On the Internet."

"Nah, I don't read that bullshit. I've got a great idea for you."

"Yeah?"

"Yeah. We miss you, buddy. Me and Seth, the kids. Uncle. What do you think about getting out of Denver for a while?"

I tightened my grip on the envelope. Getting out of Denver? I started to jog, going from the desk to the door and back.

"Can't. I've got things to do here."

"Like what?"

"Loose ends," I said. A fine sweat broke out on my brow. "Gotta do some things."

"Loose ends? Slow down there, buddy, I can't understand you."

"I've got stuff going on out here. I can't leave; I need to make some things happen."

"Matt? Listen, I really want you to come out here. Take a real break, take it easy."

"I can't leave!" I snapped.

"Hey, sure you can. You take your time and then come on out here. Uncle's cabin's been empty all spring, and all summer so far. You can—"

"Stop it!" I shouted, my voice rising hysterically. Nate had to know about Hannah. He was trying to pull me away from her. Fuck, he'd spoken to the reporter. Maybe he spoke to Pam.

"Buddy, where are you? Are you in your apartment?"

I rushed to the hotel windows and snapped the curtains shut.

"Why do you want to know?" I whispered.

"Matt? I can't understand you, hang on. Let me—"

I ended the call and flung my phone onto the bed. Fuck, was Nate in Denver? Was he coming to stop me?

I left the hotel in a cold sweat. I drove into Boulder, watching my rearview mirror carefully and sticking under the speed limit. I held the manila envelope on my lap.

Please, please, please be there tonight. Time was running out. I could feel it.

I drove right into one of Colorado's capricious summer storms. Perfect. The wind pushed at my car and the rain pelted against my windows so that I couldn't hear myself think. Fuck, at least it wasn't hail.

I parked on Pearl Street and tucked the envelope under my hoodie. Memories washed over me as I jogged to the alley where the DYNAMITE sign shone like a beacon. I laughed and paced the narrow backstreet.

God, I wanted to pat myself on the back. I had a good plan here. My brainstorming paid off. Chrissy was the key. Chrissy liked me. She would take my envelope to Hannah, I knew it.

The rain stopped and the night air cooled sharply. I hovered around the entrance to the club. I checked my watch. 11 P.M. Chrissy was probably inside.

A beefy-looking bouncer emerged.

"No loitering, pal."

"I'm waiting for a friend."

"Oh, yeah, you got a friend in here? Get in or get lost."

I had planned to catch Chrissy going into work or leaving, but maybe the bouncer had a point. I could find her inside. Fuck, though, I didn't want to see Hannah's sister topless.

"Okay," I mumbled, patting my pocket.

Shit. I left my wallet at the hotel. The bouncer glowered at me.

"Get lost, ya bum," he said, advancing.

I darted up the alley and pressed myself against the brick wall out front. No way, I didn't need another round of assault charges, and I didn't need to be filing them either.

Hours passed as I waited out front. I jogged sporadically to keep warm. I shivered and sagged against the damp bricks.

Fucking Colorado with a cold night in August.

Around 3 A.M., a familiar voice jolted me from my stupor.

"I'll see you tomorrow," Chrissy called, her voice echoing down the alley. "Ha! Pretty sure I won. Try harder, girl."

I would have recognized her voice anywhere. It was Hannah's voice, just a touch huskier. Relief rushed through me. Fuck, I wanted to cry. This was it.

Chrissy stalked out of the alley. She made a beeline for a streetlamp.

"Chrissy!" I shouted. I pulled out the manila envelope and hurried toward her. She turned. A huge grin split my face. "Hey, it's me! Matt!"

Chrissy was rummaging in her purse. I pushed back my hood. A plume of pepper spray erupted in my face.

"Fuck!" I cried, twisting away. I clutched my face. The envelope flew from my hands.

"Fuck you, you douche bag!"

I heard Chrissy's heels clacking away from me. I gasped for air. My skin was on fire. My nose and eyes and throat burned. When I opened my eyes, the world blurred around me.

"My envelope," I wheezed.

I got on my hands and knees and began to feel around on the sidewalk.

"In the puddle, bro," someone said. I looked toward the voice. I made out a lanky figure holding a phone. Was he filming this?

My hand splashed onto the sodden envelope.

Chapter 22

HANNAH

I stopped reading the news about Matt after the pepper spray video went viral.

It was pulled from YouTube the same weekend it appeared, but by then it was everywhere. One site posted it under the title M. PIERCE TRIES TO SUBMIT MANUSCRIPT TO STRIPPER. Even *Fit to Print* linked to the video.

I didn't talk to Chrissy about it. Really, there was nothing to say.

With July behind me, I knew I had to focus on making some sort of life without Matt. Until then, I half hoped and half feared he would force himself back into my life, but that was a dream. He could never make it right.

I scrolled through my pictures of Matt and wondered who the hell he was. A beautiful man. A stranger. A liar. A global bestseller. An author I had admired for years.

Had I ever really held him in my arms? Did I dream our time together? Like a ghost, he slipped away from me.

With a new phone number, I only got calls from my family.

My new in-box was empty except for e-mails from Pam.

According to Mom, Matt's nighttime drives past the house stopped.

I wondered what had been in the envelope Matt tried to give Chrissy. I watched the video as many times as I could stand it. I have to admit, it *did* look like a manuscript.

Whatever it was, it sat in a puddle for over a minute while Matt reeled and groped around on the sidewalk. It was probably ruined.

And Matt . . .

My beautiful lover on his hands and knees, with no one to help him. His intentions were probably ruined, too.

We were finally, truly over.

At work, I blazed through the tasks Pam gave me. I never wanted downtime. I worked through my lunch break and brought work home. When my eyes ached from too much reading, I hit the gym and ran on the treadmill until I wanted to collapse.

And that's what I did. I went home, collapsed, woke up, and headed to work.

The hollowness inside of me didn't shrink. It expanded until it seemed to press at the limits of my being. I became less than a shell of myself. I was a fine limning—a suggestion of Hannah Catalano.

One day, I thought, I wouldn't even be that.

I understood how people fall apart.

I understood how dangerous it is to let someone become your whole life, and how powerless we are to prevent it. *Never deny me,* Matt once said. As if I had a choice.

Pam plopped a manuscript onto my desk at the end of August.

It was rare for Pam to hand me anything; usually I picked through the slush pile myself or found the day's work waiting on my desk.

I slid out the manuscript. *The Surrogate,* no author.

"What's this?"

"A manuscript," she said drily.

Ugh. No Mercy Pam. Yes, I could see that it was a manuscript.

"Right," I said. "So . . . I'll give it a read?"

"That's the idea." Pam lingered. "Oh, it's . . . by a local lady. She has this marvelous habit of not putting her name on her manuscripts."

Pam leaned over and scribbled *Jane Doe* on the top page.

I stared at her in disbelief. Holy fuck, was Pam actually letting me read a manuscript by one of her authors? This was a far cry from the slush pile. This was real agent work.

"Pam, I—"

She held up a hand. "Don't imagine your opinion is vital here. Just read the manuscript. I need confirmation of what I already know to be true."

Pam breezed out.

Okay. Confirmation . . . of what she already knew to be true. That sounded bogus. I flipped the title page aside.

One of two things had to be happening here. Either Pam wanted to bump me up to the next level of work (and didn't know how to be nice about it), or Pam actually needed a second opinion on this manuscript (and didn't know how to be nice about it).

Either way, I would view this as a test and not let my head explode.

Two hours later, I was still reading the manuscript. My other paperwork was shoved aside. I slouched in my chair and propped my feet on the desk. And I was definitely not reading at work pace. I was reading at pleasure pace, lost in the story.

The Surrogate told the story of a future Earth where, for the right price, people could escape life's pain. Exams, divorce, jail time, dental work, messy breakups, *anything*—no one had to live through it, thanks to the Isaac Project.

The project began as a medical breakthrough in palliative care, and it ended as the most revolutionary venture since the World Wide Web. A client simply downloaded his consciousness into a sleeping cell and uploaded the consciousness of a surrogate, a professional who lived in his body for the duration of the pain.

Once the assignment was complete, the client returned to his body and carried on with a pain-free life.

Really, the novel told the story of one particular surrogate—a jaded workaholic who'd spent more time in the bodies of others than in his own eighty-year-old body. The surrogate had no personal life to speak of. *He was hollow.*

That is, until one job changed everything.

The surrogate was uploaded into the body of a wealthy executive. His assignment was to confront his client's wife with his affair and desire for divorce.

Except the surrogate couldn't do it.

He looked through his client's eyes, saw his wife, and . . .

. . . knew that he wouldn't hurt this woman for any price. Never before had the pain of his clients—cowards and escapists, all of them—contained such wonder as she possessed.

This beauty would haunt him.

I flew into Pam's office.

"This—" I blinked and cleared my throat, lowering the pages I was brandishing.

Pam was giving me a death glare. "Hi, Hannah, thank you for knocking."

"Sorry, I—"

"Go on." Pam sat back in her chair and sighed, gesturing with her pen. "Let's hear it, since you can't seem to contain your zeal."

I smoothed my skirt and took a breath. I was stunned. Damn, I had just barged into Pamela Wing's office like I owned the place. That wasn't what shocked me, though.

For the first time in nearly two months, I had forgotten my misery.

I had forgotten my hollowness.

I needed more of this story.

"This is . . ."

"As ever, Hannah, your eloquence astounds."

"It's very partial," I stammered.

"Keenly observed. The author assures me she has another twenty pages on the way."

"I'd like to read them. If that's all right with you." I gazed out the window. If I met Pam's eyes, she would see my desperation. "The . . . protagonist. It seems obvious he'll hijack the body of his client, you know? And . . ."

I felt Pam's eyes on me.

". . . And that's an interesting quandary. So much is unstated here." I swallowed. "The cultural commentary on our attitude toward pain and escape. And consumerism. The Thoreau epigraph about desperation is pretty perfect, too. This feels really relevant. I mean, people *do* lead lives of quiet desperation, until something or someone comes along and—" I clamped my mouth shut.

Fuck. Okay, how did this become me spilling my guts to my boss?

Pam raised a brow. She looked curious, not deadly.

"I think you're right," she conceded. "It's relevant. We'll talk more about it when we've read the next pages."

I turned to go, pausing outside my door.

"Ms. Wing?"

"Hm?"

I lifted the manuscript.

"You don't really represent speculative fiction, do you?"

"No, but I make exceptions for my established authors."

Established authors.

So it was true; Pam was letting me read something remotely important.

For the first time since Matt and I parted ways, I imagined how it would feel to be a partner with Pam and Laura. That was my dream. At least, it was the old Hannah's dream.

"It's not without flaws," I said after a beat. "Mostly small conceptual oversights that need explanation. But it's . . ."

I glanced at the manuscript. Did my subjective opinion mean anything here?

"Ms. Wing, it's the most compelling thing I've read all year."

Chunks of *The Surrogate* arrived weekly throughout September. I read them like a junkie getting my fix. I'd never really liked science fiction, but *The Surrogate* didn't read like science fiction. It was a love story.

Just as I'd anticipated, the surrogate pursued his client's wife, but not in the body of her husband. Not initially. He contrived reasons to meet with her in his own aged body and in the bodies of other clients. He met her as a man, a woman, a child . . .

He loved her through every face of love. To her, the faces must have seemed like façades, but one continuous truth joined them.

Finally, the surrogate schemed his way back into the husband's body.

My eyes raced across the page. God, where was this going? Body theft was a crime punishable by death, and anyway, what was the surrogate thinking? Did he plan to seduce the woman from her husband's body? She didn't even know him!

The scene was getting insane. The surrogate was about to go to bed with the woman he loved, and he was pretending to be her husband. It was impossibly wrong, and yet I wanted it to happen. Later he could explain, later, but now—

"Hannah Catalano?"

Someone was standing in my doorway. The air went out of my lungs. That voice, that tall frame. I yanked my feet off the desk and nearly tipped over in my office chair.

Oh, my God, it was—

Not Matt.

But it was!

It was Matt plus a few years and black hair and a friendly smile.

The man advanced, his hand thrust toward me. He was dressed in a stylish dark suit. I stumbled to my feet and shook his hand.

"Yes, hi," I said.

The man's likeness to Matt derailed me. I stood there blinking owlishly at him.

"Nathaniel Sky. Call me Nate."

I plunked into my chair.

"I'm sorry," he said. "I gave you a shock."

Gave me a shock? More like a violent blow to the heart. I was looking at Matt's brother. Memories of Matt went off like fireworks in my brain. My eyes watered. The way Nate was smiling, his graceful carriage, his imposing presence—it was all Matt.

"Well." He cleared his throat. "I won't take much of your time."

"S-sorry, I . . . sorry. Yeah, no, um, sit, please . . ."

Wow, English.

Nate chuckled and tilted his head. The gesture was so Matt that I had to turn away.

"I've come to ask a favor, Hannah. Can I call you Hannah?"

I nodded. Safe to say, coherent sentences would not be forthcoming.

Nate ignored the chair. He moved around my desk and his heavy hand came to rest on my shoulder. Thankfully, the touch was genial and comforting, not one of Matt's touches.

Matt's touches . . . demanding, desperate.

I removed my glasses and rubbed at my eyes. I couldn't believe, after almost three months, how much raw emotion I felt.

"I didn't come here to bring you pain," Nate said quietly. I ventured a glance at him and he smiled gently. "I've heard so much about you. I wouldn't have come if I had any other option. I need your help. You must know this is about Matt."

I blinked rapidly.

"How is he?" I whispered.

"Not good." Nate shook his head. "Not good, Hannah." He turned and walked to the window, gazing down at the street. I studied his back while I collected my wits. Jeez, the gene pool was seriously skewed in the Sky family's favor. Go figure.

"He's drinking. I don't know how else to put it." Nate's voice was low and full of feeling. "Hannah, he's my brother. He's my little brother . . ."

It was weirdly comforting not to be the only person at a loss for words.

We were both silent for a while, fighting our emotions.

"What can I do?" I said at last.

"Maybe nothing. I don't know. I could always pull him back from these ledges. Not this time." Again, Nate shook his head. He was so somber; it was like we were talking about a dead man. I shuddered and my heart lurched. How bad was Matt?

"Where is he? What's happening?"

Nate turned and met my eyes.

"I knew you would help," he said. "He told me so much about you. I knew you had to be—" Whatever Nate was going to say, he let it go. A Pam-like efficiency came over him. This, I could see, was far easier for Nate than emotion.

"Good," he said. Had I agreed to something? "He's staying at our uncle's cabin in upstate New York. I got you a one-way ticket to the nearest airport and a rental car. Anything can be moved, date-wise, but I don't see why—"

"Wait, what?"

Nate produced a folder from his laptop bag and began spreading documents on my desk. He looked earnestly between me and the papers, his dark brows raised.

"Hm? I've cleared your schedule with Pam, don't worry. She and I have spoken. We all have a common interest here, which is—"

"Excuse me? Look, I—"

This had to be a joke. Incredulity was quickly replacing my fear. Matt's brother just sauntered into my office and was now strong-arming me into flying to New York to rescue Matt's alcoholic ass (that was doing God knows what in some random cabin), and oh, before I even agreed to this crackpot plan, he'd talked to *my* boss and cleared *my* schedule—

". . . some spending money," Nate was saying, "travel expenses, anything you need above and beyond the car and the ticket. All my contact information is here. I insist you keep the change, as I know this is something of an inconvenience."

I turned my deer-in-the-headlights look on the envelope Nate was pressing into my hands. Thoughtlessly, I rifled through the bills. Brand-new Benjamin Franklins. Okay, I was counting. One thousand, two thousand, three thousand—

"Five," Nate murmured.

My head shot up.

My God, this wasn't for travel expenses. This was a bribe.

Nate moved toward the doorway, leaving the money in my hands and the travel information on my desk. I was paralyzed with anger. That was fortunate for Nate, because otherwise I would have brained him with my stapler.

"I'll be in touch," Nate said. "I'm staying in the city for a few days. Call me if you have any questions. Hannah, I knew you would help. The way Matt spoke about you . . ."

There it was again, that guileless vulnerability. This asshole loved his brother, at least, who also happened to be an asshole.

Briefly, I envisioned Matt and Nate sitting together and discussing me. Conspiring? Was this a ploy to send me running back to Matt's arms?

No, no way. Matt was drinking. Matt was in trouble. I needed to think.

"You're both the same," I fumed.

Nate glanced over his shoulder.

"Of course we are." He smiled and shrugged. "We're brothers."

Chapter 23

MATT

The Finger Lakes are wine country.

Fuck, they even have this thing called the Seneca Lake Wine Trail. You go around the whole goddamn lake hitting up wineries until you pass out. It's like a hall crawl for cultured adults.

Granted, I wasn't about to hit the trail. I did hit up a few wineries, though. I'd borrowed my brother's bike, a silver Icon Sheene, and I tore all over Geneva like a maniac.

Not caring is really damn liberating.

I kept the cabin stocked with wine, bourbon, and Dunhills. Nate stopped pestering me around the middle of September—thank God. He'd had a damn good idea, me getting some time alone in nature or whatever, but I didn't need him to mother-hen me the whole time.

So I was drinking again. So what? I forgot how much I loved it.

And fuck, I wrote *Ten Thousand Nights* drunk off my ass. It's still my most popular novel. I could write *The Surrogate* wasted, no problem.

I wrapped myself in an afghan and sat out on the porch. I made my weekly call to Pam.

"Matthew." She sighed.

Why did she always have to be such a bitch? I was starting to expect her oh-no-it's-Matt-again tone, like 'Damn, too bad I have to talk to my most famous author.'

"Yeah, sorry to rain on your goddamn parade," I slurred.

Silence.

"I mean fuck, Pam, it's not like I'm fucking nobody. Last time I checked—"

"It's the time, Matthew." Her voice was quiet and faraway. I looked at my phone. It was 4:00 in the morning.

"You're two fucking hours behind me! God, Pam, also, fuck, work on my schedule. I'm the next fucking Balzac. What about Proust? He used to—"

"Matthew, what do you want."

There was no question mark at the end of Pam's sentence. That bitch. She knew she had me by the balls because she had Hannah.

I spit a mouthful of Riesling over the rail. I needed a bottle of beer. Better yet, I needed a bottle of Woodford Reserve.

"You *know* what I want. What does she think? I'm writing like you always ask, but you're never fucking h—"

"She loves it." Pam stifled a yawn.

Okay, Pam had probably been asleep—like I fucking cared. She deserved this. She ratted me out to the reporters. Her and Bethany, maybe even Nate. I'd had time to think and I finally figured they were all in on it. They knew about me and Hannah. They tore us down on purpose.

Why, I didn't know, and it didn't matter. You can't trust anyone.

"I swear," I growled. "Tell me more."

"She . . . she really empathizes with the narrator, the surrogate."

"Why?"

"I don't know, Matthew. We work together, we don't do psychoanalysis."

"Oh, fuck you, Pam."

I ended the call. Fuck her. I drained my bottle and dropped it, watching it roll across the porch. What a gorgeous fucking night. Cool and dark, windy and quiet. All I needed was a cigarette. Or that bottle of beer. My Ambien was kicking in, though. God, I loved that feeling . . . like a balloon rising and expanding in my head.

I woke up drunk.

Jesus, why did I sleep on the porch? I was fucking freezing, wearing only boxers, and sore as fuck, slumped over in a wicker chair.

I flicked through my phone. Huh, I'd talked to Pam. God, she probably called me in the middle of the fucking night. She was always calling, always harassing me.

I shuffled into the cabin and took two shots of bourbon. I gulped down three glasses of water. Damn, that did me exactly right. Headache gone, stomach settled, hands steady.

I refreshed Laurence's water and topped off his food dish.

"Perfect morning," I told him. I hummed as I dressed. Mm, it felt good to drink. I'm an all-day all-night drinker when I drink. I do nothing by halves.

My mind whirred along as I brushed my teeth, popped a Xanax and a Lexapro, and collected my latest pages from the kitchen table. I was writing everything by hand. Only fucking way to write. Why did I ever use a computer? Pen in hand, hand to the page, it's godly.

The morning was chilly. I lit a smoke and headed out, leaving a few windows open and the front door unlocked. Uncle's cabin was in the middle of goddamn nowhere.

I strolled up the gravel road to my nearest neighbor, a little farm called the Patch where people came to pick fresh vegetables and buy eggs. My typist was the farmer's wife. Fuck, I couldn't be bothered typing out my own stuff, and this lady looked like she could use the change. I paid her ten dollars per typed page.

We had a rough start—she kept fucking up the formatting and couldn't make out my handwriting—but after about a month we got going smoothly. I wrote, I took the pages to Wendy, I bought some vegetables, I picked up the pages, I paid Wendy, I mailed the pages to Pam, rinse and repeat.

I never went online. I hadn't even brought my laptop to the cabin. The Internet was a mess of gossip about me, and it was part of how Bethany took me down. And it was how I met Hannah. Now its unreal, anonymous spaces, the programs and sites where we connected, the laptop screen glowing like a window to another world . . . could only bring me pain.

"You got pages for me?" Wendy smiled, the corners of her eyes wrinkling sweetly.

She was crouched in a ring of wire mesh with a horde of fuzzy chicks teeming around her. When she saw me, she wiped her hands on her jeans and climbed out.

"Yeah, fifteen or so," I said.

I hovered near the pen. I didn't like to look Wendy in the eye. Hell, I didn't like to look anybody in the eye. Eye contact is too intimate.

Wendy understood that. She got me. She also didn't care about the perpetual booze on my breath—not that I could tell, at least.

She took the pages and rubbed my shoulder. She had dry knobby hands.

"All right, hon," she said. "Would you look at these little guys? Just look at 'em."

"Yeah, they're sweet. God, they're cute." I ran a hand through my hair. I needed a shower. I should have taken another two shots. "I'll look at the animals for a while. That okay?"

Wendy laughed.

"Matt, I told you to stop asking. You come see 'em anytime. I'll be in the house."

"Mm, thanks. Thanks, Wendy."

I watched as she moved toward the old farmhouse. Morning sunlight fell across the white clapboard. Here and there the paint was peeling. The grounds were unkempt, patches of garden braced by scruffy grass and dirt.

Perfect. This place was perfect. I stepped into the chick pen.

"Hey, guys." I crouched and reached for the chicks. They swarmed away from me, making me laugh. "You little jerks. You're all fat. You're all going to be ugly in about a month, all scrawny and gray. Come here."

The tiny endless peeping of the chicks was breaking my fucking heart. I would probably cry when I got into the barn. That's what I usually did.

Finally, I captured one of the chicks. I cupped its body to my chest.

Little bird, I thought. *Soft, warm little bird.*

I wandered around visiting the animals and talking to them. I fed the goats and looked into their weird rectangular pupils. I stroked my hand down a pig's leathery back.

In the barn, a tabby darted away from me.

I glanced around. There was no one in sight, just me and the old black Percheron. I drifted over and he came to the edge of his stall. He knew this routine. He lowered his lumbering head toward me and I hugged him around the neck.

"Hey, pal," I said, my voice thick. I wasn't sad or anything. Mike said that crying is a cathartic release and sometimes it has nothing to do with sorrow.

The horse's huge body made the stall door creak. His neck was pure muscle. I ran my hand down his snout.

"You're big and strong," I whispered.

Even in the cool morning, the barn was warm. The smells of hay and feed permeated the air. I pressed my face into the horse's neck and tears began to slip from my eyes.

"Matt?"

I whirled.

Ah, fuck. Wendy's daughter stood in the doorway smiling at

me. I could never remember her name. Hope? Grace? Something wholesome and forgettable.

"Mm. Fucking hay allergies," I muttered, rubbing my eyes.

"Oh, yeah, those'll get you." She lifted an empty bottle. "We've got a new baby cow. You ought to see him."

I shoved my hands into my pockets and looked away as the girl came closer. She looked twentyish and was very striking—black silky hair, freckles, blue eyes. She wore her hair in a long braid down her spine. I saw her pretty much every time I came to the Patch, but it never dawned on me that she might be seeking me out.

"Yeah, I will," I said. "I'm making my rounds."

"Mom's already working on your typing. You know, she really loves doing that. She won't let me read it, though."

The girl came to stand before me. She seemed too close, but then again, I was drunk—lost to that space-time shit.

"Well, yeah," I mumbled. "It's kind of private."

"No big deal." The girl chuckled. She rose onto her toes and wrapped her arms around my shoulders. Her breasts brushed my chest. "Matt?" she whispered.

I didn't move. I felt like a lump of clay. Her arms were cool and slender, and I was aware of her pressing closer. Her breath tickled my neck. How strange. I felt nothing. I stood there listlessly and stared at the barn wall.

"Why are you so sad?" the girl said. "You're so sad. Let me try to make you happy."

A cold, familiar smirk distorted my lips.

"You think you can?" I said.

"I know I can. I'll take care of you." The girl's hands moved down my back. No fire sprang up in their wake. I only became aware of my pronounced ribs and the ridge of my spine. Huh. I'd have to pick up some eggs while I was here. More fat, more protein.

The girl began to undo my jeans. I let her, gazing down impassively as she worked. She gripped my soft cock and I saw her brows knit. My smirk twitched.

After massaging me ineffectually for a minute, the girl dropped to her knees. I had to hand it to her—she was determined. She licked along the soft organ and sucked at the tip. When she glanced up at me, confusion flashed through her eyes.

My cock had zero interest.

I shrugged, and then started to laugh helplessly. The girl turned red.

"Nice try, kid," I said.

I tucked my member away, did up my jeans, and strolled out of the barn. Turns out laughter works as well as tears.

I scrambled two eggs when I got back to the cabin. I pushed them around on my plate, washing down small bites with bourbon. Somehow, the booze and pharmaceuticals kept my stomach full. I tried to eat throughout the day, but most nights I ended up puking.

No big deal; nausea comes with the territory.

I wrote for a few hours, and then I got too drunk to see straight. I'd hit a roadblock in *The Surrogate.* My protagonist was about to make love to the woman he spent half the novel chasing. I wanted to write a steamy sex scene, but the words weren't flowing.

The images weren't flowing.

Usually I could sit back, imagine a scene, and transcribe it. Not this time. I kept thinking about Hannah reading it. I wanted to write it for her.

I tried to reconnect with the passion we used to feel. In my car, in the field, in her room, in my bed. The images were sterile. Hands on skin, mouths locked.

Fuck. What was happening to me? And why was I having Pam feed my novel to Hannah anyway? There was no point. Three months had passed. Hannah and I were definitely over.

I could barely remember the sound of her voice, the smell of her hair.

She had become an idea.

I sent my story to Hannah the way people pray—casting my plea into the ether. A plea to be understood. Looking for the signs.

I woke on the couch. At some point, I had changed into loose pajama pants. The cold bit at me and I let it. So much of my life now was dumb penitence.

After taking two shots and a Xanax, I called Mike.

Mike was still a decent psychiatrist, even if I didn't trust him. He'd set me up with meds before I flew out to New York. I called him from time to time. A thirty-minute call to Mike cost me a hundred bucks, but the money didn't matter.

"Hi, Matthew. How are you doing?"

"Fine. You know, good. Is it a good time?"

"Yes, sure."

I heard a door close.

"Look, who transcribes your notes?" I said.

"Matthew, we've been over this. I—"

"No, I know. But Hannah's mom, she does that, you know? The transcription stuff. And I was thinking, if she types your notes . . ."

Mike was one of very few people who didn't cut me off when I rambled. Granted, my rambling worked in his monetary favor. I still appreciated it.

"You know, that would be bad for me," I said. I began to prowl through the cabin. Shadows pooled on the floor. I had no idea what time it was or even what day. I lost whole weeks to the rhythms of drunkenness. "There are things I want to say. But no one can know. It gets onto the Internet and everywhere."

The Mike–Hannah's mother connection evaded me. I thought about it a lot. There was Hannah's mother and the medical records. There was Mike, my psychiatrist. They might be conversing, but how could I ever find out?

"I take our physician-patient privilege very seriously, Matthew. Also, as I have mentioned, I dictate my own notes with a voice recognition program."

"Ah, right. That's right. Do you make notes about these calls?"

"Yes, I make short notes about these calls. Let me ask you a question, Matthew."

"Shoot."

"Are you taking the Zyprexa I prescribed?"

"No, not really. It makes me sleepy. I take the Xanax."

"I would like you to hold on the Xanax and try the Zyprexa. These fearful suspicions you're exhibiting should be—"

"Fine, whatever. I'll try that."

I smirked and rolled my eyes at Laurence. Classic. Mike was trying to accuse me of paranoia. He did that every time I got close to the truth.

"Anyway, Mike, I have a problem. Basically . . ." I bounced the ball of my foot against the wall. "I can't get my prick up." I laughed and resumed pacing.

"Okay, help me with specifics," Mike said. I was grateful for his clinical tone. "Are you having trouble sustaining erection or achieving erection?"

"Achieving, I guess."

"How long has this been going on?"

"About three months. I don't know, maybe two. Since I left Denver."

"Have you attempted intercourse and found yourself unresponsive?"

I thought about the girl in the barn.

"Um, not really." I winced. I needed another drink. "Look, all I know is, I used to wake up with wood almost every day." I ground my teeth. Goddamn, I wasn't about to tell Mike how Hannah could get me hard just looking at me, how her voice made my cock perk up, how I hardened instantly in her hand.

My throat started to burn. I rubbed my jaw.

"I just need some fucking Viagra," I snapped. "I need to get off, all right? I need the release. I'm going crazy."

"Medication is an option," Mike said, "but I can't prescribe treatment to a healthy young man without doing a workup first. Erectile dysfunction is often the result of organic—"

"Meeting over." I ended the call and tossed my phone onto the couch.

A healthy young man.

Maybe Mike had a point. Maybe my dick would be more interested in life if I stopped drinking myself into oblivion. Somehow, though, I doubted it.

I opened a bottle of beer and sat at the kitchen table. I ran my pen along the spiral ring of my notebook. I could skip the sex scene, come back to it later. But how would I handle the rest of the novel? The sex wasn't exactly incidental to the plot. Fuck.

I'd deleted the pictures of Hannah from my phone months ago. I didn't deserve to have them, and I knew she wouldn't want me looking at them. Still, I tried to remember them as I moved a hand between my legs.

I tried to remember that first time when we were strangers on the Internet.

Hannah. You should let your robe hang open.

And the second time, when I saw her picture and grew hard looking at it.

The third time, in a motel in Montana.

God, you're perfect. Lie down. Put the phone near your ear. I want you to have both hands free.

I remembered her dark, heavy hair strewn across my thighs. Her fingertips brushing my cock for the first time. Her mouth, the bend of her knee. The sunlight on her eyelashes.

Beneath my hand, my cock didn't even twitch.

I hurled my bottle across the room. It crashed into the wall, and beer and glass rained down. Laurence bolted to the corner of his cage with a loud thump.

"Sorry," I mumbled. "Fuck, sorry Laurence."

I shoved my notebook away. I stood and went down, my ankle twisting under me. The pain was a blessed relief. The floor rose to meet me and I tumbled right through it, down into the river of forgetfulness.

Chapter 24

HANNAH

My flight out of DIA was delayed, which gave me more time to wonder how totally I'd lost my mind.

It didn't, unfortunately, give me time to back out. Not with Nate shadowing me like a bodyguard. The asshole had neglected to mention that his travel plans included us flying east together and then driving five hours from Newark to Geneva.

I was looking at nine hours of quality time with Matt's brother.

As if this weren't awkward enough.

"Hannah, please," Nate said, trying for the twentieth time to extract my carry-on from my shoulders. I grasped the straps of my backpack.

"I've got it," I snapped. I shot an acid look at Nate, and he frowned. Ugh, I felt instantly penitent. These rich . . . arrogant . . . presumptuous . . . good-looking assholes! How could they be so infuriating and so pitiful at the same time?

Pity and fury: the same emotions I felt when I thought about Matt.

Matt, the man I was going to rescue.

It was the first weekend in October, which had given me

about one week to mull over Nate's request. And I did pretend to mull, though my decision was made the moment I heard Matt was drinking.

I approached Pam about the time off. As usual when Pam didn't want to discuss something, she barely looked up from her computer.

"Yes, it's fine, Hannah. I've already spoken with Nathaniel about it. I'll be in LA that weekend and Laura is in Chicago. We'll shut down the office."

"The thing is," I said, "I'm not sure how long I'll be gone. It might take longer than one weekend. I don't really know."

"Yes, it's fine. It's all fine, Hannah. Believe it or not, I can survive without you."

Pam glanced at me. Fuck, she probably thought I was fishing for a paid vacation, which I definitely was not. Thanks to Nate, I had five thousand extra dollars in my bank. I wondered if Pam knew about that. I wondered if Matt knew. Maybe it was Matt's money.

Ugh, these conspiracy theories had to stop.

"Great, okay. I'll . . . I'll e-mail you if it looks like I'll be gone for more than a week, but I don't think that's going to happen."

"Fine. Sounds good, Hannah."

Pam's tone and posture said I was dismissed. I lingered by her desk until she was forced to glare at me.

"Yes, Hannah?"

"Have you been in touch with Matt?"

I thought I saw something pass through Pam's expression, but it was gone before I could decipher it.

"Yes. He's still my author. We communicate from time to time."

"How is he?"

I closed my eyes; I didn't want to see Pam's withering glare.

That woman is a shark, Matt once told me, but Matt was a tiger and Nate was a hawk. They were all dangerous. They all lived in the rarefied air of the successful and, now more than ever, I felt like a child.

A child in the dark.

I kept wondering—how dare they? How dare Matt use me and lie to me? How dare Nate swoop in and bribe me into helping his brother? How dare Pam treat me with such cool indifference when I was going to save her bloody author?

God, but I was in love with Matt.

My heart quickened as I stood in Pam's office and felt the anger and heat of my love. I didn't need five thousand dollars to go to him. The money was an insult. And I wasn't doing Pam a favor by going to him. And he sure as fuck didn't deserve me going to him.

I was going to him because I loved him and because love is unstoppable.

"He's seen better days," Pam said quietly.

My eyes flickered open.

Pam wasn't glaring. Her expression had softened and she wore a small frown.

"He becomes someone else, Hannah. Someone I don't know. He's difficult to know as is, but—" She ran her fingers over the keyboard. Emotion made her restive. It did the same thing to Matt; it did the same thing to Nate. I felt triumphant in my simple ability to be human.

"But you tell me." Pam cleared her throat. "You go out there and you tell me how he is."

I blinked and nodded.

"I will," I said. "I promise."

I hurried out before the waterworks started. Pam needed me. So did Nate and Matt. Why couldn't they admit it?

I packed on Thursday after calling Nate and agreeing to his plan. He did a poor job of concealing his relief. I tried to return his money, but he shut me down. He told me to pack for cool weather. He told me he would give me a lift to the airport.

It wasn't until he picked me up that he told me we'd be traveling together. *Asshole.*

Our flight boarded forty minutes late.

Nate grinned as I stowed my backpack and gawked. I stretched out my legs.

"Is the legroom to your liking, Miss Catalano?"

I blushed.

"I've never flown first class."

"Ah. It really is the only way to fly."

I glared out the pill-shaped window. Yeah, the only way to fly if you can afford it.

I wanted to chatter as we took off and hit waves of turbulence—I'm a nervous flyer—but I'd given Nate the cold shoulder one too many times. He closed his eyes and zoned out as the cabin rattled.

I studied his face.

Again I was struck by his resemblance to Matt. Nate's hair was black, though, and Matt's was the color of sand with brilliant highlights and darker shocks. I remembered the feel of those silky strands sliding through my fingers . . . while we kissed . . . while he went down on me.

Fuck.

I was not going to New York to leap into Matt's bed. I was going to New York to try to help him, and then to get on with my life.

When I thought Nate was dead asleep, I pulled out my copy of *The Silver Cord.*

I'd been rereading Matt's books over the last three months. Contained within his sentences, coded in his words, was the man I loved and all the secrets he'd kept from me. Reading the books was like hearing his voice. His wit, his sarcasm, his mercurial moods, and then his unusual forlorn wisdom—it was all there.

On Friday morning I had telephoned Pam to ask if there were any new pages of *The Surrogate.* Jane Doe's writing arrived like clockwork on Thursdays, but we hadn't had an installment for two weeks. I was hoping for pages to read on the plane. There was nothing, though, and no explanation from Pam.

How annoying. The author was stalled on a scene I was dying to read, and dreading, too. The sex scene.

Nate flipped over the cover of my book.

"Nate!"

I jumped, jerking it away.

"Sorry, I wanted to see what you were reading."

I shoved *The Silver Cord* into my backpack.

"Now you know." My face heated.

"Yes. That's one of my favorites of his."

I peeked at the immaculately dressed man beside me. I was flying comfortable in leggings and a teal tunic top. Nate was flying like a Wall Street executive in a gray suit and golden tie with an Eldredge knot so perfect that I wanted to stare at his throat.

When Nate wasn't annoying the hell out of me, he intrigued me. What did he do? I'd noticed his heavy wedding band. Did Sky men cheat on their wives, or just their girlfriends?

"Is it true?" I said. "That it's sort of . . . about your family?"

"Yes." Nate smiled at me. I frowned back at him. He had a way of smiling so warmly that my anger dissolved, and whenever he spoke to me he gave me all of his attention. It was unnerving. At present, he'd angled himself toward me and appeared oblivious of the several flight attendants ogling him. "I take it you read as much online?"

There was none of Matt's cynicism in his voice, just frank curiosity.

"Well, yeah. I . . . followed the news for a while."

"I can't blame you."

I thought about *The Silver Cord* while Nate watched me patiently.

"So you guys were very religious growing up?"

"Yes, very."

"I wouldn't have guessed it," I muttered. I slapped a hand over my mouth—fuck, I did not mean to say that—but Nate only laughed.

"Think about our names—Matthew, Seth, Nathaniel. All biblical. Our parents took us to church twice each Sunday. Our uncle, not so much."

"Your parents," I murmured.

"Yes. Their loss was very hard on Matt. He was young. Old enough to remember them, too young to really understand. I still don't think he understands. He feels pain like no one I have ever known, and always has. He's such an emotional creature."

I watched Nate, silently willing him to go on. After a moment, he did.

"I remember once we were on vacation in Maine and our father went into a cave, and he disappeared from view. Matt . . ." Nate smiled thinly. "He plopped himself down on the sand and cried so hard. He thought our father was gone. He was inconsolable, even when Dad came out. All day these huge tears were standing in his eyes and I could see"—Nate gestured to his eyes—"I could see that it meant something more to Matt, our father disappearing into the dark. It was more than fear. It was like a betrayal to him."

"Every small separation echoed a vaster good-bye," I said quietly. It was a line from *The Silver Cord.* My favorite line.

"Yes, exactly."

"Did he always want to be a writer?"

"Oh, I don't know. He would say no. He rarely talks about it, though I once heard him say that the only thing he hates more than writing is not writing." Nate chuckled. "After he left graduate school, I thought he would be a drunk for the rest of his short life. But he wrote—and the writing became his addiction."

Until now, I thought.

"Yeah, I see. Thank you."

"You're welcome, of course. Between the Internet and *The Silver Cord,* it seems you know quite a bit about me and mine."

I ducked and pretended to be searching for something in my backpack. How awkward. It was one thing to snoop into Matt's life in the anonymous privacy of the Net, and quite another to be sitting next to his brother and discussing my research.

"Yeah, I . . . I guess."

"Fair enough, Hannah. I know quite a bit about you and yours, too."

My stomach twisted. How much did Nate know? How much had Matt told him?

My panic must have been obvious, because Nate quickly added, "Matt spoke very well of you and your family."

I smiled tightly.

That conversation set the tone for the rest of the trip. Nate and I had reached an uneasy camaraderie and there we stayed, skirting the obvious awkwardness of our adventure.

I kept hoping Nate would volunteer his thoughts on why Matt was in such bad shape, but he didn't. Maybe he didn't know. Was it because of me? Was it because his cover was blown? Both? I didn't seriously think losing me could drive Matt into the ground.

Nate's car, a silver Cadillac sedan, was parked at Newark.

"I live near Trenton," he explained as we put our bags in the trunk. "There are small airports between here and Geneva, but I looked into tickets and they'd really give you the runaround—down to Florida, back up to Philly, over to New York—and even then you'd need to do some driving. This is much better, and it gives us time to talk."

I clutched my backpack on my lap.

Time to talk. Awesome.

"I wouldn't mind doing some driving," I said, but as we moved through Newark in the growing dark, I became increasingly relieved it was Nate behind the wheel.

"Oh, you'll get to drive. We'll pick up your rental car when we get to Geneva."

I glanced at my phone. It was 7 P.M. Even if we made great time, we'd reach Geneva at midnight.

"I don't think rental places are open that late."

Nate shook his head. Thank God Nate was a more attentive driver than Matt. He drove aggressively, but he kept his hawkish eyes on the road and his hands on the wheel.

"I pulled a few strings, got the manager to open late for us. It's an emergency, after all."

I smirked and gazed out the window. *So you bribed him, too.* I remembered Matt trying to buy everything I laid my hands on. I had a distinct vision of Sky men plowing through life snarling and slinging money at their problems.

By the time we reached Pennsylvania, it was too dark to see. Staring out the window, I could just make out rolling farmland and fences.

"Beautiful country," Nate told me. "Very fertile. Is this your first time out east?"

"Yeah. I grew up in Colorado."

"Well, I'm sorry you can't see more. Waking up to the Finger Lakes will be amazing, at least. It's more of the same between here and there—lots of farmland around New York State."

I nodded and smiled, though farmland didn't jibe with my idea of New York.

My mind kept returning to Nate's words.

It's an emergency, after all.

Was I really the right person for this? What was I supposed to do?

We passed into New York and something changed in Nate. He sat forward as he drove. He glanced at me from time to time and began to chatter. Did I want to stop for food? *No.* Did I need a cup of coffee? *No.* Did I want the radio on, off? The heat? AC? He sped up.

"I've got you set up at Geneva on the Lake. You'll like it. I got you a suite. I'm sure you looked over the papers I gave you."

"Yeah, briefly . . ." I had also Googled the resort and then rapidly closed Firefox because I didn't want to think about how much Nate was spending on me. "You really didn't have to, I mean, it's so nice—"

"Oh, please. You're doing me a favor here, Hannah. If anything's not to your liking, or if there are hitches, anything at all, you call me. I always have my phone. And of course . . ." He adjusted the rearview mirror. He ran his fingers through his thick hair and drummed the wheel. "Of course you might want to go see Matt right away."

I watched the night outside my window, hoping to conceal the fear on my face.

I had gotten used to Nate's calm, persistent presence on the journey. Maybe I didn't want a travel companion at first, but suddenly the thought of being abandoned in New York terrified me. Abandoned with an unstable Matt, no less.

Our whirlwind romance aside, Matt and I barely knew one another.

We were strangers. Again. Still.

"Is—" I hesitated. "I mean, why—"

"Hm? If you're tired, by all means, get settled in your room, sleep. See him in the morning. I'm sure he's around. He's—"

"Have you gone to see him?" I blurted.

"Of course. Yes, of course." Nate smiled, but his smile was tight. "More than once. He's, you know . . . I'm his oldest brother. It's different. I come around and he feels like I'm babying him. It doesn't work." He laughed.

Nate's smile, his rambling, that anxious laugh—none of it was comforting.

I caught him looking at me.

"He's not dangerous, Hannah."

I felt so small. I hugged my backpack.

Not dangerous. That was easy for Nate to say. Matt hadn't blasted Nate's life apart.

"Is he suicidal?" I whispered.

"No! God, no." Nate's knuckles were white.

We drove the rest of the way to Geneva in silence. I wanted to ask Nate a million things—*When did you last see him? How do you know he's not suicidal?*—but my questions only seemed to make Nate tense, and his tension was feeding mine.

I had no idea whether I'd check into the hotel that night or go see Matt.

I was chickening out big time.

A friendly but tired-looking Enterprise employee walked me through the car pickup. Nate filled out the paperwork, asking for my signature here and there. Of course he booked me a Ford Escape and not a cheaper economy car.

The night air was freezing. Nate carried my suitcase to the car and we idled beside it, reviewing directions on my iPhone. He'd overburdened me with maps, advice, and contact information. I shivered as our conversation wound down.

Abruptly, Nate hugged me.

"Thank you, Hannah," he said, releasing me at once.

I studied my feet.

"I care about him," I said. "So much."

"I know. I know that now. He needs you."

"I know."

Hearing Nate say those words—*he needs you*—galvanized me. I was here for a purpose. I was here for the man I loved, not to hide in a swanky resort.

"I'll be in touch," I said. I squeezed Nate's shoulder and climbed into the car.

The resort was just minutes from the rental place; the cabin was just minutes from the resort, north of the tip of Seneca Lake.

I drove past Geneva on the Lake and got my bearings.

Within ten minutes, I was turning onto the gravel road that led out to Matt's uncle's cabin. I drove slowly into total darkness. My tires crunched on the country road and my high beams illuminated slices of forest.

My palms were sweating on the wheel.

Matt, my Matt. I hadn't seen him in so long. My eyes ached to see him, my hands to touch him. My whole heart reached out for him.

The driveway to the cabin amounted to two dirt ruts through wooded land. I stopped when my headlights glanced off a window. If Matt was asleep, I wanted to let him sleep.

I walked the rest of the way. The October night prickled along my arms.

Tall trees surrounded the cabin, which was a cozy midsize structure with a wraparound porch. Wind chimes hung from the eaves and tolled quietly in the dark.

I brought up my hand to knock on the door, and then I tried the knob spontaneously. It turned in my grip.

My heart stuttered as I crept into the cabin. As my eyes adjusted to the dark, I made out a kitchen table and counter littered with bottles, most of them empty.

A fly buzzed in the otherwise perfect quiet. Dishes slanted in piles from the sink and a sour odor pervaded the air.

Broken glass on the floor.

Ashtrays overflowing with butts.

Clothes and papers strewn everywhere.

Something rustled. My eyes darted to the corner, where Laurence sat in his cage. He watched me with shining eyes. I tiptoed to him. He pressed his body close to me and I smiled, touching his fur through the bars.

"Hey there," I whispered. "It's okay now. You're okay."

A metallic click sounded at my back.

I spun.

I was looking at Matt.

I was looking at the muzzle of a gun.

Chapter 25

MATT

Hannah froze so completely, it was like I had stopped time.

I froze, too. Even my hands were steady as I pointed the pistol at her head.

My God, I was hallucinating.

It couldn't be Hannah. And yet it was. The moonlight highlighted her lovely face. I caught a whiff of her sweet shampoo.

"M . . . M . . . Matt," she breathed. It was Hannah's voice in perfect replica, husky with halftones of fear.

She began to inch along the wall. I lowered my gun.

"You're not real," I said.

Hannah's dark eyes were pinned to the gun. I tapped the barrel against my thigh. Her nostrils flared.

"It's me," she said. "Matt, it's me. G . . . give me the gun."

"Give you the gun?" I laughed and waved it. "So what, I can have some horrific dream in which a figment of my imagination blows out my brains? No fucking thanks."

"I'm real, Matt. Please. It's me, I—"

Hannah reached for the pistol. I backed away, smirking.

"Oh, no you don't. This is Chekhov's gun. You know what that means, right?" I aimed at a wall, sighting down the barrel. I thought about going outside and firing a round into the forest. Fuck, that would feel good.

Hannah's clammy hand touched my forearm. Our eyes met. Too real, that touch. I moved my finger off the trigger.

"Hannah?"

"Yes, Matt, it's me. God, it's me. Help me."

She slid her hands down my arm to the gun. She covered my fingers with hers and lowered it slowly.

"Help me," she whispered. "How do I . . ."

Her hands shook on mine.

"Here. Like this."

I popped out the magazine and racked the slide. A round clattered to the floor.

Hannah flinched.

"It's okay," I murmured, locking the slide. "It's empty now."

"Can . . . can I—"

"Anything," I said.

Hannah stood so close that our hips touched. She loosened the pistol from my grip. She took the magazine and collected the fallen round.

"I'll be right back," she said. "Right back. I promise." She darted to the door. I shuffled to the window and peered out, but I couldn't see a damn thing.

My God, Hannah was here. Could it be?

And I pulled a gun on her.

And however she got here, she was probably about to hightail it into the night.

With my gun.

Fuck.

I slumped on the couch.

Was this really happening?

I began to drink from a bottle of bourbon standing on the coffee table. God, this stuff tasted seriously sickening.

I didn't hear Hannah return, but suddenly she was kneeling by my feet. She gazed up at me with teary eyes.

"Do you have any other guns? Any weapons?"

"No," I mumbled. "Unless kitchen knives count."

She let out a breath.

She reached for my bottle, then retracted her hand.

"Oh, Matt. What's happening? Look at you."

I looked at myself. I was wearing cheap boxers and tatty slippers with pompoms on them.

"These aren't mine. These—I found them here—the slippers. Not mine."

I swallowed another shallow mouthful of bourbon. I couldn't think about any of this—Hannah being here, me, the gun, anything.

Hannah smiled. A tear slipped down her cheek.

"That's okay," she whispered. "That's okay." She patted one of my slippers. "Nice and warm. You gotta keep your feet warm."

I shifted my feet on the floorboards. I stared off.

"Yeah, it's cold," I said.

"It really is. It's freezing. Let's close these windows, okay?"

Hannah stroked her hands along my face. God, I needed to shave. She tried to make me look at her. My eyes were burning. I rolled them away.

"Here, I'll get the windows. You stay put."

I nursed my bottle while Hannah drifted around, closing windows in the main room.

"Do you want to sleep? Are you tired?"

"No," I said.

"You want the lights on?"

"No."

"Okay, how about a fire? I'd like to build a fire."

I shrugged.

Hannah began to move wedges of oak from the holder to the grate. I watched her work. Wordlessly, she found matches in the kitchen and got the fire going. Then she started to load dishes into the washer.

The mess around her was incalculable. I knew she couldn't put a dent in it and maybe she knew that, too, but I sensed she needed something to do.

As for me, I remained seated on the couch.

I had decided on silence.

Silence and drunkenness.

Hannah tidied around the kitchen area, wiping down the counter and piling empty bottles into a bag. She lifted a half-empty bottle of Malbec. With a glance in my direction, she began to pour the wine down the drain.

"Are you ready to stop drinking?" she said.

I shrugged and took a swig from my bottle.

I couldn't take my eyes off Hannah.

Only as the alcohol numbed me and firelight began to fill the room did I notice how greatly changed she was. Her hair was straight and short, falling at a dramatic angle around her face. Her cheeks were hollow, her high cheekbones standing out. Her whole body was slimmer.

I rose and took a few steps toward the kitchen.

I needed a better look at her.

Hannah paused, watching me.

What was that expression on her face? *Was she afraid of me?*

What an awful thought.

I stopped where I was, standing at the edge of the kitchen area, and Hannah resumed emptying bottles into the sink.

My gaze trailed up her ankles and calves. Her leggings left nothing to the imagination. She wore a loose long top that just covered her bottom.

The old possessiveness stirred in me, but I didn't move. Three months ago, I would have lifted her shirt and squeezed her ass. It was mine then—mine to look at and touch.

Hannah edged past me. She ducked her head and drew in her shoulders, trying to make herself small.

Yes, she was afraid of me. Of course. Why wouldn't she be? I was a drunken stranger who pulled a gun on her moments ago. And now I was hovering around staring at her body.

I turned to watch her collect bottles from the coffee table and floor. She paused by the fireplace and pulled out her phone.

I advanced.

"Who are you texting?" I growled.

Her eyes went round. They looked so much larger in her hungry face. She was still beautiful, though. The weight she had lost somehow made it easier to read her expression. It was as though, with nothing spare on the stage, she became pure emotion.

"Nate," she said. "Your brother."

I barked out a laugh.

Nate, of course. Nate with his grand ideas.

I began to pace, kicking bottles and clothes out of my way.

"Nate, fucking Nate. He sent you here?"

"He asked me to come." Hannah slid her phone away.

"Well, isn't that fucking sweet. And here you are. Good of him to warn me. You know, a heads-up might've been nice."

"He thought you would be angry. He thought you might leave. I think he was right."

I glowered at Hannah.

She ignored me and continued emptying bottles. I tightened my grip on the neck of what would soon be my last bottle of bourbon.

"I hope you're happy; you've poured about a thousand dollars in wine down the drain."

"I'll pay you back. You have to stop drinking, Matt. Everyone's worried about you."

"Everyone, huh?"

"Pam, your brothers, your uncle."

"What about you?" I tipped the bottle to my lips. I was drinking too much, too fast. I leaned against the back of the couch as the room swayed.

Hannah's eyes were wet again. Fuck, I wished she would quit crying.

"No one is as worried as I am," she said.

She plunked the bag of bottles down in the kitchen and disappeared into my bedroom. I closed my eyes. I heard her moving through the cabin, shutting windows.

She returned with a few more bottles, which she emptied and tossed. She cleared the booze from my fridge and freezer and swept broken glass from the floor into a dustpan.

Her eyes landed on the kitchen table. It was littered with pill bottles and papers.

"Those are mine," I said.

"I won't get rid of anything else." Hannah moved toward the table. I thought I might fall if I let go of the couch, and besides, the game was up.

The game had been up for a while now.

Hannah examined my prescriptions.

Fresh tears rolled down her face as she lined up the bottles.

Firelight fell across the table, illuminating my notebook and piles of loose pages. Hannah picked up the first pile. I watched her face as her expression changed.

Emboldened by the bourbon, I wanted to demand to know why she had never returned my zillions of calls, texts, and e-mails. Why, if she was so worried, did she leave me alone this long? Why? Why couldn't she forgive me? And why couldn't I forgive myself?

I was still too scared to ask.

If Hannah really couldn't forgive me, I would never find my way. She left me alone in the riddle. I needed her because I loved her—or I loved her because I needed her. Why had the feelings turned to a maze? Now I was lost in the dark. In my dreams I ran paths walled with high hedges. Always the leaves brushing me like laughter. Always the long night.

"I couldn't . . . get you to hear me," I said, speaking carefully so I didn't slur.

"So you did this?"

She lifted the handwritten pages of *The Surrogate.* I nodded.

Hannah was silent a long while. I could see her thinking . . . a parade of questions, answers, realizations. She must have looked like this when she first learned I was M. Pierce.

Finally, she set down the pages. She came toward me. This time, I was scared.

I closed my eyes and braced myself against the couch. Hannah slipped the bottle from my fingers. I heard her set it on the floor.

She hugged me from behind, folding her hands over my heart.

God, that soft skin . . .

"You are always deceiving me," she whispered.

I clasped the couch with both hands.

"Always, Matt, always speaking to me from any mouth but your own. Don't you know that I love you? I see you under all your lies, and I always find you."

I opened my eyes and rolled back my head, staring at the vaulted ceiling. I wouldn't let these brimming tears fall.

Hannah's fingers skated over my chest and stomach. Desire's dark eye cracked open.

"Hannah . . . I can't."

"Can't what?" She kissed my back. Her open mouth lingered against my bare shoulder. She bit down gently and held my hips.

"I can't write the scene," I mumbled. *I can't get it up.*

"I was waiting for that scene. I've been living on your words. Why can't you write it?"

"I can't feel it. The feelings, I can't . . ."

I dug my fingers into the back of the couch. God, how humiliating. I would have broken away from Hannah if I didn't feel sure I would fall.

She moved sinuously against me, kissing a trail up my neck to my ear. She stood on her tiptoes and tugged at my earlobe. I moaned softly.

"I can't," I pleaded. "I can't."

"Shhh, Matt. It's okay now, it's over. I'm here and I'll never leave you."

Hannah crushed her breasts to my back. She pressed a hand to the front of my boxers. I gasped. For the first time in months, heat surged into my loins.

"Ah, fuck," I groaned. "Hannah . . ."

I began to rub my cock against her palm. She whispered sweet nothings in my ear. The sense of the words fell away; all that remained were her hot breath and encouraging voice.

Soon, I was straining against my boxers. Hannah slid them down. Her fingers curled around my shaft and she cupped my balls. I gazed down in disbelief.

Nothing less than this was enough.

I humped into Hannah's hand frantically.

"I haven't—" I stammered. "I won't last."

"It's okay, Matt, it's okay."

The firelight flashed on our skin, dyeing us amber-orange. The silence of the cabin closed around us. Hannah matched my desperate rhythm with her hands.

"Oh," I sighed, "oh . . . oh."

With a cry like a sob, I came into her hand. I sagged against the couch. Hannah moved off, discreetly wiping her hand clean, and returned to embrace me. I wrapped an arm around her.

"I'm tired," she said, kissing my neck. "It's late. Can you sleep?"

"Mm."

I leaned my weight on her. Fuck, I was really feeling the alcohol.

As we passed my bottle, Hannah plucked it up and helped me toward thc kitchen.

"Last one," I said, eyeing the bourbon.

"Then you do it."

My hand shook as I poured the amber liquid down the drain.

Hannah didn't know—how could she?—what this meant for tomorrow.

As she helped me into the bedroom, I glimpsed a pendant

resting near the hollow of her throat. It was bright against her pale skin.

"The lock," I mumbled. More like three of the locks; I was seeing triple. Still, I knew exactly what it was—the padlock necklace I bought for Hannah in Estes.

"I got it engraved," she said. She brought my hand to the smooth metal and I traced a finger over the letters . . . *H* . . . *M.*

Hannah.

Matt.

I collapsed onto the bed and reeled into darkness.

Chapter 26

HANNAH

I woke with a start. The bed was cold. The room was dark and quiet, and it took me a moment to remember where I was: in a cabin in Geneva, New York.

Under the bathroom door, I saw a strip of light.

God, Matt . . .

I sat up against the headboard and gathered the quilt around myself. Was he sick, or just using the bathroom? Did he have a secret stash of alcohol in the cabin? I stared into the darkness and tried to empty my mind.

Inside, I could feel the chipped fragments of my heart. My poor, beautiful lover . . . what had agony done to him?

He was twenty pounds lighter, at least, and his eyes were wild and glassy. His handsome features were scruffy with stubble. His hair grew long down the back of his neck.

Worst of all, though, was the total absence of his proud spirit. Shuffling around the cabin, refusing to meet my eyes . . . he was broken.

My intentions dissolved when I saw him. Why did I think I could keep my distance? Why would I want to? Love is relentless.

The bedside clock read 5:12 A.M. No wonder I felt like a train wreck.

I slid out from under the sheets and pulled on my tunic top. I had pajamas in my suitcase, but my suitcase was in the car and I'd had no desire to step away from Matt last night, even after he face-planted into bed.

I didn't want him to wake up alone. Not ever again.

I padded to the bathroom door and listened.

"Matt?"

Silence.

I knocked gently.

"I'm fine," he said, his voice quiet. It sounded like he was on the floor. I crouched and flattened both hands to the door.

"Are you sure?"

"Mm, I—"

I heard scuffling, then silence.

Last night, watching Matt breathe greedily in his sleep, I wondered if I should be worried about alcohol poisoning. Worry gnawed at me again as I listened through the bathroom door.

"Matt? Are you sick?"

"Hangover," he said, "it's nothing."

His tone definitely said, *Leave me alone.*

He was probably puking his guts out.

Sure enough, I heard more scuffling followed by retching. The sounds were hoarse and painful. I nuzzled closer to the door. Typical Matt, suffering alone.

Why did he hide from me?

By now he should have known that not even a loaded gun could drive me away.

I was fully awake, so I began to pace around the bedroom. I pulled on my leggings. I made the bed. I'm a productive worrier.

The toilet flushed, but Matt didn't emerge.

I roamed through the cabin and did a little more cleaning, gathering laundry and emptying ashtrays. I changed Laurence's

water and fed him a few raisins. Poor little guy, the things he must have seen . . .

My eyes strayed toward the kitchen table with its stacks of pages. I felt a familiar stab of betrayal. I thought of Matt and Pam, conspiring to get *The Surrogate* to me. A love story. A lie story. I remembered how I felt at the cusp of Matt's unwritten sex scene: I wanted it to happen, the deception didn't matter.

Was Matt trying to manipulate my feelings about what he'd done, or was he simply trying to explain himself?

My heart wasn't made of paper. That was fiction. This was my life.

I was making my way back to the bedroom when I heard a cry.

"Matt!" Fuck this hiding bullshit. I barged into the bathroom.

Matt cowered in the corner, hugging himself and staring at the floor. The smell of vomit hung in the air.

"Oh, God, baby," I whispered, kneeling at his side and stroking the hair back from his brow. His whole body shook. He was soaked with sweat.

"Hannah. Hannah . . ."

He clasped my arm. I had never seen such fear in his eyes. His gaze darted around on the floor, where all I could see were pale tiles with gray speckles.

"Matt, it's okay now, listen to me, it's okay."

Every time I brushed back his hair, a fresh sheen of sweat sprang up on his brow. I touched his neck. His heart was racing. My God, what was this?

"Xanax," he chattered. "Get me one. Get me a Xanax. In the k-kitchen."

"Matt, I don't think—"

"Hannah!"

I scurried to the kitchen. Okay, Xanax. Get a Xanax. Maybe Matt was addicted. Fuck, maybe that's what this was. Fuck. Did he need some kind of fix? Was he doing more than drinking himself to death?

Panic made it impossible to focus. My hands knocked against the table and scattered pill bottles. Fuck, fuck, fuck. Which was which? Why did Matt have all these fucking pharmaceuticals anyway?

Finally I found the Xanax. I shook out one blue oval and ran back to Matt, who was gripping the sink. Water dripped from his hair. He grabbed the pill, chewed and swallowed it, his face twisted in disgust.

I hovered at his side. He smiled grimly at me.

Oh, God, I despised my emotions right now. Tears gathered in my eyes and I dashed them away. Fuck, I couldn't stand to see Matt—a man who always seemed so smug and in control—this frightened.

He splashed water on his face. He drank from his cupped hands. I tried to rub his back, but he flinched from my touch. His skin was on fire.

"Matt, what can I do? What's going on? This—" I hesitated. This didn't look like any hangover I had ever seen.

Matt shrank into the corner again. He opened his mouth, then lunged for the toilet, clinging to it and gagging. There was nothing in his stomach. Nothing but water, bile, and a blue swirl of crushed Xanax.

"Ah, fuck," he groaned.

Violent shivers racked him.

I caught his hand and squeezed it.

"Matt," I said helplessly.

He seemed to be struggling with himself. After a space, he pulled himself to his feet.

"We have to . . . g-go to the hospital," he said. He searched my eyes, which were the size of plates. "It's okay, Hannah, b-but we h-have to go. Th-this is withdrawal."

Matt's grip on my hand was weak.

His words sank in slowly.

Alcohol withdrawal. I should have guessed, but I had never

witnessed it. I had no idea. God, I didn't know a single real alcoholic.

Until Matt.

"Yeah, okay," I said. I needed to be strong right now. I needed to be calm. "Okay, the—"

"Get m-me in the c-car," Matt prompted, lurching toward the doorway. "Your ph-phone. Geneva General."

Matt's anxiety was contagious. My heart began to hammer and my hands shook. At least I had something to do besides hover and panic.

I helped Matt through the cabin and out onto the porch. He vomited over the rail.

He was still wearing boxers and those sad old slippers. I couldn't look at the slippers. I could *not* break down right now.

I boosted him into the car as best I could. Matt slumped in the seat. I dashed back to the cabin for my flip-flops and purse.

Geneva General Hospital was less than four miles away. I propped my phone on my thigh and studied the directions as I backed out of the drive too fast, thwacking branches.

I squeezed Matt's shoulder. "It's okay now," I said. "We'll be there in eight minutes. Five minutes. I love you, Matt."

If Matt heard me, he gave no indication. He was crumpled against the car door. He flinched with each bump in the road and his shallow breath hitched, but I wasn't about to slow down. I drove like hell, swerving and spraying gravel. My headlights bobbed crazily in the morning dark.

"It's okay," I kept saying, "it's okay," staring between my phone and the road. Fuck the dark. Fuck these road signs!

"Here!" I turned sharply onto North Street. Matt swayed. "Sorry, I—" I glanced at Matt and slammed on the brakes. My scream filled the car. Matt was convulsing, his eyes rolled into the back of his head and his arms and legs jerking spastically.

I floored the gas. The tires screeched.

By the time we reached the hospital, Matt had stopped seizing.

I didn't know which was worse—the spasms or this deathlike stillness.

Another seizure shook him as I hurtled out of the SUV. I sprinted past the ambulance bay. Eerie white light lit everything. *Oh, God, thank God, thank God for this place.* I realized I was praying as I ran. *God, don't take him! God, please, he's mine!*

I burst into the ER.

I must have said the right words, explained things right. All I could hear was my fear grinding and screaming. My heart was in the car with Matt.

I watched as the paramedics dragged him onto a stretcher. His beautiful body was lifeless. Then he started to seize.

Strangers surrounded the stretcher. I tried to get to Matt. They ran the stretcher into the hospital and I rushed after them. I collided with a nurse.

"My boyfriend!" I shrieked, reaching after him. *My boyfriend?*

"Hon, listen to me." The nurse held my shoulders. No way could I get past this lady; she was solid and Germanic. "We need you here right now. What's your name?"

"Hannah. Hannah Catalano."

I glanced around for the first time. An old man and a younger couple sat in the lobby. All three pairs of eyes were on me.

"Okay, hon, what's your boyfriend's name? Did he bring ID?" The nurse led me behind the front desk. Right, this was the desk clerk. I'd just seen her, and I nearly climbed over her desk screaming about Matt.

I dropped into a bony aluminum chair and hugged myself. *Matt, oh, God, Matt.*

For the next fifteen minutes, I fielded questions and filled out paperwork, half of which I couldn't complete. Every other question was a reminder of how little I knew about Matt.

At least I wasn't bawling. Fear and hollow dread held back my tears.

"What are they doing? Can they stop the seizures? Is—"

The nurse rebuffed my questions with more of her own.

"He's very dehydrated. Do you know how long he's been drinking? How many times has he detoxed in the past?"

I don't know. I don't know. I don't know!

Detoxed in the past . . .

I remembered the way Matt's hand shook when I made him pour out his last bottle. I wanted to scream. He knew this would happen, didn't he? He'd been down this road before, probably more than once.

Around 6 A.M., the nurse released me.

"I'll call you in as soon as he's stable," she promised.

I shambled into the lobby.

People came and went. The fluorescent lights hummed steadily.

I Googled "alcohol withdrawal" on my phone and skimmed the results.

Life-threatening condition.

Drinking heavily for weeks.

Agitation, seizure, delirium tremens . . . can be fatal.

When I held Matt last night and he came into my hand—was it the last time? And if I lost him now, how was I supposed to live?

I scrolled through my contacts.

Mom, Dad, Chrissy, Jay, Pam, Nate.

I should call Nate. Where was he anyway? Maybe he spent the night in Geneva, though I doubted it. He probably drove home and passed out.

"Hannah?"

The desk clerk smiled down at me.

"You can go see him now. Down the hall, he's in the first bed on the left."

My terror burbled back up.

"Thanks," I said. I grabbed my things and jogged down the hall to the ICU. I blinked rapidly against the sanitized whiteness of the hospital. Everywhere I looked I saw monitors and beds and curtains. I heard low voices and a periodic groan. Doctors and nurses moved to and fro purposefully, ignoring me.

First bed on the left.

No one stopped me as I slipped into the curtained-off space.

Matt lay on a hospital bed, the head inclined. Velcro straps tethered his wrists and ankles to the rails. He had an IV in one arm, a catheter in the other. His drip bag was half empty. He was asleep, or maybe unconscious. A monitor blipped his stats.

I swallowed and crept closer. The weight of sorrow crushed my chest. I made this happen. I made him pour out all his alcohol. I made his system fly into panic. I made him start drinking in the first place.

Someone had dressed him in a pale gown with blue spots and socks with rubber paw-shaped grips. A tube snaked out from under his gown. I touched his chest.

"Matt?" I whispered, but I knew he couldn't hear me.

There was a pamphlet by his bed: *Physical Restraints and Your Rights.*

I kept one hand on Matt's body as I found my phone and made a call.

I listened to the ringtone.

Just when I thought no one would answer, I heard a click, then Nate's groggy voice.

"Hi, Hannah, everything okay?"

I began to sob.

Chapter 27

MATT

Nate set the plush manatee on my chest and I touched it reluctantly.

It was velvet soft with black plastic eyes. I stroked it as I glared at the wall.

"A stuffed animal." I smirked. "What does she think I am, a child?"

Nate shrugged. "I can't say as to that, though you do a damn good job of acting like one."

Nate was brusquer than usual. Than ever, actually. I hugged the stuffed animal to my chest.

"What the fuck is your problem? You've been a shit all week. I'm lying in a hospital bed, cut me some slack."

Nate dropped into the chair by my bed and steepled his fingers. He looked at my untouched breakfast.

"I would like to know how you propose to get out of here without eating, Matt."

"I have no appetite. You can Google 'withdrawal.' It's kind of a common symptom."

Nate sighed through his nose. He closed his eyes and leaned

back in the chair. God, if he didn't look like a long-suffering saint right now. I rolled my eyes.

"You know," I said, "you could just send Hannah in here unannounced and try to get her to feed me. That sounds like exactly the kind of humiliating thing you'd put me through."

"Don't think I haven't tried, Matt. Unfortunately, she was so crushed when I told her you didn't want to see her that it would be ridiculous to try to send her in now."

"I don't want *her* to see *me.* There's a fucking difference."

"Oh, tell that to her!" Nate rose and began to pace. I had never seen him so agitated. He was always the calm one, the kind one. "Besides, she's done enough of my dirty work."

Dirty work. That hurt.

"I'll see her when I'm out of here," I mumbled. "When I can get out of this damn gown and shave, feel more like myself."

"You and your godforsaken pride. I'm pretty sure she's seen you at your worst."

"Yeah, thanks to you," I snapped.

Nate and I glared at one another. My fucking asshole of a brother. Freshly showered, in a tailored suit, he definitely had the upper hand. I played with the manatee's flippers.

"I had no other choice, Matt. And you know what? She worked. I'm only sorry I dragged the poor girl into this. You pulled a gun on her, you insane son of a bitch."

I winced. Mm, so Hannah told him about the gun.

"Yes, she told me about that," Nate said, weirdly prescient. "And before you ask, I have your gun. And you're not getting it back."

"Is she here?"

"Oh, yes, as usual, she's sitting out in the lobby like a goddamn orphan. She wanted to deliver that to you personally." Nate jabbed a finger at my manatee.

"Don't touch her," I said.

"Excuse me?" Nate's eyes flared.

"What have you guys been doing?"

"Cleaning up *your* mess. Taking care of *your* rabbit. Packing *your* belongings."

I nodded vaguely. So, my stay at the cabin was over. I was going home, but home to where? Home to Uncle or home to Denver? Or would Nate try to ship me off to a rehab facility? I felt strangely neutral on the matter.

In fact, I couldn't think of a damn thing I wanted, besides Hannah. And even Hannah was unknown territory. The thought of her filled me with embarrassment and guilt.

"Can I leave?" I said.

"Eat your breakfast."

Only Nate could talk to me like that. Only Nate could make me feel like a child.

I pulled the tray over and began to poke at the omelet I'd ordered. I thought of Hannah sitting in the lobby, waiting for Nate. Waiting for me. A spike of anxiety melted under my meds. Fuck, I was heavily medicated. It had been five days since I arrived at the hospital. I had my own room and I was off the IV, but the nurses and doctors still watched me vigilantly.

My omelet was cold and rubbery. I scooped another piece into my mouth. I tucked my manatee under my arm and looked at Nate.

I wasn't trying to look pitiful, but I must have, because his expression had done a one-eighty.

"Goddamn it, Matt." He came to me and clasped the back of my neck, leaning in and pressing his forehead to mine. He smelled like cologne and autumn. Like the outside world. My big brother. I shut my eyes against the prick of tears.

"Why am I so fucked-up?" I whispered.

"Hey, little guy, you're not fucked-up." He stroked my neck. "I love you, buddy. Your brother loves you."

My throat constricted. Was he trying to make me cry? I squeezed the manatee.

"And Hannah loves you, Matt. She really loves you. Can't you see that?"

Nate straightened and turned away suddenly. He brought a hand to his face.

"We're bringing you home today." He cleared his throat and got control of his voice. "You need to make a meaningful effort with your breakfast, show that your system is bouncing back. The doctor is going to check you. The psychiatrist wants to check you out, too. Be nice, okay? And you *have* to promise to take your discharge meds, whatever they are."

"I promise, I will." I chewed another bite of my mealy omelet.

"All right, buddy. When they're through with you, I'll fill out the discharge paperwork. I've brought you some clothes, too."

Another swell of panic ebbed in my chest. My blood was pure Librium. I was thinking about the clothes I had at the cabin. I didn't have much. When I packed in August, I wasn't worried about looking good. But now? Now I was going to see Hannah.

"Warm clothes?" I ventured.

Nate was at the door. He must have heard the anxiety in my voice.

"A few things of mine." He smiled back at me. "And a razor."

My doctor was a young Indian man. I saw him once or twice a day. He called me Mr. Sky and had a knowledgeable and pleasant bedside manner.

"You have eaten your breakfast, Mr. Sky. This is good."

I smiled and nodded. It was true; I had cleared the hateful tray with its processed omelet, cup of bland fruit, orange juice, milk, and toast. And I felt sick to my stomach.

Dr. Parikh listened to my heart and looked in my eyes.

"Mr. Sky, you must be continuing to take the Librium for seven days. I will prescribe for you a tapered dose. You will be having seizures if you do not take it. You must not be drinking."

"I won't be drinking," I promised.

The doctor spared me any further admonitions. We shook hands.

"You must take care of yourself, Mr. Sky."

The psychiatrist on call was a tall woman with papery skin

and gray-blond hair. She lowered the rail and perched on the edge of my bed.

"Will you consider moving from here to an inpatient rehab?" she said. "I strongly recommend it. We have connections with New Mercies. Their thirty-day inpatient treatment program gives you the best chance to stay sober as you transition."

Be nice, Nate had said. I rubbed my mouth to keep from smirking.

"I'm fine," I said. Right, I'm awesome—I just detoxed for the hundredth time and I'm lying here clinging to a stuffed manatee from my lover whom I refuse to see.

My lover.

I closed my eyes. The night Hannah appeared in the cabin and pulled me off . . . it was lost in a haze of alcohol. I remembered the pleasure, though. Goddamn, that girl . . .

"Matthew? Are you feeling all right?"

I glared at the psychiatrist.

I opened my mouth to threaten her with my uncle's lawyer, a New Yorker who razed lives like it was his job (it was), and then clenched my teeth. *Be nice.*

"I have good support from family and friends," I said. "I won't be drinking."

The psychiatrist hassled me for the next ten minutes. She asked if I felt suicidal. She even asked if I felt homicidal. Thank God she didn't know about the gun incident. She reviewed my medications and the tapered Librium dose.

"When you sign the release-of-information form, we'll fax your notes to your psychiatrist in Denver. You should schedule a follow-up with him as soon as you get back."

"Sure," I said. Fuck. I was going to be drugged dumb for the next week, maybe longer.

Finally, she left.

Nate returned, beaming. He said the doctor and psychiatrist had okayed my release. He left a duffel bag of clothes at the end of my bed.

"Come on out when you're ready. I'll be just outside."

God, I could have kissed him. He'd lent me dark gray Armani Collezioni corduroys and a forest green V-neck cashmere sweater. I changed quickly, luxuriating in the feel of real clothes against my skin.

In the bathroom, I had to grip the counter. The room tilted like a skiff on chop, then righted itself. Damn, I was weak. And I didn't look so hot. I washed my face, shaved, and avoided my reflection as much as possible. He wasn't helping psych me up to see Hannah.

Nothing was helping.

I held the plush manatee and sat on the edge of my bed. I must have sat there for a good chunk of time because Nate appeared, smiling uncertainly at me.

"Hey, buddy, looking good."

"Oh, yeah. Thanks." I smoothed a hand down my soft sweater.

"You got everything?" He picked up the duffel bag and scouted around. He glanced at the manatee clutched in my hand. "Got your little friend there?"

"Yeah."

"Paperwork's done, I just need your signature."

"Okay."

I stood carefully. Nate wrapped an arm around my shoulder and led me out. I don't know if I had ever been more grateful. I scribbled my name on two papers, and the nurse behind the desk wished me luck. Nate guided me to the lobby. I stared at the tiles.

"Here he is!" Nate announced with forced cheer. I didn't look up. In the high shine on the floor, I saw a shape approaching. Fuck, I was still wearing my hospital bracelet. I yanked at it.

Hannah's feet—shearling boots—poked into view. I glanced at Nate. He'd moved off, but he was watching us with open curiosity.

Hannah touched my arm. I met her eyes quickly. Dark, liquid, full of concern.

"Thanks," I said, lifting the manatee.

Shame pressed down on me like the weight of the world.

"Do you like it?"

Hannah cupped her hands around my hands. A memory flickered in the dark: Hannah lowering the gun.

"Yeah, it's soft . . ."

We stood like that for a while, me fiddling with the manatee and Hannah stroking my hands and wrists. A familiar electricity passed between us. Skin to skin.

Nate, probably having established that I was a few sandwiches short of a picnic, ushered us outside. Cold air swirled around me. I sucked in a stinging lungful. October on the East Coast . . . so alive. I wished for a clear head, but no such luck—our first stop was the pharmacy.

We picked up my meds and Nate made me take the first dose in the parking lot. He bought a Sprite from a vending machine, popped it open, and placed the correct pill in my hand. I tried to angle myself away from the car.

"Hannah's watching," I hissed.

"Take it."

I swallowed the pill and shoved the soda back at Nate.

"You might try making eye contact with her," he said.

"I *am* trying."

I climbed into the back of Nate's car and Hannah smiled at me. I smiled in her direction.

Laurence was in his cage on the front passenger seat. He shuffled uncertainly as the car moved. There was, Nate explained, no need for us to go back to the cabin. He and Hannah had packed everything and cleaned the place.

I thought of Wendy and the farm animals.

"What's the matter?" Hannah whispered.

"I had . . . some vegetables. In the fridge."

"We had to throw some out. We ate as many as we could."

Anger gripped me as I imagined Nate and Hannah cooking together. I held my manatee and glared out the window. Hannah held my hand.

The Librium came on strong as we hit the highway. I listed against the door. Hannah pulled my head onto her lap and I curled up across the bench.

"We are we going?" I said quietly.

"To your brother's house."

"Then where are we going?"

"Where do you want to go?" She ran her fingers through my hair.

"Wherever you're going."

"Then you'll come back to Denver with me. I'll take care of you, Matt."

I fell asleep to the feel of Hannah's fingertips on my face.

I woke to my nephew's shrill voice. "Uncle Matt Uncle Matt Uncle Matt!"

My nephew is an unholy terror. I sat up in time to see him throw himself bodily at the car. Nate laughed and climbed out.

Maybe dealing with eight-year-old Owen was how Nate learned to deal with me.

"Wow," Hannah murmured. She was looking out the window, up the sloping lawn toward my brother's house. I felt another twinge of anger—and jealousy.

First they were cooking together, now she was admiring his suburban monstrosity. Was this the kind of thing Hannah liked? I followed her gaze to the house, a two-story brick-front beast that sold new to Nate for a cool million.

"We could—" I rubbed my jaw. "I could—" Fuck these drugs, tangling my thoughts. What was I trying to say? We could get a place like this? Oh, please.

Nate opened my door and Owen launched himself across my lap. Valerie was hurrying down the driveway to meet us, pulling Madison by the hand.

My niece is a quiet, bookish girl, thank God.

I carried Owen out of the car. Everyone was staring at me.

Everyone. Nate, Valerie, my niece and nephew, Hannah. I wanted to melt.

We exploded into awkward greetings. Valerie hugged Hannah, then me. I kissed her cheek. My niece hugged me obligatorily. We shared a look that said, *I know the feeling.*

"Hey, Val," I mumbled. "Hey, Maddie." I set down Owen and he latched onto my leg. I had to walk-drag him up to the house.

I never let go of my manatee, and I never let go of Hannah's hand.

It was 3:00 in the afternoon. Valerie made some noise about dinner.

"I'm not hungry," I mumbled. I felt like death. The potpourri odor and purple scheme of Nate's house turned my stomach.

Hannah and Madison were deep in conversation about the *Inheritance Cycle.* I shook off Owen, who proceeded to tear through the house screaming like a banshee, his voice echoing off the high ceiling.

Nate moved ahead of me with the suitcases.

"I'll put you two down here," he said, heading to the basement. "That okay?"

"Mm."

"Maddie wants to look after your rabbit. She's been dying to meet him."

"Sure," I said. Better Madison than Owen.

The basement was fully finished with its own bedroom, kitchenette, full bath, and TV area. Like I cared about any of that. All I wanted was to be with Hannah.

Nate rubbed my back and we traded glances.

"I'll tell Hannah where you are," he said, and I nodded. I knew, as I had known for years, that I had the best older brother in the world.

Chapter 28

HANNAH

Nate detained me on my way to the basement.

"Hannah. I'm not sure if we'll get to talk again. You know, without Matt looming." He waved a hand and laughed. He looked apologetic.

Over the last five days, I sensed that Nate was giving me the brother test—making sure I was good enough for Matt, or insane enough. Casual conversations about my job or interests turned to grilling sessions, after which Nate was aloof and broody.

And as we'd cleaned the cabin, Nate periodically surveyed the wreckage and announced, "This is the way Matt is." His tone was always the same—uncompromising, almost proud—and I caught his meaning perfectly.

This is the way Matt is; take it or leave it.

Nate didn't realize that I was already all in.

Then, when Matt refused to see me in the hospital and I stayed on helping clean the cabin and pack, Nate's attitude started to change.

He began to talk openly about Matt's substance abuse.

I learned that Matt had detoxed half a dozen times before.

He'd been in and out of hospitals and rehab. He'd also been to court more than once for drug possession, public intoxication, and drunk driving, always handily evading charges with the family lawyer.

Nate told me endless anecdotes about Matt. Funny stories. Scary stories. I drank it all in. I understood that Nate loved Matt desperately, and so we had something in common.

I paused with my hand on the basement door.

"Sure," I said, "what's up?"

I'd spent the last thirty minutes locked in conversation with Matt's niece, then Nate's wife, and finally admiring Owen's Lego collection. I was itching to get to Matt.

"Oh, nothing particular." Nate loosened his collar. The guy ran on mysterious funds of energy. After a week of flying, driving, cleaning, and packing, he didn't even look tired. "I've seen him go through this, you know. It's important that he take his meds."

"I know. I'll make sure he does."

"It won't be easy for a while, Hannah. He usually needs some time to snap out of it."

"The drinking?" I frowned. I was not equipped to rehab Matt, much as I wanted to.

"Oh, no. I doubt he'll drink. That was very situational."

Very situational. Very much my fault.

"What I mean is, he may not seem like his old self for a while. I'm sure you've noticed some of that already."

I nodded.

"And he's not your responsibility," Nate went on. "I'll arrange tickets for you two tomorrow, if I can, but if that's too soon—" He frowned. He was having a rare struggle with words. "Rather, you've done all I hoped, Hannah. More than I hoped. Please don't feel—well, you know I can keep him here for a while. I would do it happily. I would do anything for him."

Nate was staring up at the large arched window above the front door. Afternoon sunlight warmed his face. Looking at him—his patience and seriousness—I knew that he meant what he said. He would do anything for Matt.

And still, I didn't doubt for a moment where Matt would be happiest.

No one could love him like I loved him. He belonged with me.

"Tomorrow is perfect," I said. I fully planned to reimburse Nate for the last-minute airfare, somehow. "The sooner we get back to our lives, the better."

"My thoughts exactly, Hannah. I'll move forward with the tickets, then. You can run it by Matt, if you don't mind. And thank you, again. He's lucky to have you."

Nate kissed my cheek. The brush of his lips was so formal and chaste, but all I could think of was Matt's jealous stare. He'd hit the roof if he saw this.

I closed the basement door behind me.

I expected to find Matt asleep, but when I got downstairs I heard the shower running. Our suitcases stood in the bedroom. I prized off my boots and paced the plush carpet.

Valerie seemed nice enough, but holy hideous decorating scheme. She'd turned Nate's mansion into a dollhouse.

The shower ran . . . and ran as I paced.

I cased the kitchenette. There were sodas, fruit, and sandwich stuff in the fridge. That would do if Matt got hungry. Should I make him eat? God, I had no idea what I was doing.

I began to undress, laying my jeans and sweater over my suitcase. I shimmied out of my bra and thong. I didn't need a shower—I had one that morning—but I needed to be with Matt.

I let myself into the bathroom. Steam filled the spacious interior.

The girl in me got giddy looking at that bathroom. Valerie's princess décor may have failed in the house, but it worked like magic here. The rugs were lush, the towels fluffy and huge, and the sink brimmed with candles, lotions, and perfumes.

I shut the door loudly to announce my presence. When I drew back the shower curtain, I found Matt standing under the water, staring lifelessly at the drain. Our eyes met; he rolled his away with doglike diffidence.

He may not seem like his old self for a while.

I stepped into the shower and eased my body under the spray.

"I guess we both like a hot shower," I said, my mouth near his ear.

He grimaced and looked away.

I didn't need anyone to tell me that Matt was mortified. I had seen him at his lowest. He would never willingly show me that.

I also didn't need anyone to tell me that Matt was happy to see me. His grimace notwithstanding, I felt his stiffening member touch my leg. I brushed against it and watched his eyelids flutter.

Between guilt and desire, he was static. I took his hand and brought it to my breast. He squeezed gently and I moaned.

God . . . that touch, did he know what it did to me?

"Matt, touch me. I've been desperate for you, please."

My hands devoured his body. I cringed as I felt ridges of bone.

For the pure pleasure of it, I ran a bar of soap along his skin. I slicked my fingers up his back and lathered shampoo into his hair.

Gradually, Matt began to touch me.

He was cautious at first, caressing my shoulders, arms, and sides. He watched his hands, never my eyes. His cock hardened between us. When I touched it, he covered my breasts.

He lifted them and circled my nipples with his tongue. He touched me as though he'd never touched me before.

His fingertips danced over my sex. I groaned and tried to grind onto his hand, but nothing could rush him. He touched me wonderingly; he spread my folds and fingered me as I panted. My God, I couldn't bear this slow torture.

At last, we stumbled out of the shower. I gripped the edge of the sink and gazed over my shoulder at Matt. Wet curls were plastered to my neck.

I hoped I looked half as good as Matt, who looked like a sea god come to shore. Water coursed down his hard body. His golden treasure trail glistened. Was I under the influence of Valerie's décor?

Matt held my hip and positioned his head against my slit. He started to tremble.

"It's okay," I whispered. "Please, I need it . . ."

He entered me with slowly deepening strokes. I bit my lip to suppress a groan. If I let go, everyone in the house would hear me.

Frantically, I wiped a patch of fog from the mirror.

Matt stared at our reflection as he bucked into me. His body couldn't disguise its need. His thrusts grew brutal and his eyes burned as he watched.

"Oh . . . Matt," I gasped, bracing myself against the counter. "God, don't hold back."

Matt was unusually quiet. No dirty talk tumbled from his lips—not even a moan.

He was transfixed by our reflection. I saw him watching my breasts, their heavy fullness bouncing as he slammed into me. Color flamed my cheeks. I remembered the first time, when he yanked up my top and fondled me in plain view of my house. Where was that man?

He looked down at our bodies.

"Tell me," I panted. "What do you see?"

Matt opened his mouth, but nothing came out. Disappointment crashed through me.

He usually needs some time to snap out of it.

I knew I wanted too much too soon, but I was addicted to Matt's dirty mouth. I was addicted to the way he humiliated me in bed.

Spurred by my rising crescendo of pleasure, I rocked back into his thrusts. I found my voice and started to babble.

"Your cock," I stammered. "I feel it, Matt . . . deep between my legs."

"Hannah . . ."

My name was a whisper on his lips.

"Tell me, please, talk to me—"

"Mm . . . my dick," he gasped. I moaned in need and encouragement. "Fuck—take it. I'm watching you take it. Ah, fuck, I'm watching your tight little pussy—"

I let go of my dignity; the rush of passion tore it away.

"Give it to me, Matt, fuck me, come in me—"

"Fuck, Hannah!"

Matt's hands snaked around me. His strong fingers found my clit and rubbed it, tickling the nerves, making my body explode.

We came together and collapsed against the sink.

Afterward, Matt was inert again. I wrapped a towel around him and ruffled his hair with another. I had hoped that sex would knock his head clear all at once, which was ridiculous. Nate was right—Matt needed time. And I could be patient.

I kissed his mouth. He kissed me back halfheartedly.

"Tired," he murmured, shuffling out of the bathroom. I watched after him in dismay. He *did* look tired, and with good reason. His body had been through a punishing ordeal. Fuck, maybe I shouldn't have coerced him into sex. What was wrong with me? I pressed the heels of my hands to my eyes. Hannah, grow a brain!

I grabbed an orange and a bottle of water from the fridge and hurried to the bedroom. Matt lay belly down on the quilt. He was wearing black boxers, and the manatee I had given him was nestled into his side.

I swallowed the lump in my throat.

"I brought you an orange."

Silence.

I set the fruit on the bedside table. His pill bottles were there.

"Have you taken these? I think"—I fiddled with a bottle—"I think you're supposed to take this twice a day."

Matt held out a hand.

"Um, yeah, okay, so—" So don't fuck up Matt's meds. Oh,

God. Which was which? Tapering dose . . . highest dose. After some fumbling, I set a 25 mg capsule in Matt's palm. He washed it down with the bottled water.

"Sorry," he said after a space.

I patted my body dry and climbed naked onto the bed. I stretched out beside him, hugging him and fitting my curves to his skin.

"No apologies," I said.

"It makes me sleepy. Can we talk?"

"Of course we can talk."

"I messed up. With you."

"No apologies," I repeated. "I'm not sorry I met you."

"I tried to stay away. At first, I tried."

"You couldn't have." My chest tightened reflexively at the thought of a life without Matt. I gathered a breath. Time to sound like an idiot. "Can I tell you something?"

"Mm."

"Matt, I—I don't think I could have stayed away from you. Not in this lifetime." I traced my fingertips over his back. "I love you. You know I love you."

"Why?"

It helped that Matt's eyes were fixed on the wall. Those penetrating green eyes . . . I couldn't have said these things to them.

"I think I've always loved you," I whispered. "I felt something since we met, since we first started writing together. It was like I had loved you without knowing you, and the love was in me, waiting to happen. So you can't apologize, Matt. It's you I love. There's no why about it."

Matt rolled to face me. He met my gaze—finally—with obvious difficulty. We watched one another.

"You and Nate . . ."

"He's been a perfect gentleman," I said.

"Yeah?" Matt searched my expression drowsily.

God, was he actually worried about this? I sighed and cupped his cheek.

"Matt . . . I don't want a perfect gentleman."

"What do you want?"

"You."

For the first time in months, I watched Matt's gorgeous face light up with real laughter. It was soft, enervated laughter, but it was laughter. I wanted to cry.

"Not a gentleman." He chuckled, his eyes slipping closed.

"Definitely not a gentleman," I murmured.

Chapter 29

MATT

Hannah and I had an unspoken understanding.

I would live with her in Denver.

"Here it is," she said, smiling at an unassuming corner building.

I paid our cabbie and wedged Laurence's cage off the seat. I dragged our suitcases onto the sidewalk.

The apartment complex was small and, frankly, hideous. Flimsy balconies jutted from brown brick. Inside, we had to lug our bags to the second floor.

"I haven't . . . had much time," Hannah said as she let us in.

What had Hannah been doing for three months? Her apartment was a shell. I set Laurence's cage on the floor of the family room. Family room? Living room? With one lamp and a "table" that consisted of plywood and cinder blocks, it was hard to tell.

I wandered through the empty rooms. There was no kitchen table. I found two plates in a cupboard. Another smaller room was entirely empty.

Only Hannah's bedroom showed signs of life: books, a mattress on the floor, a calendar on the wall. I cleared my throat. She was hovering in the doorway, watching me.

"It's . . ." I scanned the space for a single redeeming quality. "Ah, got nice high ceilings."

Hannah burst into laughter. She hugged me tight and I lifted her off her feet.

"You're here, Hannah," I said into her hair. "This is the only place I want to be."

It was true; I couldn't stomach the thought of my sprawling, modern, lonely apartment. I didn't even want my furniture and appliances. I wanted to start fresh with Hannah.

"I've been stalling on the décor," she admitted. "But now I'll make it really great. I'll cook, too. Fatten you up." She poked my ribs and I smirked.

"Fatten yourself up while you're at it."

"Oh, right." She toed the floor. "Kind of lost my appetite . . . in the craziness."

"Mm. You cut your hair, too." I fluffed the layered curls at the back of her head. They were heavy with product. Hannah blinked up at me. "I like it, bird. I like it a lot."

She exhaled in relief.

I roamed through the apartment some more, feeling like a ghost. I couldn't get hold of my moods. The highs were sharp; the lows were deep. Was it the Librium? I felt totally dislocated. Hannah trailed after me, perhaps feeling equally lost.

"What?" I murmured. She was staring at me again. I knew for a fact I didn't look stareworthy. My wardrobe, at the very least, needed to be fetched posthaste. I was wearing old jeans and a blue thermal turtleneck.

"It's just . . . it's surreal. I mean, M. Pierce is walking through my apartment."

"Matt Sky," I corrected her, "your fucked-up asshole of a boyfriend."

My words were not intended to make Hannah beam, but I

think all she heard was *boyfriend.* She launched herself into my arms again and I kissed her hard. My heart protested with a fluttering rhythm. God, I was weak. I'd nearly collapsed after the sex in Nate's basement. How humiliating.

"Baby, I—"

Hannah had one leg hooked around my ass and was rocking into my groin.

"Yeah?"

"I . . . I think I know exactly what this place needs," I said, easing her back.

"What?"

I ran my fingers over the drywall, which was pale and smeared with stains.

"A little color," I said, smiling down at her.

A little color turned out to be an understatement.

Over the next week, when I wasn't sleeping off my meds, Hannah and I painted the apartment. I let her choose everything—and pay for nothing. She was crazy about bright colors.

We painted the main room turquoise, the kitchen yellow, the bedroom blue, the bathroom pink, and the "office library writing room," as we dubbed it, lettuce green.

Hannah tried damn hard to stop me from buying everything. I countered by threatening to buy anything she looked at, literally.

In an antiques shop, I caught her laughing at a clown lamp.

"Really?" I said, raising a brow. "Kind of the stuff of nightmares, but since you won't tell me what you *do* want . . ."

"Matt!" She peeled after me as I stalked toward checkout with the lamp. She yanked at my arm. "Okay, okay! Not that, this!"

We covered the scratched hardwood with bright area rugs. We hung Restoration Hardware lamps in every room—vintage birdcage chandeliers, the Foucault Iron Orb—and busied surfaces with knickknacks, accent lamps, and candles.

Oh, yeah, we got surfaces.

I let Hannah choose a kitchen island from Williams-Sonoma

and a handsome circular table and chairs from Ethan Allen . . . along with a turquoise Quincy bed frame, teal end tables, a claw-foot tub, arched mirrors from West Elm, a deep-buttoned velvet sofa from Couch, and what felt like one of everything from Anthropologie.

Anthropologie seemed to be Hannah's favorite store. We bought dozens of their hand-painted plates, the Rivulets quilt and shams, a vintage dresser, lace curtains, patterned pillows, animal-shaped wall hooks, and new knobs for everything (including Laurence's hutch).

By the time we were done, the apartment looked like a gypsy caravan collided with a psychic's tent. Nothing matched. I mean, nothing. No two knobs were the same, no two pillows or bookshelves or picture frames.

And Hannah loved it. And I loved seeing her happy.

We wrote THE NEST in letter-shaped coat hooks by the front door.

We laughed a lot while we decorated. We goofed off a lot. I think I was almost happy, except when Hannah had to go to work.

I followed her around as she showered and dressed.

"My sweet shadow," she said, kissing me slowly before slipping out the door.

I was anything but sweet in Hannah's absence. The Librium dragged me into a nap, after which I ranged through the apartment feeling sick.

Writing was out of the question.

Hannah paid special attention to our "office" furnishings, making me choose the desk and transition my whole library over, but that didn't inspire me to write.

Nothing did.

More often than not, I avoided the room. The only thing I actually wrote was a letter to Wendy. I thanked her for her transcription services and included a check. *Severance pay,* I called it. I apologized for my hasty departure and promised to visit one day.

Another loose end tied up. What now? I felt like a dog waiting for his master to come home. Five o'clock rolled around and I stood on the balcony watching for Hannah.

Once, I got it in my head to follow her to work. I thought I might feel better being closer to her. I trailed her into the agency and deposited myself on a bench in the lobby.

Pam found me there, of course.

"Matthew." She looked at me quizzically. "How wonderful to see you."

"Mm. Hi, Pam." I picked at the cuff of my sleeve.

"Are you—" She glanced around the empty lobby. "Did you need to see me?"

"No, just sitting."

"Ah." Pam blinked and nodded.

God, go away, Pam. I was counting down the seconds until she asked about my writing, but she never did.

"Well, it's great to see you, again." She pat-squeezed my shoulder. I was starting to hate that gesture. Nothing says *I view you as an invalid* quite like the shoulder pat-squeeze.

As if the run-in with Pam weren't enough, a tour group appeared in the lobby a few hours later. They were mostly college-aged, probably a creative writing class.

I angled my body toward the wall.

The tour guide's voice began to drone.

"The Granite Wing Agency is one of Denver's literary landmarks. It was founded—"

"Oh, my God!" a student enthused. I heard footfalls approaching. A young woman came to stand practically on my feet. "Are you—? Oh, my God. Can you—? Oh, my God, it's M. Pierce."

The tour group closed in like a school of piranhas. I was off the Librium by then and my Xanax was at the apartment. Basically I was fucked.

M. Pierce, M. Pierce, M. Pierce. It was all I could hear.

Little did those assholes know, my pen name had become a source of major anxiety for me. I never wanted to hear it again. It reminded me of losing Hannah, and it made me feel like I was losing her again.

"Please," I mumbled, my ears ringing.

Even the tour guide was soliciting my attention.

"Leave him alone!" Hannah's voice echoed through the lobby. I was on my feet facing the corner, my head in my hands.

Hannah collided with the cluster of students and body checked the young woman into a wall. She threw her arms around me.

"Baby, come on."

She guided me out of the building.

After that, I rarely left the apartment.

Hannah was careful never to ask about my writing, though sometimes I saw her rifling through my pages. She probably assumed I was writing on the computer. I let her think so.

We watched movies together, my favorites and hers—*Legends of the Fall, Wonder Boys, Good Will Hunting.*

We read aloud to one another.

Hannah tried to teach me how to cook. Pan-fried pork chops ended with me lying on the kitchen floor, covered in flour.

On Halloween, we went to her parents' house and handed out candy, watching the trick-or-treaters from the porch.

Chrissy "apologized" for macing me in the face. ("You deserved it," she said. "I know," I told her.)

We fucked all over the apartment—in the shower, on the couch, in bed, against walls. I knew I wasn't the same, of course, and I knew Hannah felt the change.

For one thing, silence replaced my rapacious dirty talk. Hannah had to coax the words out of me. And for another, I couldn't bring myself to get rough with Hannah.

Maybe I still felt guilty. I don't know.

I kept waiting for something to click into place, but it wasn't happening, and the more it didn't happen, the more nervous I got. How long would my tame lovemaking satisfy Hannah?

She didn't say a word about it, but she struggled to inspire me. She went strutting around the apartment in nothing but a thong and bustier. She cleaned in a skirt, no panties, and bent over every available surface. She slept naked, too. Each morning I woke with a hard-on pressed against her soft skin.

God, I was lucky.

And fuck, I was unhappy.

When Hannah left for work, she took all of my happiness with her, and the void left in me was my essential misery.

I woke to an empty apartment on Saturday.

I loped through the rooms in a state of mild panic.

"Where's Hannah?" I asked Laurence.

I tried her cell. It rang and rang and went to voice mail.

I threw on a bathrobe and stood out on the balcony, watching the street. The November sunlight was deceptive. I shivered and paced.

I was still out there at noon, probably looking like a bum, when Hannah came striding up the sidewalk. She spotted me on the balcony and waved.

"Go inside!" She laughed. She was carrying two bags. "It's freezing!"

I shuffled inside and waited for her on the landing. Hannah took the stairs two at a time and kissed me on the mouth.

"Hi," I said through the kiss.

She giggled as I tried to get her against the wall.

"In!" she huffed, slipping away from me. I followed her into the apartment and helped her out of her coat. I loomed, trying to get a look at her shopping bags.

"I called. Where were you?"

"Making secret purchases." Hannah darted to the bedroom and returned with only one bag. From it, she produced a box of gourmet cupcakes. They were piled high with icing—more icing than cake. I smiled as she pushed one on me.

"Happy birthday, Matt," she whispered.

I blinked, reeling for a beat. *Birthday*? My watch and phone were in the bedroom. I glanced at the kitchen calendar. November 9.

"Holy shit," I said.

"You forgot your own birthday, didn't you?" Hannah took my face between her hands and kissed me longingly. Without looking, I slid my cupcake onto the counter. I pulled her close.

"I think I did," I murmured, kissing my way down her neck. She pushed my bathrobe off my shoulders. Hannah was wearing a form-fitting sweater dress and leggings. The outfit showed off her beautiful body.

"I have another present for you." Hannah took my hand and pulled me toward the bedroom. I gazed at her ass as it swayed from side to side.

I knew I was about the get the blow job of a lifetime.

Until Hannah started going through her other shopping bag.

She looked uneasy.

"Can you take off your boxers?" She glanced at me.

"Um . . . yeah." I slid my boxers down my legs. Suddenly things were awkward. Hannah was fully dressed and I was standing there semihard, totally naked, and not a little confused.

She wrestled with some packaging and withdrew a blindfold from the bag. *Oh.* Hannah and I hadn't tried anything kinky since . . . well, since four months ago when I tied her to my bed. Did she think I could do that now? Could I?

"I see how it is," I said, laughing nervously.

"Do you?" There was a glimmer of mischief in Hannah's eyes. She slid behind me and told me to close my eyes, then she tied the blindfold onto me.

"Okay, maybe I don't see." I grinned and held the footboard. Blindfolded blow job. I could definitely get into this.

Hannah guided me over to the bed and I stretched out on my back. My cock twitched in anticipation. God, I wanted to feel her hot tongue on my dick . . .

If only I could *say* that.

I heard Hannah's clothes hitting the floor. My senses intensified in the absence of sight. I could smell Hannah's honeysuckle perfume and a few of our candles. The warm air of the apartment seemed to gust over my skin.

"You look so good," Hannah purred. She climbed over me and I sighed as her creamy skin brushed mine. She drew my wrist toward a bedpost. My grin faltered.

"Oh, really?" I chuckled as she began to tie me to the bed.

"Yes, really." Hannah's breasts brushed my face as she worked, tying my wrists with soft cords to the upper bedposts. I mouthed at her nipples blindly.

"Not yet," she whispered, lifting them beyond my reach. Fuck . . .

She tied each of my ankles to the bottom bedposts. I swallowed and tried to move. Damn, Hannah tied a good knot. I was spread-eagle and nearly immobile.

No lover had ever bound me before. I always cracked the whip—literally *and* figuratively. And truth be told, I wasn't sure how much I liked this.

Hannah straddled my torso.

"Do you want to suck on me, Matt? Do you want to taste my skin?"

"Mm . . ."

"You have to tell me exactly what you want."

"Your breasts."

I felt Hannah hovering over my face. A stiff nipple rubbed at my lips, but when I moved to suck it, she moved away.

"Please," I whispered. Instinctively, I tried to yank my arms free.

"Please what?"

"Let me . . . suck on your nipples, come on."

I was rewarded with a pert nipple between my lips. I gasped and felt my cock thickening. I sucked hungrily at Hannah's breast, biting down and tugging to make her yelp.

Crazy girl, she had a lot more coming to her if she kept this up.

"The other," I snarled. "Give me the other."

Hannah obliged me and I swirled my tongue over her other nipple.

"All right, that's enough." She moved away. I turned my head on the pillow and stared into the blackness of my blindfolded eyes.

The mattress shifted.

Suddenly Hannah's sex pressed against my mouth, smothering me.

"Mm!" I groaned and began to lap at her slit.

She tasted like desire, and she was hot and soaked.

"Oh, God, Matt," she panted. I pictured her sitting astride me, her pussy resting on my face. Her fingertips tweaked my nipples and I jerked on the bed.

"Touch me!" My words came out muffled against Hannah's cunt. She rubbed it over my face, smearing her arousal on my nose and lips. I fucked her with my tongue.

At last, Hannah's fingers wrapped around my cock. She flicked her tongue over my tip. I tried to thrust into her mouth, but I couldn't move.

"What do you want?" Hannah lifted her sex from my face. I breathed raggedly.

"My cock, God—suck it, Hannah."

Hannah wriggled her tongue against the tiny hole in the head of my cock.

"Ah! God, please," I whispered. "Suck my cock, please . . ."

Was I not saying something right? I wrenched my arms and legs helplessly. My erect member throbbed, aching for stimulation.

Hannah giggled and climbed off of me. She left me panting on the bed. Holy fuck. I licked my lips, tasting her musky sweetness.

"I was just getting you ready," she murmured. "I'm not going to tease you on your birthday, Matt, but I needed you hard. Are you ready?"

"Fuck, yes," I snapped. How the hell did I look? I was ready for anything. Her mouth, her pussy—I just needed Hannah on my dick.

I heard some indeterminate rustling. A cold hand grasped my cock. I hissed and tensed. Hannah began to stroke me, spreading a copious amount of lube along my shaft. It trickled over my balls and I moaned.

"Baby, it's—"

"Shhh." Hannah stilled my lips with a clean finger.

She climbed over me and positioned my sex. My slick tip slid along her crack, stopping in the dimple of her anus. I flexed my thighs, trying to push my cock up toward Hannah's pussy, but she held it steady against the puckered entrance of her ass.

"Happy birthday, lover," she whispered. She began to lower herself. I felt my cockhead spreading an improbably tight ring of muscle. I tensed from head to toe.

"What—what are you doing?"

The reply from Hannah was a long, low moan. I trembled in my restraints. My God . . . she was going to take me into her ass.

"Oh, fuck," I grunted. My breaths grew shallow. "Oh . . . oh . . ."

All at once, my head popped into Hannah's ass. She cried out—and I cried out, thrashing helplessly. It felt so good, it almost hurt. My heart drummed in my chest.

"More," I pleaded.

"More of what?" Hannah said, her voice strained but even. "Tell me. Tell me everything. Never deny me, Matt."

Never deny me.

I'd said those words to Hannah months ago.

"Your ass," I growled. "Mm . . . Hannah, get on my dick."

"God, Matt . . ."

Hannah lowered herself inch by agonizing inch. I could do nothing but wait—and as I waited, I felt my tongue loosening. I couldn't deny the incredible eroticism of the moment: Hannah making me fuck her ass for the first time, my strong body helpless.

"Fuck, God, your ass," I moaned. "Your tight ass, you want my cock inside it, Hannah?"

"Yes," she breathed.

At last, Hannah sat on my groin, my dick deep inside her.

"Comfortable?" I gasped. "God, Hannah, my beautiful slut . . ."

"So full . . ."

"That's r-right," I growled. "Now ride my dick."

Trying to call the shots while bound should have been an exercise in frustration, but Hannah obeyed me. She loved to obey me. And I loved to call the shots.

She began to bounce on my cock, the tight grip of her ass stroking me hard.

"Fuck!" I writhed. I wanted to squeeze her tits. I wanted to spank her ass.

Lube squelched in the silence and Hannah's cheeks slapped at my thighs.

"Faster, fuck," I panted. "Nn . . . make me come. Listen to your ass, Hannah, fuck . . ."

"Oh, God, oh, God . . ." Hannah's pace became frenzied. I jerked in my bonds. She reached behind her cleft and cupped my balls, fondling them. I gasped as jets of cum shot from me.

"Hannah, I'm coming!" I moaned. "God, Hannah—"

Hannah's bottom milked out the last of my desire. I began to struggle at once, baring my teeth like an animal. So help me God, I would tear these silly cords.

"Untie me . . . *now,*" I growled.

Chapter 30

HANNAH

I bound my broken, beautiful Matt, so sad and silent.

I unbound my tiger.

When I slid the blindfold off his head, his eyes were electric. A frisson of fear passed through me. Fuck, was he angry?

"H-happy birthday," I mumbled again, my hands trembling as I untied his ankles. Ankles first, hands last. I wondered if I should flee to the bathroom.

Matt said nothing. He watched me with his smoldering stare. As I freed his feet, he flexed his legs and dug his heels into the bed.

For months, I longed to see this very heat in Matt's eyes . . . the dangerous unpredictability I loved. But now? Now I felt the double edge of it—the fear that was so real and exciting.

"I . . . I've been . . . planning that for a while," I said. I massaged Matt's ankles, delaying untying his wrists. "I hope . . . that was okay."

God, Matt looked exquisite. My eyes trailed over his body. His chest rose and fell with deep breaths; his lean arms were taut with muscle. I wanted to ride him again, and again and again. I wanted to flick my tongue over his deliciously sensitive nipples. I knew that drove him crazy. I knew it made him hard.

"Wow, I . . . made a mess, huh?" I glanced at the lube coating Matt's groin. My backside mustn't have looked much better. "Maybe . . . I'll grab a washcloth real quick."

"Hannah." Matt's voice was low with menace.

"Oh, right, sorry . . ." I crawled toward the headboard. Every manner of irrational fear came to me as I untied Matt's hands. Was this off-limits, binding Matt? Fuck, why hadn't I asked? Was he going to get up and walk out?

I got one of his hands untied. I half expected him to grab me by the throat, but he only rolled his wrist.

"Last one . . ." I loosed Matt's other hand.

He sat up in a flash. Steely arms hauled me onto his lap.

"Hannah," Matt snarled into my ear. He plunged two fingers into my ass and I yelped. I tried to wriggle off his hand, but Matt pinned me in place. "You must be very pleased with yourself. Do you like it, having my cum in your ass?"

His long fingers stirred and I squeaked. Matt was right; I was proud of myself for taking him like that—and I was also sore.

"Can't hear you, darling. You need a third finger in this very capable ass of yours?"

"No!" I panted. "Er, yes! I mean—"

Matt trembled with laughter. God . . . there it was, the breathless, cynical laughter that made my insides melt.

"No what, Hannah? Yes what?" Matt poised a third finger against my ass.

"No . . . no more, please. I . . . yes, I—" I warmed. "I like . . . having your cum in my ass."

"Ah, God, Hannah." Matt eased his fingers out of me. He began to stroke the curve of my bottom. Reflexively, I pushed it out for his touch.

Everything was different. Everything. The way he caressed me—so possessively, with such satisfaction—and his voice in my ear, exultant with power.

My heart thrilled. My eyes watered. He was back, God, he was back.

"Such a sweet ass." Matt sighed, squeezing my rump. "You're a good girl, Hannah, so good to take my whole cock. Were you scared?"

"Yes." I hid my sheepish smile against his neck.

"Mm, I bet. You did well. You made me come hard. Are you ready to help me again?"

Again?

Before I knew what was happening, Matt banded the blindfold across my eyes. He jerked my hands behind my back and bound them together. Disoriented, I tumbled from his lap.

I lay in a painful, awkward position on the mattress as he began to pull on my nipples.

"God! Matt!"

The store of darker desires, which Matt had suppressed for months, seemed to break over me all at once. He was hasty and starved. There was no logic to his motions.

He twisted and tugged on my nipples, slapped and squeezed my breasts. I squirmed on the sheets and moaned, my arousal spiraling upward.

"Yeah?" Matt laughed. "How is this, Hannah? Just right?"

He pried my legs apart and slapped my sex. Fuck! The sting of pleasure echoed through me. He bit on my clit. He dragged me off the bed.

On my feet suddenly, I swayed against Matt.

"Matt," I panted. "Where—" *Where are we going?* The words died on my lips as Matt pushed me forward. He left me a moment—I heard water running as he cleaned himself hastily in the bathroom—then returned and guided me out of the bedroom.

For a split second, I envisioned Matt fucking me on the balcony. *No way*! But he turned me into a room that smelled of old books.

Ah, my lover's writing room, where he was doing zero writing.

I heard a whoosh of papers. Matt forced me forward. Cool, smooth wood pressed into my breasts. I was bent over Matt's desk.

"Stay put," he murmured. Matt padded away and left me with my pumping heart. Every part of me loved this—the waiting, the exposure, the pain and degradation—and I never stopped to ask why. I knew better. Desire is arcane.

Matt's footfalls returned, moving up the hall. I felt his presence when he entered the room. The air stirred. Papers whispered against the floor.

Without hesitation, he gripped my hip and a hard strap hit my ass.

"Fuck!" I cried, jerking violently. "Matt!"

I scrabbled to get away. The leathery band came down again, cracking against my skin.

Holy fuck, Matt was spanking me with a belt. I couldn't process the pain fast enough to feel the pleasure.

"You've needed this for a while," he growled. "I won't stop until you stay still and take it. Yield to it, Hannah—you love it. You're dripping wet."

To my total mortification, I realized Matt was right. Desire oozed from my sex.

God, but it hurt! My breasts were smashed against the desk; my ass was burning. I gulped in a few breaths and willed my body to stillness.

Yield to it. Stay still and take it.

I could do this.

"God, baby," Matt moaned.

I went limp. I sagged against the desk and let the belt's blows come down in that merciless rhythm. My pussy throbbed and I felt a string of wetness sticking to my thigh.

"Oh, Hannah . . . fuck, fuck."

I heard Matt unraveling as I lay there. God, he adored this. Bolstered by his approval, I began to moan and spread my legs.

"Uhn! More," I panted.

"Hannah, goddamn," he hissed. "God you're good, you're so good."

The numbing lashes of the belt ceased. In the same second, Matt's cock filled me. I knew what he wanted and I gave it to him. I lay motionless over the desk, taking it.

Matt found my clit and rubbed it furiously as he fucked me. He took me to the edge of ecstasy. No, he forced me to the edge. And when he drove me over it, I screamed his name.

Matt exploded into my spasming body.

Afterward, we stumbled into the shower. I was dazed and flushed from head to toe, and Matt was grinning like the Cheshire cat.

Best sex of my life: bent over a desk and belted. Who would have thought?

As we showered and toweled off, Matt's emerald eyes followed me. He made me conscious of my every motion. My tiger . . . always watching me.

When I went to pull on yoga pants, Matt smirked and shook his head.

"This," he said, handing me a tiny ivory baby doll that barely covered my ass. "For the rest of the day."

My blush turned up a notch.

Matt dressed in pale lounge pants. We sat on the couch eating cupcakes and laughing. He couldn't believe my gall, he said. He meant my birthday present.

"Hey, neither can I!" I dabbed frosting on his nose. His eyes darkened. Oh, damn, I loved that look on his face . . .

Around dinnertime, Matt disappeared into the office.

When I went to see what he was doing, I found the door closed.

Hmph.

I sulked for a while, sitting in the main room and petting Laurence.

I didn't know that I had just met my writer.

Over the following week, I met the damn writer again and again. Matt seemed himself, the sex was amazing, but he grew restless when I melted into my afterglow.

"Going to check on something," he'd say, or, "I'll be right back."

When I went looking for him an hour later, I invariably found the office door shut. Sometimes I heard him pacing, but mostly he was silent.

My cooking occasionally lured him out.

I would turn from the stove and bump into a looming Matt—jump—and then laugh helplessly. God, he was adorable.

"I smelled something," he'd say, brushing past me to poke around.

I had him for ten minutes as he wolfed down dinner, then I lost him to his prose.

While Matt wrote, I spent my own time reading and working on yoga. I came to look forward to those private hours. Time together and time apart, didn't every relationship need both?

Though I was powerfully curious about Matt's writing, I knew better than to pester him. I figured he would volunteer what he wanted me to know—which turned out to be very little.

Sometimes, before I went to work or after I got home, Matt paced and spoke animatedly about writing in general.

I loved to hear him then. I loved to see him lost to me, strange as it sounds, and consumed by his passion. He talked to have it out with himself, arguing points I wasn't contending, and he stared into the heart of a fire I could not see.

My lover was a writer. He was a writer first and my lover second.

On the last Friday in November, I found Pam waiting for me in my office.

I shrugged off my coat and glanced at my watch. Whew, I was on time. No matter how long I worked for Pam, her presence put me on eggshells.

"Morning, Hannah."

"Ms. Wing." I smiled.

"I need you to read these manuscripts." She tapped two thick envelopes on my desk. "Laura thinks they have promise, but I haven't got time to go through them."

"Sure thing. Is that all?"

"For now." Pam moved toward the door. "Oh, and when you're done with that . . ."

"Hm?" I looked up. Pam was grinning at me. Yikes, playful Pam was decidedly scarier than serious Pam.

"Well, if you get the time, I have the latest offering from Jane Doe."

My eyes widened. Pam laughed, obviously gratified.

"Pam!" I whined.

She stepped into her office and returned with a stack of pages. I snatched them. There was no doubt in my mind that Pam already ransacked the pages, but I didn't care.

I shut out the world and read hungrily.

It was *The Surrogate,* of course. It was the complete manuscript.

The story darkened as I read, and more than once my throat tightened with grief. The surrogate's lover found out his secret and abandoned him. I felt Matt exorcising his turmoil in the prose. Only a few people would know the truth of this fiction.

If I had wondered at Matt's agony in the cabin in Geneva, now I knew. For him, the loss of me was *a presence . . .*

. . . a hole in his life that should not be filled. It was over, and it could not be over because he could not forget. She would become all that emptiness. In that, there was a comfort.

Nothing lasts forever, and nothing ever ends.

I scrubbed the tears from my eyes. I wanted to fly home to Matt, but I'd only put two hours on the clock. Fuck.

Matt's novels notoriously ended on low notes. *The Surrogate* was no exception. It closed with the surrogate on the run.

I gaped at the final line.

He disappeared off the cold grid, into the river of dreams.

What did that vague-ass sentence mean? Did the surrogate kill himself? What?

I stormed into Pam's office. She was laughing before I got there.

"Okay, Hannah, what do you think?"

"I think he's a dick! And I hate literary fiction!" I jabbed the manuscript at her. "God, it's like . . . he spends every novel getting you by the balls, only to tear them off!"

Pam raised a blow. I blinked.

"Why, Hannah, I didn't know your opinions could be so . . . explicit."

"Sorry, I—"

"Quite all right. Matthew's view of the world is dark. But you know that, don't you? I took you for a fan."

I folded my arms and tried to think objectively. Pam was right. I had loved Matt's fiction . . . before I had loved Matt.

Now?

Now I saw him every day—Matt in slippers, Matt after sex, Matt sniffing around the kitchen—and I couldn't bear to think he housed such strange sorrow.

Sad things seem truest to me.

His words. More of his words.

"Pam, I—"

"Go on," Pam said. She nodded at her door.

"I was . . . going to ask for an early lunch."

"Take a day, Hannah."

I wanted to hug Pam. Except never.

I gunned it home.

Matt was sequestered in the office, of course. I flung the door open. By the look on his face, my intrusion shaved a year off his life, but a smile quickly replaced his surprise.

"Hannah, hey." He rose from the desk. "What did you think? I gave Pam—"

"I know," I said. I buried my face his shoulder. "Matt, it's too sad."

He chuckled and hugged me.

"But Hannah, you know I think—"

"I know! I know. You think life is sad." I drew back enough to search Matt's expression. "But are you happy?"

His brows lifted.

"Of course I am. How can you ask me that?"

"I don't know. Your writing, that story . . ." I blushed. Had I read too far into Matt's fiction?

"Hannah." He lifted my chin. He stroked my cheek and feathered a hand through my hair. "I have you. I'm happier than any man has a right to be."

"That's all I need to hear," I whispered. "Every day."

"Oh, suddenly she has demands."

Matt defused my maudlin mood with a swift smack to my ass. I yelped and laughed.

As we held one another, my head on his chest and his chin in my hair, my gaze wandered to the desk. His notebook lay open.

"Are you starting something new?"

"Mm."

"What is it?"

"Our story," Matt said. He tilted his head and regarded me carefully.

"Our story?" I frowned. I could hardly handle *The Surrogate.* I knew I couldn't handle Matt turning us into a tragedy.

"It's a love story, Hannah."

"How does it end?"

Matt's gaze was suddenly inscrutable.

He hiked up my skirt and lifted me. I wrapped my legs around his waist.

"It never ends," he said, and he carried me out of the office.

EPILOGUE

M. Pierce Writes from the Grave

FEBRUARY 3, 2014

AARON SNOW, staff writer

Critics are grudgingly offering praise for *Night Owl,* the Internet phenom turned e-book, which reached the top of Amazon's fiction bestseller list last weekend.

The alleged author, W. Pierce, has openly styled himself (or herself) after the late Matthew Sky, a reclusive writer who published under the pen name M. Pierce and kept his identity a secret throughout most of his literary career.

Just months after Sky's death rocked the literary world, W. Pierce's *Night Owl* began circulating on the Internet.

"It's a publicity stunt," said Pamela Wing, Sky's former agent, "and one of the lowest order. His or her unoriginality aside, W. Pierce is making a platform on Matthew Sky's death. No reader should support that, and no critic should take it seriously."

Fans of the Sky novels have slammed W. Pierce's imitation of Sky's style and crass representation of his person.

Given the grisly and unusual circumstances of Sky's death, other fans have taken a different tack. Days after *Night Owl* was released, one fan tweeted, "This isn't LIKE Sky, this IS Sky. 'Nothing lasts forever, and nothing ever ends.'"

To be continued . . .

ACKNOWLEDGMENTS

A few thanks—

To Betsy Lerner and Jennifer Weis, the lions at my gate, to the team at St. Martin's Press, to the poet Alan Shapiro, and to Michael Downs.

Thanks also to Jhanteigh Kupihea, Lisa Jones Maurer, Maryse of maryse.net, and Aestas of aestasbookblog.com.

My heartfelt thanks go to the book bloggers who supported *Night Owl* with reviews, interviews, giveaways, and more. You cannot all be named here, but know that I am in debt to you.

Finally, a warm thanks to my readers. My books, of course, are for you.

DEAR READER,

Did you enjoy *Night Owl*? I would love to hear your thoughts. Please consider writing a review. I read all my reviews and I greatly appreciate the feedback.

If you are reading on a mobile device, check out the last

page of this book, where you can rate *Night Owl* and share your rating on Facebook and Twitter.

You can follow me on Twitter at @mpiercefiction.

You can read about my upcoming books at mpiercefiction .com.

Thanks for your support.